As he cantered toward the gates, looking up at the ramparts, a solitary figure drew his eye. A woman.

Her hands braced on the stone wall. She was staring down at his men from the bridge, stoically watching the seizure of her home. He recognized her instantly—Her Royal Highness, Princess Cwen. She was a vision of beauty set against the backdrop of a bland gray sky.

Never before had a woman made such a remarkable impact on him, and he took the opportunity to openly study her. Unsurprisingly, she looked forlorn, hauntingly beautiful, loose tendrils of her long dark hair fluttering in the wild late-summer wind, the jewels in her defiant crown twinkling in the fading afternoon light, and Njal felt a strange thud of awareness pound through him. He hadn't been able to stop thinking about her since he'd come face-to-face with her on the battlefield earlier today, when she had called a halt to the fighting, surrendering herself to him.

Now, as if she could sense his gaze on her, as if he'd willed her to look at him, she glanced his way and their eyes connected.

Author Note

Thank you so much for choosing to read *The Viking's Princess Bride*.

A terrible war is coming to Jorvik. Norse leader Njal Salversson wants to wreak revenge on the Northumbrian king who destroyed his settlement in East Anglia. The king is injured in battle and his daughter, the widowed Princess Cwen, surrenders. Njal will now take the fortress and crown to secure a permanent foothold here for his people—and his place in history. His terms? Peace will come with his marriage to the Saxon princess... They will rule the kingdom together.

Princess Cwen knows the only way she can save her people is to marry the Norse leader. He is devastatingly attractive, but she can never give in to her desire as she hides a terrible secret—one that would destroy the monarchy, her family and her beloved son.

I love writing an enemies-to-lovers story—especially when the hero and heroine fall for one another the moment they set eyes on each other. Yet Njal and Cwen are at war, on opposing sides, sworn to hate each other. When they agree to a marriage of convenience, they are forced to grow closer while trying to create stability in Jorvik and Bamburgh (two of my favorite real-life locations—if you haven't visited, you should!).

I hope you enjoy reading it as much as I enjoyed writing it.

You can contact me at sarahrodiedits@gmail.com or via @sarahrodiedits. Or visit my website at sarahrodi.com.

THE VIKING'S PRINCESS BRIDE

SARAH RODI

Harlequin
HISTORICAL

If you purchased this book without a cover you should be aware that this book is stolen property. It was reported as "unsold and destroyed" to the publisher, and neither the author nor the publisher has received any payment for this "stripped book."

Harlequin
HISTORICAL

ISBN-13: 978-1-335-53997-7

The Viking's Princess Bride

Copyright © 2025 by Sarah Rodi

All rights reserved. No part of this book may be used or reproduced in any manner whatsoever without written permission.

Without limiting the author's and publisher's exclusive rights, any unauthorized use of this publication to train generative artificial intelligence (AI) technologies is expressly prohibited.

This is a work of fiction. Names, characters, places and incidents are either the product of the author's imagination or are used fictitiously. Any resemblance to actual persons, living or dead, businesses, companies, events or locales is entirely coincidental.

For questions and comments about the quality of this book, please contact us at CustomerService@Harlequin.com.

TM and ® are trademarks of Harlequin Enterprises ULC.

Harlequin Enterprises ULC
22 Adelaide St. West, 41st Floor
Toronto, Ontario M5H 4E3, Canada
www.Harlequin.com

Printed in U.S.A.

Sarah Rodi has always been a hopeless romantic. She grew up watching old romantic movies recommended by her granddad or devouring love stories from the local library. Sarah lives in the village of Cookham in Berkshire, where she enjoys walking along the River Thames with her husband, her two daughters and their dog. She has been a magazine journalist for over twenty years, but it has been her lifelong dream to write romance for Harlequin. Sarah believes everyone deserves to find their happy-ever-after. You can contact her via @sarahrodiedits or sarahrodiedits@gmail.com. Or visit her website at sarahrodi.com.

Books by Sarah Rodi

Harlequin Historical

One Night with Her Viking Warrior
Claimed by the Viking Chief
Second Chance with His Viking Wife
"Chosen as the Warrior's Wife"
in *Convenient Vows with a Viking*
The Viking and the Runaway Empress
Her Secret Vows with the Viking

Rise of the Ivarssons

The Viking's Stolen Princess
Escaping with Her Saxon Enemy

Visit the Author Profile page
at Harlequin.com for more titles.

For the Prosecco Hags—Bethan, Charlotte, Emily, Louise, Millie and Victoria. Thank you for all the support, understanding, love and laughter.

Chapter One

*874,
Northumbria, England*

The large black wooden gates to the besieged fortress slowly opened, like reluctant, trembling wings.

At last.

Njal Salversson determined this would be the Northumbrian king's final flight—but would his Saxon enemy flee, or would he fight?

Starve the roots and the crop dies—Njal's late father had taught him that, back when they had first arrived on this isle, content to live a simple farming life. Now he felt each one of the long years that had passed in his weary, aching muscles. But he'd never forgotten the man or his words.

Njal and his men had been starving Jorvik for weeks now, cutting off the city's supplies and any contact with their allies. He knew they must be dangerously short of food and water, leaving the king no choice but to finally open the gates and ride out to meet him.

Njal and his men lay in wait, lined up on the meadows outside the city, watching as legions of Saxon soldiers piled out of the defensive walls, their gleaming armour glinting in the afternoon sunlight as they formed ranks, while archers took up their positions on the ramparts, preparing for battle.

So Ælfweard did mean to fight.

The ground trembled with the thunderous sound of Njal's own army, his warriors' swords and axes hammering against their shields, building up to a great crescendo to rally their courage and strength. But Njal felt no fear. Since the massacre of their Norse people who had come to settle here, he had drawn his sword over and again. He had seen his men through two years of fighting across these lands with grit and fierce determination, and finally, today, they would wreak revenge on the Saxon king for the slaughter of their kin.

Njal raised his sword in the air. 'For vengeance!' he roared.

'For vengeance,' his men repeated.

And he pressed his heels into the sides of his trusty steed and led his men in the charge.

A horde of heathen beasts thundered towards the Saxon army like a dark, treacherous wave. Huge ferocious-looking men on horseback bore down on them, causing the ground and Cwen's knees to quake. Anger and war-paint were etched on the Norsemen's faces, their sinister spears raised as they surged forwards.

These pagans could only want one thing—the end of the king's reign. They had been at war these past few years, and it seemed these beasts would not stop until they'd brought total devastation to the Saxon city and annihilation of the people of Jorvik.

'Hold your ground!' she heard the king command his men, as horses and their riders jostled either side of her in terror. Cwen slammed down her visor even further, disguising her face, blending in with the soldiers surrounding her. The king would not approve of her being here. But she refused to sit at home to await her fate, not when she was just as good a fighter as any one of these men. She had to help. She wanted to be a part of her people's future, or witness their demise. And if it came to it, she was prepared to die alongside them.

She clasped her sword tighter. Her heart thumped in alarm as the wind whipped up, screeching across the meadow just as the great heathen army crashed ferociously into the rows of soldiers in front of her. The sound of metal clashing against metal, groaning, grunting, thrusting swords and axes clattering into shields resounded all around her. All thoughts fled, and her fight instinct took over. She must do all she could to protect her people. The monarchy. Her heir and son. And she lashed out, taking on one opponent, then the next.

She had never seen fighting like it. These heathens weren't men—they were animals. They knew no mercy—and they were already gaining ground, even though they were outnumbered at least six to one. As the battle raged on, she was thrown off her horse, the force of impact momentarily winding her, but she quickly righted herself, found her feet and threw herself back into the fray once more.

In the middle of seeing off several dangerous opponents, Cwen became aware of a warrior approaching the king and engaging him in combat. He looked wild and formidable, and when their swords clashed, she knew, instantly, their ageing monarch was no match for the heathen's strength. As she struck down her latest opponent she watched in horror as the towering brute delivered a blow meant to kill and the king crumpled to the ground.

With a cry of distress, she covered the distance between them just as the beast raised his weapon, ready to strike again. 'No! Father…'

Trying to get free of the Saxon men tackling him, Njal looked past them to see his brother, Ove, raise his sword once more, as if to make certain the king had taken his last breath. With a surge of strength Njal dispatched his opponents before charging on, reaching his brother just in time. He gripped Ove's arm and pushed him backwards to prevent him from delivering his final strike.

'*Nei, stǫðva!* No,' Njal commanded. He had instructed the men to merely wound the king, and his commanders to take Ælfweard and his most trusted soldiers as hostages. Death was too good for a man like him; he wanted Ælfweard to suffer, to know what it felt like to have everything he cared about taken from him, just like he had done to Njal and his brother.

Ove wrestled with him, set on his course. 'I want blood,' he raged. But Njal was older. He had always been the stronger of the two and there was no getting past him.

Finally, with a growl of dissatisfaction, Ove gave up the fight, lowering his sword, but not before giving Njal one last frustrated shove, cursing him. 'I don't understand you. Don't you want this to be over?'

Njal turned back towards the Saxon soldiers, huddled round their wounded monarch on the ground, watching on in disbelief as Ælfweard fell unconscious. He placed a steadying hand on his brother's shoulder. 'It already is.'

One Saxon had rushed forwards, taking control over all others, pushing through the throng of men. They'd dropped to their knees beside the king and tried to pull him up, cradling Ælfweard's shoulders in their arms, unwilling to see him die.

Removing their helmet, long, dark braided hair tumbled down over slender shoulders—and Njal reeled. He realised in disturbed shock it was a woman, and he was momentarily stunned. What was she doing here, amidst the brutality of the fighting? The battlefield was no place for a lady, and certainly not one of such beauty. She was like a rare jewel dazzling in the grey.

His hungry gaze raked over every perfect feature, as if he'd been starved of the sight of a woman. She had the darkest hair, black like the plumage of Odin's ravens, pale, smooth skin like the moon, and taut, pursed lips he had the sudden desire to brush his thumb over in a sensual caress. He felt a strange thud of awareness pound through his body. He had grown too used to the sight of blood, of death, these past years—yet she was an image to soothe all of that. Never before had a woman made such a remarkable impact on him—and in the midst of a war.

'Father,' she said, taking in the king's injuries, panicked. And Njal knew instantly that she was Ælfweard's heir, the princess Cwen. Perhaps Northumbria held even greater riches than he had ever dreamed of.

He had heard tales of her beauty, and the descriptions were nothing compared to the flawless reality, but the strength of his reaction to her troubled him. He had determined never to have his head turned by a woman again, and especially not one with Saxon blood in her veins. He had learned his lesson the hard way. Hell, he'd been suffering the consequences ever since.

The princess bent over and pressed her ear to the king's chest, listening, and when she sat up again, her smoke-grey eyes were wide.

Njal stepped towards her, his frame casting a shadow over her in the late afternoon sun, and as if she could sense his gaze on her, the change of light, she glanced up and their eyes connected. His breath hitched with appreciation. She really was stunning.

'He still breathes. Please, spare him,' she whispered.

A fist of anger clenched in his stomach. 'And why would I do that?' he said, gripping the hilt of his father's sword tighter in his hand, drawing on its strength. After all, it was her king who had started this. He willed himself to remember all that had happened in the past, at these people's hands.

'Have you no heart?' she cried.

'Where was your king's when he massacred our families? They were simple traders, settlers.' Njal's fury surged as he spoke. 'Your father allowed them to stay, under the false pretence of giving them land to farm in return for peace—and then cowardly slaughtered them as they slept.'

A crease ruptured her perfect brow. She gave a little shake of her head. Did she not know what her father had done? He thought she must.

'Did he think that his actions wouldn't have consequences? That we would just allow him to murder our families?' Njal couldn't hide the bitterness behind his words.

'No. At least you had fair warning; saw us coming—it was an honest fight, men against men, not armed soldiers against helpless women and children.'

She looked conflicted; her face a storm of emotion. 'I cannot claim to know what my father was thinking, or why he behaved how he did, but it seems you have won your vengeance. Please. Let this be the end of it,' she said, desperate.

Njal didn't want to hear her pleas. Her father had ruined his life—why shouldn't he ruin hers in return? But that was his anger talking and he knew he had to keep it in check. He had to see beyond this moment.

He looked down at the king. His wound was deep, but he might live yet, and Njal didn't know how he felt about that. He had longed for this day, to see this man suffer the same pain he had inflicted on others. Yet despite what the princess might think, Njal had never intended to take the king's life—and he was livid with his brother. It hadn't been part of the plan. Njal had known an eye for an eye would never get them anywhere. It wouldn't bring back his family. They needed to make peace—to forge a new treaty for his people to live here safely, to protect the lives of the future.

But when he returned his gaze to the princess, he thought all was not lost. Perhaps he could begin his rule here with a show of mercy. It might work in his favour.

'Tell your men to lay down their weapons,' Njal said. 'Surrender yourself—and the fortress—to me.'

She tilted her chin up, defiant. 'Give me your word you will not hurt him further. That you will offer aid to those who need it.' She boldly, brazenly, held his stare, and he knew then that she was strong—he must not underestimate her.

He gave a single nod in agreement.

Ove pushed forwards, letting out a deep roar of frustration. 'No! We must end this—he must die!' he said. 'If you don't have the strength to do what is necessary, then I will.' He launched towards the king, brandishing his sword once more, and it incensed Njal further. He turned, blocking his brother's path.

'Seize him,' he said to his men, and they instantly obeyed, crowding Ove, and his brother tried to fight them off, ranting and raving.

Njal understood his rage, after all, his brother had been just fourteen when he'd witnessed the death of their parents at the hands of the Saxons, by order of this despicable king. But still, he could not have Ove going against his command. He was his kinsman and best fighter, but he had become a law unto himself, behaving in ways Njal didn't approve of, enjoying drawing Saxon blood a little too much and taunting their women for sport. It was people like Ove who gave the Norsemen a bad name.

The men took hold of him and Njal sighed—he had a hard time relying on others as it was, he had been let down badly before, so he didn't want to be worrying about his brother's defiance too. As soon as he had secured their position here in Jorvik, Ove would need to be reprimanded. He would have to bring him under control, and fast. His brother had to learn his reckless actions impacted them all.

Turning back to the princess, he inclined his head. 'Yield, and we won't touch him. You have my word.'

Cwen slowly, reverentially, placed her sword down

on the trampled, bloodstained wildflowers next to her father's body, and there was a long moment of heavy silence as everyone—Saxons and Danes—took in the enormity of what it meant. The conflict was over, at last.

Njal could scarcely believe it. They had achieved what they'd set out to do two years ago. He had fulfilled his vow to avenge his parents' death, and the rest of his people who had died that godforsaken night. The Danes had control of Northumbria. Now he would take the fortress and his place in history. His people would be safe.

Yet in that moment, despite its significance, he couldn't move his eyes from the princess's.

It was rare for a woman to capture his interest—revenge and conquest had ruled his mind these past years. And yet, suddenly, out of nowhere, conquest of a different kind usurped his thoughts. He wanted her. Badly. How inconvenient, that he should feel this now, towards a Saxon, who was the daughter of his enemy. It was depraved. It wasn't right, and he despised himself—and her—for it.

'Put down your weapons,' the princess courageously commanded the king's soldiers, raising her voice to be heard by the men around her, and the Saxons began to follow her orders, cautiously relinquishing their swords in an incredible wave that spread around the battlefield. 'There will be no more fighting between our peoples. No more bloodshed. It ends today.'

She spoke in a flurry to the king's men. One passed her a strip of material, which she tied around her father's shoulder and upper chest to try to stem the flow of blood. Another soldier brought forward a horse, and they helped her to lift the king's limp body onto it. 'We must get him back to the fortress, to a healer. Quickly.'

And then she raised her gaze to look at Njal once more—her stare loaded with scorn. 'It would appear you have won your right to live here—your place on the throne, if never in our hearts.'

Cwen turned to leave, but Njal moved fast. He came up behind her, gripping her upper arm, taking her as his prisoner, and she gasped, swinging round to face him. 'You promised—you gave me your word you wouldn't lay a finger on him.'

'That I did,' he said, leaning over her shoulder to slap the horse on its rump, sending the rider and the king on his way. And then he leaned in to whisper in her ear. 'But I never said a word about not touching you.'

Cwen's pulse pounded in her chest as the fearsome leader of the Norsemen began to lead her towards his own animal, and she was amazed her trembling legs were still holding her up. Concerned exclamations escaped the lips of her father's men as they watched on, weaponless, no doubt uneasy about the thought of her being alone in this heathen's company yet unable to come to her aid. They began jostling with their captors, who were holding them back, and she realised with a slow unfurling of sickening dread, she was on her own.

'What do you want with me?'

Terribly tall and broad, the leader of the enemy army was not what she'd thought he would be like. His campaign of destruction had desecrated many of the east of England's villages as he'd made his way here, fighting battle after battle, draining her father's resources, and she had conjured up ferocious images of what he was like so many times. But he was so much...more. Strong and muscular, he was more powerful than any other man she'd ever seen. Dangerous. Yet she had expected him to be much older, not so close to her own age.

He had longish black hair and a thick dark beard, both streaked with silver strands, unusual for such a virile man in his prime, but it didn't detract from his looks. No, if anything, it made him more striking. His hair was tied back in a band on the top of his head, the hair to the sides shaven to almost his scalp, hardening his look.

'Where are you taking me?'

He ignored her question as he tugged her across the muddy ground and her heart was in her mouth, already regretting her decision. She had forfeited her father's throne and her future crown by surrendering—something she'd been told never to do, not under any circumstances. From an early age, it had been drummed into her to protect their family's rule and power above all else. That she must make sacrifices for their family because of who they were. But she hadn't been able to stand by and watch this man kill her father. Even though they had never got along, he was still her blood. Had she made a terrible mistake?

The truth was, this warrior was right—her father had been a cruel and cold king, ruling the country with an iron fist, and her and her mother too. She had been forced to bend to his will, foregoing her own happiness time and time again.

The king had lived in paranoid fear, obsessed that the heathen settlers were plotting against him, planning to attack—and he'd felt he needed to strike first to prevent it from happening. But she hadn't known he'd murdered them all in their sleep. Women and children too. It was despicable. It made her feel sick. No wonder more Norsemen had come, and in force, across the sea from every direction, bringing their fury with them, waging war. Her father had brought it upon them.

But that didn't help her now.

She wrestled against the Norseman's hold, slanting a glance at him as he dragged her along. His face was unreadable, like stone. He was cold, hard—and she felt his anger like a drawn arrow, ready to be unleashed. His jaw was tight, his nostrils flared—and she was acutely aware of his long fingers curled around her arm, firm, holding her fast, searing her skin through her armour.

He despised her, she realised. He hated her kind.

She wondered if she should try to escape his grasp and make a run for it, but she didn't think she'd get very far. He could easily outrun her; overpower her. But still, she dug her feet in and tried to pull back, resisting his hold, attempting to yank her arm free of him.

'Your Highness,' Njal warned, rounding on her.

She tilted her chin up as she looked at him. 'Is that still my title?'

He gave her a long, hard look. 'For now.' He had such piercing Arctic-blue eyes. They displayed a determination of the like she had never seen a man possess before.

'And what should I call you?' she said, stalling for time. Maybe she could talk him round; stop him from doing whatever he was planning to do.

'Njal.'

Njal Salversson. She had known that. It was a name she'd heard many times in her father's great hall—usually accompanied by a look of fear in the ealdormen's eyes. She could see why.

He began to walk again, taking large, powerful strides, dragging her with him, and she struggled to keep up. He was dressed in a well-worn leather mail coat and breeches, with long boots which had seen better days—testament to all the battles he had fought, reminding her he had been ruthless in his crusade of hate, unstoppable, until he had reached the gates of Jorvik. And even then, they'd camped out on the banks of the River Ouse, unwavering, cutting off the city's supplies. Many inside the walls were starving, forcing her father's hand. He could hide no longer inside the fortress walls—he'd had to fight.

She had heard stories of how some of these Danes had tormented Saxon women—was he one of those? If so, who knew what he would do to her—a princess? Would he hurt her; kill her; use her as some kind of trophy? Would she be passed from one man to another as a victor's prize? And yet, she only had herself to blame.

She had considered, when her father had been wounded, if she should take her own life, so she couldn't be used, whored by the heathens, preserving her dignity and her family name. But then she'd looked up into the Norseman's blue eyes and a flicker of something—something she couldn't explain—had made her think it might just be worth pleading for mercy. With fierce but cool control, he *had* halted the other brute from dealing her father that fatal blow.

'Where are you taking me?' she asked again, still trying to resist him.

'Home,' he said. '*My* home, now,' he taunted her. 'In

the absence of your father, you and I will discuss the terms of our victory.'

'Discuss... You mean to talk?' she said, shocked, relieved.

He stopped abruptly, turning to face her once more. 'No matter how tempting it might be to storm in here and take *everything* for myself,' he said, looking her up and down. 'I'm not that kind of man. I insist we speak in private, agree to the conditions of the transfer of power. Protest once more and I'll be forced to carry you.'

Disturbed by the thought of him throwing her over his shoulder, and wanting to keep her feet firmly on the ground, she finally relented, allowing him to usher her towards the animal. But with a growing sense of alarm she realised the man who had struck down her father had been released by Njal's men and was now following them, escorting them. The brute was almost the same size and build as his leader, had the same dark hair, but without the distinctive grey streaks, and his face wasn't so wise. She bristled as he loomed closer.

Njal, perhaps sensing her hesitation, her footsteps falter in trepidation, looked at her, then at the man. 'You will stay behind, Brother,' he said. 'Clear the battlefield and secure the Saxon soldiers.'

Brother?

'I thought we were going to share everything, as equals—even the spoils,' the brute sneered, his beady eyes raking over her, and Cwen shivered. 'Why do you get to have all the fun?'

Njal drew Cwen closer towards him. 'Put the already dying out of their misery, get aid for the wounded and bring the living back to the fortress,' he said to the man, his face stern, his voice as hard as stone. 'That's an order.'

The brute bunched his fists at his sides and cursed, violently, making Cwen baulk.

Without any warning, Njal ascended his horse, simultaneously tugging her up into his arms, and she froze. She was his captive, trapped in his embrace and overwhelmed by the sudden, unsettling impact of their bodies meeting. He deliberately pulled her back against his solid chest, her head tucked into his shoulder, and the intimacy of sitting between his muscular thighs made her squirm. Her face burned and she struggled against his hold.

'Stop it. Don't try to fight me,' he said, his arms tightening around her. 'You gave yourself up—surrendered yourself to me, remember? You're mine now, whether you like it or not.'

Chapter Two

Sat atop his fatigued horse, Njal tightened his grip on the princess and the reins. The last ride now... He had sent a group of his men on ahead, to secure the stronghold, but as they galloped across the plains towards the city in the rapidly fading daylight, he knew he must still be vigilant. He couldn't let down his guard until the terms of the treaty had been agreed on.

After today's great and final battle, his name would be his legacy. The eternal flame of glory would be his and he would be known for ever as the Norse ruler who conquered this green and verdant kingdom. But he had never asked for this. He had never wanted it. He'd just done what was necessary to save his people from further persecution. He had been content with his life—he would give anything to go back to the way things had been before.

'Is that man your kin?' the princess asked, giving an involuntary shudder, irritatingly drawing his attention back to her and the feel of her body nestled against his own. Even dressed in her chain-mail, she felt warm, a snug fit between his legs, and with every gallop, she was thrown back into his groin, making him groan, inwardly, at the tempting throb of desire. Then she'd wriggle restlessly, trying to pull away, before the next onslaught. It made him long for things he knew he shouldn't want. Especially not from her. But it had been years since he'd held a woman in his arms; taken one to his bed. Too long.

'Yes,' he said, aware his voice sounded strained.

'You don't seem that alike,' she said.

'How would you know?' There was a long pause before he said anything more. 'He is driven by rage and grief—still bitter about what happened here. We all are. Many of us lost loved ones that day—Ove and I, our parents. All at the hand of your father.'

He heard her suck in a breath at his words. She brought her arms up, wrapping them around her body, as if to protect herself from his scorn. But why shouldn't she feel the force of his wrath? By God, her people deserved it.

Since the day of the slaughter, it had been him and Ove against the world. If it hadn't been for his brother, he wasn't sure he would have wanted to live. And yet, the princess was right. He and Ove had experienced the same trauma, suffered the same grief, but their experiences had been different, setting them apart. Whereas Ove had been a victim, Njal felt responsible.

'I am older than he. He is only ten and six winters. There's eight years between us. I don't think he appreciated his brother becoming his guardian overnight, suddenly telling him what to do. It came as a shock to us both.'

She turned her head suddenly to glance at him, and he wondered why he had revealed that. He got a waft of her floral scent as her hair fluttered against his face in the cool early evening breeze, but not even her slanted look of surprise, her exquisite beauty, could make him forget the horrific scenes they'd encountered that morning.

When Njal had returned home to find the farmsteads of their settlement burning, bodies strewn about, the metallic scent of blood on the misty morning air, he'd felt he'd walked into a nightmare. The silence was deafening, as he realised all those he cared about had been slaughtered. He'd raced to find his parents amid the carnage and had discovered his father's body first, struck down by an axe outside their home, and then inside, his mother's body lying among the embers. As he'd dropped down to his knees, distraught, he could almost picture what had happened—his father putting up a fight, trying to defend his beloved wife and child, and his home. And Njal wished he had been there to help them. It was a deep regret.

Then, looking around, he could barely contain his panic and despair when he'd realised Ove was nowhere to be found. Ove was just a boy, and he hadn't done anything to deserve this. None of them had.

Njal had looked everywhere—on the beach, in the forest, in every burning building, until he'd slumped down onto the floor near their farmstead, all out of hope. And then, he'd heard a scratching sound, faint, barely audible, coming from under the floor. Unsure if he'd imagined it, with a racing heart he'd pulled at the broken table and the benches, ripping up the boards, and seen his brother's frightened, dirt-covered face peering up at him. He had been overjoyed to find him alive. Ove had been pale with shock and it had taken a while to get the truth about what had happened out of him, but slowly the details had started to unravel.

It had been the king's men. Their mother had seen them coming and raised the alarm, and she'd managed to hide Ove under the floorboards just in time. And he'd been lucky, because the royal soldiers had shown no mercy. They had not stopped until they'd razed the settlement and everyone in it to the ground.

Njal's knuckles were white as he gripped the reins now. 'Did you know about it—what your father did?' he asked the princess.

'A little,' she said carefully. 'My father had said the settlers were a threat.'

'To whom?' he said, his anger stirring once more.

'To him.'

Njal clicked his tongue in disgust.

At first, he and Ove had been grief-stricken as they'd buried their parents' bodies, overwhelmed by all they had lost; shocked by the barbarity that had been inflicted on them for no reason at all and unable to see a way forwards. When Ove had revealed who the commander was who'd been leading the king's army, Njal had felt sick. That maybe he could have prevented it; that he should have seen the signs. And then the anger had set in.

Ove was forced to grow up too soon, and Njal had always felt guilty for that; tried to make it up to him any way he could. But they'd both struggled to move past the tragic events of that night. It had hardened them both.

They'd embarked on their quest for vengeance, but as the months had passed, Ove had become more and more violent, acting impulsively, whereas Njal was the opposite—he felt the need to be in control, at all times.

But he'd never seen Ove with such an explosive temper like today. He felt as if the hostility between them was growing and it was like a dark cloud hanging over him.

Entering the gates of Jorvik now, Njal surveyed the scene for danger, making sure his men had taken charge. He felt Cwen tense in his arms; her back go rigid, as she watched the Norsemen secure the battlements and round up the Saxon guards. But this was nothing compared to what her father had inflicted upon them.

It was an impressive stronghold, boasting vast, high walls that seemed to house the entire city within them. It was even grander than he'd imagined, with a central hall and many buildings surrounding it.

Njal pulled the animal to a halt in the courtyard and lowered the princess from his hold, glad to have her out of his embrace for a moment so he could think more clearly. But he had determined this wouldn't be the last time he held her body against his. Descending his horse, he passed the reins over to one of his men.

Reluctantly, he took Cwen's arm again, leading her up the few steps into the main building, flanked by his right-hand man, Bjorn.

'Did you find us a room?' he asked him.

'Yes.'

'Show me.'

Cwen's head snapped up to look at him, still uncertain. Under closer inspection, and in the evening light, her intelligent, wary eyes were almost lucid grey, framed by long thick lashes. Her high cheekbones and slender nose gave a sharper edge to her round face, as did her pursed full lips, and he wondered what she looked like when she smiled. He doubted he'd get to see that any time soon. It was clear she did not want to be alone with him and right now he didn't feel like putting her at ease, instead purposefully behaving in a way she wouldn't be comfortable with. She'd said she didn't know the extent of her father's actions, but he knew she wasn't to be trusted. He must not let his attraction to her soften him.

As they pushed open the doors leading them into the king's great hall, the captured ealdormen and ladies cried out at the sight of the princess in a heathen's hold. Their wrists were bound, and they cowered closely together in fear, no doubt wondering what the leader of the Norsemen would do to them.

'Is that really necessary, to bind them like that?' Cwen gasped, looking up at him.

Njal shrugged. 'If my people weren't safe in their own homes, why would I think they'd be safe anywhere else?'

'These men and women weren't deemed able to fight. They are no threat to you.'

He stared down at her. Many a man would have trembled in her place, perhaps thrown themselves on the ground at his feet and begged for mercy, but she was standing up to him, and he admired her strength. Still, he would be the judge of who was a threat or not.

'I can't take any chances.'

He took in the incredible space as they walked across the room—the extraordinary vaulted ceiling, the walls covered with rich tapestries and hunting trophies. It was more magnificent than he had thought it would be. When his mother and father had brought him over to this isle when he was just a boy, he had never dreamed he would ever set foot inside the royal fortress, let alone take control of it.

'What news of the king?' he asked Bjorn, and he felt Cwen blanch beside him. Did he still live, or had he deprived the princess of a father as her king had done to him?

'He lost a lot of blood. He is being tended to in a chamber at the back of the hall. The queen is at his side. We have men standing guard on the door.'

Njal nodded and turned back to Cwen, forcing her to walk once more. 'I know the concern—and anger—you must be feeling that he has been injured.'

'Spare me your pity,' she bit.

But for the first time today, he detected a slight wobble in her voice—a sign of her vulnerability. What had rattled her—the news of her father, or seeing her people being bandied about by his men? Or perhaps getting back to the fortress and discovering that after today, nothing would be the same again.

'You forget yourself, Highness—he only lives because I am allowing it. Don't tempt me to change my mind.' Then he inclined his head. 'You must admit, a man who behaves the way he does doesn't deserve to lead.'

'And you do, I suppose?'

He felt a muscle flicker in his jaw. He had never set out to rule, but when his settlement had been attacked, Njal's life had changed overnight. His father had been the leader of their people, and suddenly, his brother and the other remaining men and women were looking to him. Those that were left were all homeless; frightened. As rumour spread that up and down the coast Norse settlement after settlement was being burnt to the ground,

Njal had known they would never be safe here unless they took action. That they had to fight back. And he'd known what he must do. What his father would have expected of him.

His father had been a great man. He had brought their people over here in longships, selling them his dream—promising them a better life with fertile land to toil. Njal had known he must fight in his memory, and for what his father was trying to build here for their people.

Now he had won. But taking in the twin thrones sat on a raised dais dominating the great hall, he was all too aware his victory came with more responsibility, and he made no move to seat himself in one of them.

'Your father's reign was one of terror and tyranny. I can't be any worse.'

As Njal's man led them out of the hall and down the corridor, Cwen saw a fire was lit inside one of the state rooms up ahead, crackling in the hearth, and Bjorn stopped outside.

'Will this suffice?'

'Yes. Leave us,' Njal said.

A prickle of apprehension trickled through her, and she jumped when the door banged shut behind them.

Finally, Njal released her from his hold and she walked over to the hearth to warm her hands, giving her something to do and a reason to get away from the intimidating warrior. He dominated the small space—this man who had darkened her dreams—and the more distance there was between them, the easier she found it to breathe.

She looked around for a weapon, something she could

use against him if she needed to, and spotted the poker hanging next to the fire. That would have to do, if it came to it.

This Norseman had her seriously on edge—and the fact she could still feel his grip on her arm, the unsettling heat of his muscular body pressed against her back from the ride here, wasn't helping.

'What is this place?' he asked, walking around, picking up some of her father's scrolls and inspecting the trinkets on a central wooden table.

'One of my father's rooms.'

He halted what he was doing and looked over at her directly, giving her his full attention. Her heart skittered. 'I do understand your father's mistakes are not your own,' he said. 'And I will take that into account when I decide what is to happen next.'

She swallowed, willing her fingers to stop trembling.

'You were next in line to your father's throne?' Njal asked.

'Yes.'

'And he would have let you rule?'

'You ask because I'm a woman?' she said, feeling a shaft of anger tear through her. 'Yes,' she spat. She had no doubt her father wished she had been born a son, but he would still rather see his own blood on the throne than anyone else. 'I am more than capable.'

'I don't doubt it. I saw that today on the battlefield. Although I am surprised he let you fight, putting you in danger.'

'He didn't. He bade me stay at home, but I went anyway. I wanted to be there, to be useful.'

He raised a single, perfect dark eyebrow. 'Do you often disobey orders?'

'Only when I disagree with those who would seek to wield power over me. And my father has tried to control my actions my whole life.' She bit her lip, surprised, wondering why she had revealed something so vulnerable to him—to this man she loathed and feared. She must do better; be more careful around him, especially where her feelings were concerned.

He came around the table to sit on the edge of it, crossing his arms over his formidable chest. His piercing, penetrating gaze was disturbing. It was as if he was trying to see inside her, to understand her. She knew he must be strategic, for it was his tactics that had led his army to this point today, so she determined to keep her wits about her.

'It was never my aim to claim power in Jorvik, to be king, but to secure a permanent foothold for my people here. Somewhere they can live without fear. Unfortunately, I have come to realise that will only happen if I rule,' he said. 'But I understand the benefits to be gained from alliances—and peace.'

'Your words of reconciliation seem at odds with your reputation as a warrior, known for violence and war. Our people have likened you to your Norse god Týr.'

He lowered his arms and came off the table towards her. 'What do you know of the Norse gods?'

'Only a little,' she said, moving round the table, putting the furniture between them. 'I spent some time reading about them, to try to understand more about my father's enemies.'

'Then you'll know that although Týr had power over

victory in battles, he also strived for peace. Do you want to be queen?'

'One day. I have been preparing for it my whole life. But to speak of it is treason while my father still lives.'

'He is fortunate my brother didn't kill him. If he survives his injuries, I shall keep my word and be merciful, but I cannot allow him to continue to rule. You, on the other hand…'

Just then, the door was pushed open, diverting their attention, and a little face peered around it. Leof… No!

Cwen's blood ran cold, immediately fearful for her child's safety. She had told him to stay hidden. But the boy ran into the room before she could stop him.

'Mother!' he cried, waving his wooden sword around in front of him.

'Leof, you should not be here!' she said, scolding him, rushing forwards, trying to stem the sudden surge of panic coursing through her veins.

But Njal reached him first, stepping between them, scooping up the boy under his arms.

Leof's maid, Eadhild, burst through the door after him, and when she saw Cwen and Njal, she looked between them, horror-struck, her face ashen. 'I am so sorry, Your Highness. I just couldn't hold him back. When he heard your voice…'

'Get out,' Njal said sternly, making Cwen and the maid wince. And Eadhild didn't need to be told twice. She pulled the door closed just as quickly as she had opened it, causing it to shudder in its frame.

Njal held up the boy, giving him a thorough inspection, as Leof wriggled in his grip. And Cwen felt afraid—more frightened than she had on the battlefield when her father had fallen, or even when she'd seen her people bound. To see her boy in the arms of this imposing warrior...

She approached them both, holding out her arms, reaching for the child.

'Please, don't hurt him.'

Njal scowled and turned his gaze on her. 'I would never hurt a child, like *some*.'

She could tell he meant her father, and she knew he must still be furious about what had happened to his own family. He might decide to find new ways to take his revenge. Would he spare her boy? 'Give him to me then,' she whispered.

He looked back at Leof, moving the boy onto his hip and relieving him of his toy weapon, placing it down on the table. 'He is your son?'

'Yes. And much too wayward,' she muttered, chastising Leof again.

'Like his mother, perhaps?' Njal said, cocking that eyebrow again. 'He looks just like you.'

'People often tell me that.' And she was glad of it—that he had the same dark hair and grey eyes as she did; the same pale skin.

'I came to protect you, Mother,' Leof said, struggling in the warrior's hold.

Njal grinned, and Cwen's stomach tightened in response. It changed his whole face. He was incredible—intimidating, formidable, but also fascinating, and she couldn't tear her gaze away from him. She didn't know what was the matter with her. She didn't want to think him attractive—he was a monster, or so her father had said.

'Did you come to fight me, Boy?'

Leof tipped his chin up, in the same way she often did. 'Yes.'

Njal's smile grew wider, and it did nothing to ease her nerves. 'I like your courage. It'll stand you in good stead later in life.'

'Please…' Cwen whispered.

Njal shrugged, and after giving the boy a final look, he set the child down and Leof raced over to her. She crouched and pulled him into her chest, tightly, momentarily relieved, but excruciatingly aware of the warrior's dark gaze still watching her.

'How old?' Njal asked.

'Five.'

'And his father?'

'Dead.'

He stared at her, nodding. 'Rumours travel fast through the settlements. I remember now, the men said you'd lost your husband—that you were widowed this past year.' His eyes swung back to the child. 'But I didn't know about the boy. This…changes things.'

She sank her teeth into her lower lip.

'You see, here in this room, we now have three claimants to the throne, two Saxons, one Dane. Two who have cause to want me dead,' Njal said, gesturing to them both.

She stood, placing her hands on Leof's shoulders, tucking him close to her legs. 'We are no threat to you.' And yet even as she said the words, she knew that if Njal was to set them free, given the chance the Saxon ealdormen might plot to remove Njal from his newfound power; to place her father, or her, even her son back on the throne…and now she realised he knew it too.

He studied her carefully. 'I need to make sure of that.'

She felt her knees tremble. 'I see.'

Now that he had found out about another heir to the throne, would he arrange to have them both killed? She drew Leof closer still, as she watched the warrior walk back towards the fire. He braced his hand on the wooden mantel. He looked up at the tapestry of their kingdom on the wall, deep in thought.

'It is my intention to bring our people together, not create more conflict.' Finally, he dropped his arm, coming away from the fire, and took a step towards her, a plan clearly forming in his mind. 'So you will stay here in Jorvik, where I can keep watch over you.'

She shook her head. 'My father would never agree to stay, not as a prisoner with you ruling over him.' He was much too proud.

'No,' he said, closing the distance between them. 'You misunderstand me. I am not talking of your father. I will allow him to retire to the country, to live out his days under strict guard—a merciful sentence for the things he has done. But you, you will remain here.'

Her eyes widened. 'As your captive?'

'No, as my wife.'

Chapter Three

Cwen took a sharp intake of breath. 'You can't mean…?'

'We will marry. It is the only way I can be sure of your family's—and your people's—allegiance. To stop the intense persecution of my people. It is the only way to ensure the rightful succession of power.'

He seemed so cold, so controlled, as if he was talking about a battle plan, not a marriage.

'No!' she said, shaking her head, so aware Leof was listening to this, and wondering what he was thinking. 'I can't! I won't! Why would I *want* to marry you?'

The tension was heavy in the air as Njal placed his hands on his hips. 'You are set to lose everything today—your throne, your title, your family… But I am not the savage you think I am. I do not want to see that happen. If we marry, you would get to keep all of that, and rule the entire kingdom in your father's stead, by my side. Would you rather face exile, or death?'

'What kind words from my supposed future husband,' she said bitterly, the enormity of what he was asking of her slowly sinking in.

He was giving her an ultimatum, she realised, and she raised her hand to her temple, suddenly feeling light-headed. Sick. She couldn't believe what he was suggesting. Another enforced marriage. Yet this time she did not even know the man. Worse, they were enemies. Their people had caused each other so much pain.

'But you despise me,' she said, shaking her head.

'I imagine the feeling is mutual. But this is about more than you and me. It is about the salvation of both our peoples. And we will both make this sacrifice—for them. Do this, and you will secure protection for all of your family, the boy included,' he said, inclining his head in the direction of Leof, trembling at her heels. 'Say yes, and I will release your subjects—I will guarantee no harm will come to them.'

Had he planned this all along? Surely not. She had not seen it coming. Could she go through with it?

She had never thought she would marry again, let alone to a Dane—a man from the north, known for their barbaric, brutal ways. She had married for duty once before—given as a gift by her father to the son of one of his allies.

She had always hoped she would marry for love. But it was not meant to be. Instead, she had been forced to agree to a political alliance. She had known Feran since childhood. She hadn't cared for him in a romantic way, or he her, but she had known she had to forego love for her family. Disobeying her father hadn't been an option, and she had felt resentful and angry at first—her only saving grace was she'd got to remove herself from the king's watchful eye. She'd wanted her own home, to lead her own life. Fortunately, she and Feran had come to an arrangement they were both happy with, and she had found contentment. Then fate had intervened, and they had been blessed with a son. But when Feran had died she'd been forced to move back here, to be the property and puppet of her father once more. Although this time, he had taken more of an interest in her boy than her, shaping and moulding him to sit on the throne one day.

'What of my son and his title?' she asked, gripping Leof's shoulders tight.

Njal glanced at the child again, and to her surprise, he hunched down, lowering himself to Leof's level. 'Do you like it here in Jorvik, Boy?'

'Yes.'

'What do you like about it?'

Leof shrugged. 'The river. The fishing. Not the constant fighting, or the lack of food. I'm hungry. But it's home.'

Njal smiled—and she wished he wouldn't, it did peculiar things to her body. 'We'll get you some food, don't you worry about that. I like to fish as well, although unfortunately I'm a lot more skilled at the fighting. I was born a Dane, but my parents brought me over to England when I was younger, and I like it here too. Now I view it more my home than anywhere else. Perhaps you could show me the best fishing spots sometime.'

The boy nodded. 'All right,' he said, wary, looking up at Cwen for approval. He placed his hand in hers. 'But only if Mother can come too.'

Her heart felt as if it could burst at his open display of loyalty.

'That is up to your mother and the choices she makes,' Njal said, rising back up to his full, towering height. '*I would never separate you. But you must go back to your maid now, while we finish talking here.*'

They watched as Leof walked over to the door and tentatively pulled it open, giving them both one last look, still concerned for his mother.

'I won't hurt her,' Njal said.

'Promise?' Leof said, hesitating in the doorway, and Cwen felt her emotions threaten to overwhelm her.

'I swear it.'

The door shut behind him and she felt the Northman's gaze turn on her again, as she furiously blinked away her tears. She could not allow herself to look weak in front of him.

'If I do this, I would need your word that my son will no longer be a threat to you—that you won't seek to remove him as my heir.'

'I give you my word,' he said, coming closer. 'Unless, that is, we should have a son of our own.'

Cwen's breath left her body. 'You mean—you expect me to lie with you? Have children with you?' she gasped, appalled.

'That *is* the expectation of every king, is it not—to have heirs to succeed them? And the aim of every marriage,' he said.

It had not been important in her first.

She felt the room start to spin and she reached out a hand to steady herself on the table. They were strangers; adversaries, and now he was not only suggesting that they marry, but that they become lovers?

She knew he was offering her salvation. He could have already had her and her family killed. He could have slaughtered her people, just as her father had done to his. But still, he was asking the impossible—for her to be intimate with him. She just couldn't do it.

He stalked towards her, watching her closely, as if wondering at her objections, and her stomach tightened in response. She knew she must not give anything away. She had to protect herself, her son, her secret.

'What's the matter?' he said, coming towards her. 'It's not as if you haven't been married before. Slept with a man before.'

'But you are a Dane.' And yet, that simple fact didn't seem to be dampening her intense, visceral reaction to him, the awful and peculiar excitement she felt when he came near her.

'So?' His eyes narrowed on her. 'Are you afraid of me?'

Did he want her to be? She refused to give him that satisfaction. 'I'm not afraid,' she lied, shaking her head.

Her dishonesty had always been critical to the survival of those she loved, knowing keeping the truth hidden was best for the monarchy and the realm. She had once made a promise that her secret would never be disclosed, and it was especially important now, when her family were at their most vulnerable.

He came closer still. 'You do not like me?' he asked, his lips curling upwards, a wicked glint lighting up his eyes.

'Why would I? You're the man who has brought an army to our door, who has seized my home for himself. Perhaps my father brought this upon us, perhaps we deserved it. But still, I don't know you!'

He reached out and took her chin in his hand, lifting her gaze to his, and his touch sent a disturbing bolt of heat through her body. 'That is easily rectified,' he said, his eyes darkening.

She wasn't sure what he was intending to do and in a sudden panic, she reached out for the poker, gripping it in her hand and holding it up, brandishing it at him.

'I don't *want* to know you!' she said, stepping away, the backs of her thighs hitting the table. She was terrified at the traitorous feelings racing through her body. 'We are the opposite, you and I. We are as different as day is to night. As right is to wrong.'

'As dead is to alive?'

She shuddered at the underlying threat, moving around the room again.

He raised his eyebrow. 'I'm intrigued—do you mean to kill me now, when your father has tried for two years without success?' He took a step towards her. 'When I have spoken about nothing but peace?'

'Don't come any closer.'

'Put that down,' he said, his voice lethal.

'Stay where you are,' she threatened.

He ignored her, coming closer still, bearing down on her. 'I don't want to hurt you, Cwen, I promised your boy.'

'I said stop.'

'And I don't tolerate disobedience or deceit.'

'I mean it,' she said.

'So do I.' And he grabbed her, making her gasp, wrestling with her for the makeshift weapon, covering her hand with his. 'Give that to me.' His body pressed against hers, backing her up against the wall, and she froze.

'Think about your next move very carefully,' he said. His voice was deadly.

She felt her chest rising and falling unsteadily, and saw a muscle flicker in his temple. She knew she had riled him. But he'd made her afraid by getting so close.

He prised her fingers off the metal and she let the poker slip from her hand onto the floor. She went to struggle, to get away, but he gripped her wrists, holding her fast, lifting them up and pinning them either side of her head against the wall.

He stared down at her, and she felt her whole body tremble.

She knew he was angry, and yet she was more concerned by the way her body was responding to his; the feel of his chest; his thighs holding her in place. And that he wasn't showing any signs of letting her go.

'Is it even lawful?' she whispered. 'A Saxon and a Dane marrying... Isn't it wrong?'

Surely all the feelings sparking through her body weren't right?

'Are you not a pagan?' she asked.

'I am still fascinated by the Norse gods. I always will be. But I had a Christian upbringing. I was baptised.' His warm breath whispered across her face.

She shook her head. 'How can that be?'

'My father came here to make a better life for us. He fell in love with this country. We all did. So much so, he turned to your god instead of ours. So yes, it is lawful. Is that the last of your concerns?'

'Hardly!'

And he grinned.

'I don't understand why you would want to do this,' she breathed. 'What's in it for you?'

'I would have thought that was obvious,' he said, in a slow, deliberate way, his eyes dipping to the rise and fall of her breasts, and she felt another responsive rush in her stomach; her face heat. 'I gain a wife of royal blood—

someone who has the trust of the ealdormen, and the people, who will help to secure my place here and bring peace to Northumbria. With you as my queen, they will accept me as king more readily.'

For some absurd reason, his answer disappointed her. He was just like her father. He saw her merely as a diplomatic tool, someone who could help him get what he wanted—lands, power. That was what was truly important to him. But what had she been expecting him to say?

'So you're willing to go through with it, without knowing anything about me?' she said. 'All for the desire of the crown? It is a heavy burden. It comes with a loss of freedom. Self-sacrifice.'

'I think I can cope.'

He gently pressed himself closer to her, and she turned her head. He leaned in towards her neck, drawing in her scent, and she gasped, as a sudden, powerful need surged through her. When he raised his head, his eyes stared down into hers. 'And that's not my only desire.'

Suddenly, the door burst open, and their heads turned in unison to look.

'Sorry to interrupt,' said his man, Bjorn, looking perplexed when he saw them, taking in the intimate scene. 'But you're needed in the hall. It's urgent.'

Cwen immediately pushed at Njal's chest with her hands, staggering away from him, her face mutinous. But he still gripped her wrist.

He bent his head to whisper in her ear. 'We're not done yet. We will finish this later.'

As they raced down the corridor, Njal had to admit, it was an unusual place to meet the woman who would become your wife—in the midst of a battle. And yet the thought had been growing in his mind all afternoon. He hadn't been able to stop thinking about her beauty since he'd pulled her into his arms on the ride back to the fortress.

He knew he shouldn't want her. He had sworn off women, determined to never love again—for love could be used against you in the most appalling ways. But he did have needs, needs that had to be sated.

He had been so close to kissing her back there. All he'd needed to do was bend his head and press his lips against hers... If she hadn't attacked him with that poker, he might well have done. But her rebellious actions, and the challenge in her pale grey eyes, hadn't put him off. Instead, they'd sent a shaft of heat right down to his groin, making him hard, and for an incredulous moment he felt his body lean into hers. She was too much of a temptation. But just as his face had hovered over hers, his man had rushed into the room.

'There's a situation,' Bjorn said now, distracting him, and he tried to focus on his man's words as they strode along the passageway. He hoped they would help to stamp out his desire.

'What is it? What's happened?'

'It's your brother...'

As they pushed open the wooden doors into the hall, Njal's heart sank. Taking in the scene, he felt Cwen tense beside him, and an uncomfortable, bristling sensation crawled over his body, cooling his heated blood. Ove had taken up position in one of the thrones, his long legs curved disrespectfully over the arms, while he spouted orders and demands at the Saxon ealdormen, who were still tied up. Some had been forced down on their knees, while others were running around fetching him ale, or scrubbing his boots. Njal's men were awkwardly watching on, as if uncertain whether they should be stepping in, trying to stop this from happening.

Njal had been afraid of this. He'd been aware that once they took the fortress for themselves, bringing them power they had never known before, it would only serve to further bring out the brute in his brother.

He clenched his fists. Why was Ove being so destructive, behaving like this? He was both embarrassed and concerned about him in equal measure.

As the door thumped shut behind them, everyone turned to stare at him and the princess, wondering what would happen next, and a hush descended on the room.

If his father was here now, he would have known what to do; how to deal with it. Ove had worshipped him, as had Njal. And yet, he was glad his parents weren't here to witness this. They'd be ashamed, as was he. And yet he could only blame himself; how could he not see Ove's shortcomings as his own failure, for he had raised him these past two winters—Ove was his responsibility.

There had been a time when Ove had looked up to him, wanted to be like him. Where had he gone so wrong? It weighed heavy on his heart.

He'd tried to protect him, keeping him from difficult choices—decisions he and his men had had to make that determined if others survived or died. But he wondered now, had keeping him from that caused this opposition to authority; his desire for power?

He'd let him get away with far too much for far too long. He'd been too lenient. He always made excuses for him, because of what they'd been through. But enough was enough. He couldn't tolerate this here. Now was a time for stability, not more disturbance.

'It seems you're in my seat, Brother,' Njal said, leading Cwen through the throng towards the dais, trying to keep his temper in check. 'I thought I said keep order, not create chaos.'

'And like I said earlier, why should you be the only one to enjoy yourself?' Ove replied.

'Well, your fun is over now.'

Njal's men appeared relieved to have their leader back, and with one nod of his head, they drew closer, their hands on their swords. 'Do not force me to make you get down from there, Ove.'

He sent him a look that said don't cross me.

Ove sneered, taking in the advancing warriors, and perhaps realising he wouldn't win this argument, he reluctantly lowered his feet and stood. Njal rolled his shoulders, trying to release some of his tension. Good, at least he was backing down. There had been enough fighting—he did not want to be at arms with his brother too, especially not in front of his men and the Saxon nobles, or Cwen. He needed to appear in control.

As Ove went to walk past him, Njal gripped his shoulder and leaned in to speak in his ear.

'You went against my wishes today. Any more behaviour against my word will not be tolerated. Is that understood?'

Ove threw him off.

'What's going on with you?' he asked. 'We have achieved what we set out to do. We have avenged their deaths.'

'How exactly? The king still lives.'

'But we have toppled him from power. He can never hurt anyone else,' Njal said.

'*I* did that!' Ove roared. 'I did what you could not. I wounded him, bringing a halt to the conflict. Me! And I would have ended him, for good. Now you're basking in *my* glory and stealing *my* rewards,' he said, slanting a glance at Cwen.

'You want the princess for yourself?' Njal asked, his anger rising.

He wasn't sure what disturbed him more—his brother's desire for power or his interest in Cwen. And a peculiar sliver of possession darted through him. Usually, he would give his brother whatever he wanted, but he couldn't give him this. The princess was his.

He put his hand around Ove's shoulder and led him over to the side of the room.

'If I am to have it my way, she is to be my wife, Brother.'

Ove's eyes widened. 'You intend to make an alliance with the very people who murdered our families? That sickens me. Mother, Father—they would be turning in their graves. I don't understand,' he said, his brow darkening. 'If you want her, why not take her and be done with it? It's just desire—only fleeting. You can do something about that. And once you have, these feelings will disappear. Why do you need to marry her? She's the enemy. The worst of her kind.'

Njal never acted on instinct. He liked to have a plan, to think things through—and be meticulous in his execution. So had he gone mad from desire, like Ove suggested? He didn't know the princess, yet he had just demanded to marry her on impulse, guided by the strength of one look on the battlefield that had left an enduring impression—a lust that needed to be sated.

She had spirit and he wanted her—so badly, he was willing to tie himself to her in marriage to make her his. But was he once again allowing himself to be led by passion when he couldn't trust her?

Njal knew he had to question his own instincts where women were concerned—his opinion couldn't be relied upon; he had got it so very wrong in the past. If he hadn't been so caught unawares by a woman before, he might have been able to save his family. And his brother was right—there was nothing stopping him from taking Cwen to one of the back rooms now and having her. Apart from…he wanted to do this right. And despite the desire he felt for her, this union *could* help their people. The princess had the support of the people. She was strong. She would help him unite the kingdom. That was what was most important here.

He would also be a fool to release two heirs to the throne of Northumbria. Even if the princess wasn't like her father—and he hadn't yet made up his mind about that—there would be no end of plots from the Saxon nobles to overthrow him and reunite Cwen or her son with the crown. No, he needed to keep her close, for strategic purposes, and where was closer than beside him, on the throne and in his bed?

'We must look to the future—be strategic,' Njal said. 'You are much too reckless, Ove, you think with your sword and nothing else.'

'I think with my sword because that is all these people

deserve,' Ove said. 'To feel the tip of my blade. I want them all dead.'

'It won't bring our family back.'

'No, but it'll make me feel better, to show these people what we're capable of.'

'Or we show them mercy, which is a lot harder to do. We show them we're capable of reasoning and negotiation—peace over fighting. We cannot be at war for ever. It is no way to live. That's not the life Mother and Father would have wanted for you, or me.' He placed a hand on his brother's shoulder again. 'And I do not want to fight among us.'

Njal sighed, wondering how he could get through to him. 'Do you remember the story Father told us about the giantess Skadi?' They would often sit around the campfire on the beach at night, sharing stories about the Norse deities. He and Ove had listened to their father in rapture.

Ove nodded. 'The one where the Norse gods killed her father?'

'Thiazi, yes. And she charged into Asgard, the kingdom of the gods, to seek revenge. She threatened to murder them all...' Njal said.

'Unless they met her demands,' Ove finished for him.

Njal nodded. 'They let Skadi pick one of the Norse gods to be her husband—one of her father's murderers, as compensation. She received the title of goddess upon her marriage...'

He remembered the tale well. Especially the ending—Odin threw Thiazi's eyes into the sky to become stars. He had thought of it often since, wondering if his own father was watching down on them. He hoped to make him proud, not appalled, as Ove had implied.

His brother shook his head. 'You could be king without her. You could kill them all and rule.'

'I could, but there would never be peace,' Njal said. 'If I marry the princess it will secure our position here. *Your* position here. I know we never wanted it, or set out to achieve it, but we can make a difference—we have power we never imagined,' Njal said.

Ove looked up at him, and he could tell his words had appeased him a little. 'I like the sound of that. And if you're king, you will ensure I will be next in line to the throne, yes?'

'You desire to rule?' he asked, shocked. He would always think of him as his baby brother, despite seeing the warrior he had become. He realised he shouldn't be surprised Ove would want power to wield, but he was much too rash to make considered decisions and lead—especially a realm of people he despised. He had the feeling it would end in disaster. And yet it sounded as if he had more of an interest in ruling than their own relationship. 'You've changed, Brother,' Njal said.

'So have you.'

They stared at each other for a long moment. 'Go, walk off your anger, while I sort out this mess,' Njal said.

To his relief, Ove didn't try his patience any further, but instead stalked away—but not before pushing over a statue near the door, sending it smashing to the ground as he made his exit, causing everyone in the hall to mutter and gasp, shaking their heads in disapproval.

Njal took a breath and turned round to face them, walking back to Cwen.

'How can you think our people would be able to live here together, side by side, after seeing that?' Cwen hissed at him.

'We will just have to set a good example,' he said, determined, set on his course.

'The time for fighting is over. Take the prisoners to the barn,' he announced to his men. 'Tonight, we remember the fallen and raise a toast to the future.' And then he looked back at Cwen. 'I will have your answer by morning.'

Chapter Four

The great hall had been set up for a feast and Njal watched as his men tucked heartily into their food. The fires had been lit in the hearths, casting a warm glow around the vast room, and everyone seemed to be in fine spirits. He had to pinch himself he was here. He had wondered if there would ever come a day where Danes would be safe in this kingdom, knowing there was such ill feeling between their peoples, but looking around the room, for the first time in a long time, he felt hopeful.

They'd brought in some of the livestock they'd seized out on the plains to be slaughtered, and the meal of stewed mutton and vegetables tasted good. It felt even better in his empty stomach. He hadn't dined like this in weeks, and the ale was flowing freely, although he had instructed his men not to drink too much. He knew they deserved to celebrate their hard-won victory, but it was their first night here and they needed to stay alert.

Cwen was sat by his side at the long table and he could feel the tension rippling off her, her body rigid, her knees pressed together. She had changed into an elegant burgundy tunic, embroidered with gold trim—a far cry from the armour and breeches she had been wearing on the battlefield—and she looked exquisite. It showed off her womanly curves; her slender waist. He'd thought she'd looked stunning before, even in her chain-mail, but now... His mouth had dried when she'd appeared back in the hall.

He was so aware of her, yet he didn't want to be. Her sweet, delicate scent reminiscent of bluebells wrapped around him, intoxicating him far greater than any ale, and every time their arms brushed, his skin burned and he noticed she pulled back.

'How is your father?' he asked. 'I trust Bjorn took you to see him?'

'What do you care?'

His eyes lanced her. 'Because whether he lives or dies, it impacts us all.'

He took the opportunity to openly study her. Her thick, dark hair had been rebraided and half pinned up, exposing the slender curve of her neck, and the jewels in her defiant crown were twinkling in the candlelight. He shouldn't like her. He shouldn't want to talk to her, touch her, or be inside her. But God help him, he did.

He would have to be careful. Right now, he had an enormous task ahead of him, to bring a rebellious kingdom under his control, and he could not allow her to steal away his focus. He had let a woman turn his head and bewitch him once before, and he had lost everything.

'Are you close to your parents?' He hadn't missed the anger that had flared in her eyes and that had lashed out behind her words earlier, when she'd told him the king had always controlled her actions.

She looked at him for the first time that evening. 'I have come to understand over the years that being my father's daughter comes with a distinct lack of freedom. A great deal of sacrifice. Since I was a little girl, I've had no choice in my religion, my movements—how I should conduct myself—or the freedom to marry who I like.'

'I see.'

Was she talking about him, or her previous marriage—or both?

She hadn't lifted her spoon once—had barely eaten anything. Instead, she was furiously twisting the silver ring on her wedding finger. Was she still grieving for her late husband? He knew the feeling of grief all too well. Did she still care for the man? He didn't like the thought—or the visions that entered his mind upon thinking of her in the arms of another. But he knew that was absurd. It had no right to bother him. Of course she had a past, as did he.

He wondered at her prickly mood. Was she worried about her father, who obviously still hadn't awoken, or his men dominating the hall? Or maybe she was thinking about his proposal. He certainly hadn't been able to get it out of his mind all evening: whether he was doing the right thing.

'But you're still thinking about my offer?'

'Was that what it was? I thought it was an order.'

'If it was, I'd have my answer by now.'

Was he being a brute, giving her an ultimatum? He had said marry him, or face banishment, or death. But no, he didn't think so, given the circumstances. He was offering her a great deal in return for being his wife, and he knew she wasn't as immune to him as she was making out. He had felt the way she'd trembled in his arms earlier, seen her eyes widen as he'd pressed against her, and her tongue dart out of her mouth to moisten her lips.

'Have you been married before?' she asked.

'No,' he said, taking a sip of his ale.

The truth was, when he was younger, he had thought that one day he might find a wife and settle down. He had always wanted children. His father had told him, often, that it was the most wonderful experience a man could have—that it had given him a purpose and a great sense of pride. He'd hoped for a deep love like his parents had. But when they had been killed, his dreams had turned to those of revenge. It had been years since he'd been with a woman. Not since Synnove.

He had been young and foolish and thought he'd been in love. They'd met at the nearby market and had struck up a conversation, but looking back now, his father had better instincts than he did. He had cautioned Njal against the relationship—not because she was from a wealthy Saxon family, but because her own father didn't approve. His father had thought it would mean trouble, and how Njal wished he hadn't been right. He had told her all about his family and their settlement during their late-night trysts down at the beach. Taking a sip of his ale now, he wondered if she'd ever cared for him, or if she'd been using him all along.

In the end, he'd lost everything because of her. And the fact he'd been making love to her while his parents lay dying—that she had known what was happening—had been the ultimate betrayal. He had struggled to come to terms with it ever since. He'd been determined never to make himself vulnerable or trust a woman again. These past few winters, he hadn't been interested in taking another woman to bed, but looking at Cwen now, he hated the fact that he was. Yes, he could see the benefits of marrying a Saxon for peace, to unite their peoples, but he resented the fact that his desire led him into making that decision. He didn't want to want her like this. And while he suddenly felt each one of those long years of abstinence in every aching, excited breath he took, at the same time, it deeply unsettled him. He must remember to steel himself against her, to focus on what was truly important for his people's contentment, and not just his own satisfaction.

'Is your heart too frozen for love?' she said, goading him. 'It must be as cold as they say, in the north, to create men with such icy hearts,' Cwen said. 'Where is it you're from?'

'A fishing village called Issvollr in Denmark.'

'But you cannot fish well?' She quirked her eyebrow. 'That's what you told Leof...'

'I love the water, but when we arrived here, it became all about the farming.' His father had promised them fertile land and a home to call their own, and that's what he'd given them. 'It might come as a surprise to you, but I used to raise animals and sow barley and rye, not fight.' He had found a great satisfaction in growing something from the soil that you could eat.

Njal had been full of wonderment for the giant skies and sandy beaches, green pastures and the uninterrupted views of the ocean. The weather had been a lot kinder than in Denmark and there was much better food to eat. He and Ove had been happy. They'd spent their days helping their parents or Njal had kept Ove entertained on the beach or in the forest. They'd been inseparable, building huge dens out of wood and fortresses out of sand. Who knew they'd ever get to live in and rule over a real one?

'I hope it was worth it?'

'At first, yes. Later, no.' He and his growing army of men had slept under canvas these past two years, moving around from camp to camp, settlement to settlement, battle to battle. He'd almost lost sight of why his father had brought them here. In some ways, it was colder than up north. He leaned back in his chair. 'Now? That remains to be seen.'

Suddenly, he felt as if their union was vital—not just to bind their people together, but for his sanity. And yet she kept toying with that damn wedding ring on her finger, reminding him she had once belonged to another.

'Do you miss him?' he asked, and regretted the question the moment it had left his lips. Yet perversely, he needed to know the answer.

'Who?' she asked.

'Your late husband.' He placed his hand over hers, his fingers running gently over her wedding ring finger, down to the cool metal ring. Searing heat shot through his body as their skin touched—did she feel it too?

She snatched her hand back. 'Yes. Every day.'

He nodded, but bitterness burned in his throat. He didn't like the way her voice turned wistful when she spoke of her former lover. But how could he be jealous of a corpse? The man was dead.

Cwen could barely concentrate. The moment Njal's hand had covered hers, his fingers circling the silver wedding band, it had sent sparks through her veins. It felt intimate, and she'd quickly retrieved her hand from under his.

'Who was he? What happened to him?'

'He was the son of my father's ally, in the north of Northumbria. His home—our home—' she frowned '—was in Bamburgh. He died in a riding accident.'

Njal nodded, as if taking that in.

Feran had never been a keen warrior, so some would say it was a blessing it happened before her father called on him to fight in the fields. He would have hated that. She had come to terms with it now, but when she had first received the news of Feran's death, she had been distraught. Although their marriage had been implemented against her will, he had become her closest friend and confidante, and even though her son was too young to properly understand, breaking the news to Leof had been devastating.

'Your boy must miss his father.'

She nodded. 'I fear he won't remember him.'

'Perhaps that's kinder. Ove and I suffered greatly, grieving for our parents.'

Njal seemed pensive, brooding—she had thought he would be gloating, celebrating his victory today, and yet he was subdued, still on guard. And she wondered if he had always been this way, or if the things her father had done, and the war that had raged on since, had made him like this—this cautious, this hard. Losing his family and his home, his feelings of security must have been shattered. Had he ever recovered from that? She could tell he saw it as his responsibility; his obligation, to keep his people safe. But none of this should matter to her, she told herself. Only, if she was going to have to marry him, if she was going to have her free will taken away once more, and be forced into another arranged marriage, it would be good to know more about him; the heart of him.

She noticed he'd washed—the blood and dirt from the battle had gone from his skin and his hair was still damp. Had he gone down to the river? He'd changed into a dark tunic, the sleeves rolled up to his elbows, revealing strange markings of blue ink on his forearms, although he still wore his leather chain-mail vest. Was he expecting more conflict? Surely no one had the stomach for it tonight?

She could tell he had the trust and loyalty of his men—they looked up to him; she had seen it in the way they had been relieved when he had returned to the hall earlier, bolstering their confidence with the Ove situation.

'Where is your brother tonight?' she said, looking around the room, realising she hadn't seen the brute, and she wasn't sorry.

Njal shrugged, his brow darkening. 'He hasn't returned since his outburst earlier.'

It had shocked her today, when Njal had said he'd raised his own brother as his son. It made him more relatable to her—that they had this huge thing in common. That they were both parents, of sorts, trying to do their best against the odds. She had recognised the confliction on his face when dealing with Ove in the hall. She knew parenting could be challenging, and her heart had softened a little towards him, seeing him try to keep his brother in check.

'I have a man watching him.'

'Is he so little to be trusted?'

'I also have a man watching you,' he said, leaning in and lowering his voice.

'Why?' she gasped, her gaze swinging back to look at him.

'For your protection—and my own, after today,' he said wryly.

She grimaced. She couldn't believe she'd tried to attack him with a poker! What had she been thinking? But she had felt desperate, frantic, as his body had pressed closer to hers—she hadn't known what he was going to do. And it wasn't a bad thing that he knew she would stand up to him if she had to. 'So I am to be a prisoner in my own home now?'

'Until we come to an agreement, yes.'

'I want to add in some conditions, before I make my final decision,' she said, evenly.

'I've already been more than fair.'

'It's about my people,' she said. 'You've been starving them for weeks…'

His jaw clenched. 'It wouldn't have come to that, if your father had come out and faced us sooner.'

'Nevertheless, they're hungry, thirsty, scared. What are you going to do about it when you release them. *If* you release them.'

'I told you I would. And if they wish, they are free to go—to leave Jorvik. If they choose to stay, no harm will come to them, but I will have their allegiance. They must bend the knee.' He put down his tankard. 'Tomorrow, you can give me the tour of the city, so I can assess any damage and secure our defences. I am willing to place you in charge of the people—see who needs aid, where there's food or water shortages. Good enough?'

She nodded, surprised he would put her in charge of anything. 'Yes.'

And as she drained her drink, Cwen was beginning to realise she would probably have to say yes to his proposal. What other choice did she have? None, as her mother had reminded her earlier. The queen was already distraught—about her husband's injury and their predicament, thinking they would be sent away from their home with nothing but the clothes on their backs, and when Cwen had told her about Njal's proposition, her mother had insisted she go ahead with it.

'You must do this, Cwen. It is the only way for us to keep a foothold here in Jorvik—to keep our bloodline on the throne. This is what your father would want.'

'And what about what I want?' Cwen had dared argue.

'Don't be foolish—you should know by now no woman gets to marry for love. I certainly didn't,' her mother had said. 'What makes you think you're any different?'

Cwen had felt the weight of the world upon her. Again. It wasn't the first time her mother had asked her to do something life-changing, for the good of the family. For the monarchy. The people. Their relationship had become strained over the years, since she'd been asked to keep her mother's secret from the world to protect the queen's marriage, her life, and it was all because of the type of romantic love her mother was saying Cwen could never have. Although Cwen wouldn't change what had passed, she still felt resentment seep through her veins, and the heavy burden of responsibility her mother had inflicted upon her—she wore it like shackles around her wrists.

Now her subjects were looking to her for reassurance, for release from their own bonds, and she would not abandon them. She had a strong sense of duty and she knew her mother was right—she would have to do this for the good of the kingdom, to keep a Saxon on the throne, and to secure her family's lineage. It was best for everyone.

But was it best for her? She felt as if a noose was tightening around her neck.

She thought about how her heart raced when Njal looked down into her eyes; how her pulse skittered when he touched her. In any normal circumstances, she imagined it would be a dream to marry a man who made a woman feel the way he did. But to her, it would be a nightmare. Because being with a man who made her feel this way, a hard-hearted man who despised her and would never understand her predicament, would be a danger to herself and her son.

'But you cannot allow the Dane to discover the truth about you—about Leof. Promise me, Cwen,' her mother had said, taking her hand. 'You will do all you can.'

She had heard all about the sexual appetites of the Danes—that they weren't easily satisfied; that they were never gentle. And Njal had been clear about his desires—she knew he was a man who could never be celibate.

He had even expressed his desire for children and the very thought filled her with dread. He wanted to see his bloodline on the royal throne. He wanted a legacy, and with her heritage and title, he thought she was the perfect candidate for the role.

Only, she wasn't. She couldn't give him what he wanted—because the simple fact was, she couldn't bear him a child.

Desperate to get away from him, to be out of his intense proximity for a while, she pushed her chair back and stood.

'Where are you going?' he asked, gripping her wrist, holding her fast.

'I'm tired. It's been a long day. I'm going to check on Leof and try to get some sleep. Where…where exactly will you be sleeping?' she asked, her brow furrowing, a blush rising.

'Is that an invitation?' He flashed her a wicked grin and her pulse raced.

'Definitely not.'

Still, he pushed out his chair and stood too.

'What are you doing?' She hated the sound of panic in her voice.

'I will see you to your chamber door.'

'Please.' She sighed, pinching her nose. 'I can find my own way. There is no need.'

'Are you always this argumentative—this wilful?'

'Yes,' she said, raising her chin.

His fingers stayed at her wrist, but she cast him off and began to walk, retreating to the rooms at the back of the hall, all too aware of him following, close behind, like a mighty hunter stalking his prey. The corridors were eerily empty and she picked up the pace, not wanting to be alone with him for a moment longer than necessary.

She reached Leof's door and peered inside. He was fast asleep, and Eadhild sat in the chair, keeping an eye on him. She was incredibly grateful to her. She gave her son a kiss on the forehead and tucked him in, so aware the dark warrior was watching her from the door. When she pulled the door to and carried on down the corridor, reaching her own chamber, she paused, shuffling her feet, uneasy about Njal knowing where she would be sleeping all night. But that was absurd. If she was going to wed him, he would need to know a lot more about her than that.

'It's been quite a day. I bet you're exhausted. Get some rest now. Lock your door behind you,' he said, going to leave. 'Sleep well.'

And his words surprised her. He was leaving? She told herself that was a good thing, and allowed herself a sigh of relief that he seemed to be retreating, back to the hall. That she wouldn't have to see him again till morning.

'Njal,' she said, calling him back, unsure why.

'Yes?'

'I am sorry—for what my father did. There is no excuse. But you must believe—I didn't know. I couldn't have done anything to stop it.'

He gave a short, sharp nod in acknowledgement.

'Do you have *no* concerns about this, about *us*—none at all?' she said.

'No,' he said, taking a step back towards her. 'You've heard my reasons. You know the people here and the way things work. You do not seem cruel, like your father, and your people look up to you. With you by my side, I do believe we could unite our peoples. They could finally have two rulers who would lead with respect, not fear.'

It was a good reason. Everything she did was to protect her son, her country, her people. She wasn't about to change that now, even if she had to put herself at risk.

But it wasn't enough.

'Plus, you're strong,' he said, coming closer. 'You aren't afraid to stand up to me, or give me your opinion. I'll need that.'

She swallowed. Would he really want her opinions—listen to her, and involve her in his decisions? He had said she could take charge of the people on the morrow. She could scarcely believe it. And yet if it was honesty he was looking for, he was speaking to the wrong woman, as she had deceived him already. Could she really have a second marriage that was based on a lie? It felt wretched.

'But perhaps the most important reason of all is the one I should have said first.' He came even nearer and she stepped back, her shoulders hitting her door. 'I think you're beautiful. I thought so from the first moment I saw you. And despite the blood that runs through your veins, who your father is, what he did, unbelievably, I want you.' Her breath stalled, his words both terrifying and pleasing her at once—and even more worrying, she felt a reciprocal rush in her stomach. 'I have to have you,' he said simply. 'And I don't believe this feeling is one-sided.'

She forced herself to laugh, but it came out a little too shrill. 'You're wrong.'

'You deny it?'

'Absolutely.'

He raised his eyebrows in mock surprise, putting his hands on his hips. 'You don't want me?'

'That is an absurd question to ask, given everything

that's happened today—these past years. The despicable things that have taken place between our families.'

'But an important one. A necessity, if we really are discussing tying ourselves together in marriage.'

He placed his hand on the wall above her head and leaned in. He took her chin in his hand and tipped her face up, so she was looking into his eyes. 'Answer the question, Cwen. Don't lie to me.'

'I—I don't know what to think of you.'

'That isn't a no.'

'It isn't a yes either!'

He grinned.

'I can't believe we're having this conversation,' she said, shaking her head, turning away from him, forcing him to drop his hand, and she began fumbling with the door handle, flustered, attempting to open the door.

'You're right,' he said. 'Perhaps in this instance, actions would speak louder than words.'

He gripped her elbow and spun her back round to face him, tugging her into his arms and before she realised what was happening, before she could protest, he bent his head. The moment his mouth covered hers, capturing her lips, she felt dizzying heat, like a wildfire spreading around her body, engulfing her in flame. She gasped at the onslaught on her senses—the woodsy outdoor scent of his skin pressed up against hers. He was so close, she could see his dark half-closed eyes watching her, as if testing her reactions.

His large hand came up to cup her jaw, drawing her closer, deepening the kiss, his thumb tenderly stroking her cheek, as his firm lips encouraged hers to open, to let him in, and she gasped as she somehow allowed his silky tongue to steal intimately inside her mouth, the lick of his gentle caresses making her shudder. She felt her eyelids softly flutter shut and her body sway as she gave into the sensations, surrendering to him for the second time today. She gripped hold of his arms, scared if she didn't, she might fall down, her body a shaking, tingling, trembling wreck. His hand trailed down her throat, and further, his thumb tenderly stroking over the sensitive exposed skin at her neckline, as he continued to taste her.

And her reaction both shocked and disturbed her. She felt her body awakening, coming to life as if for the very first time, suddenly realising it had needs—needs that had never been met—and now that she had had a taste of him, she wanted more, and she pressed herself closer against his solid, muscular chest.

But almost as soon as it had begun, incredibly, frustratingly, he pulled away, ending the kiss, leaving her breathless. His beautiful blue gaze stared searchingly down into her face. She had never been kissed like that before. And she thought that if he was so skilled to break down her defences this easily, no wonder he had taken the fortress.

'Well, I think I have my answer. And if that didn't convince you this marriage is a good idea, I don't know what will,' he said.

She looked up at him, stricken, still gripping onto his upper arms, his solid muscles flexing beneath her fingers. She released him, stumbling back, her hand reaching up to touch her burning lips. She was mortified she'd let down her guard and succumbed to his advances. 'A good idea? I was thinking the exact opposite,' she fumed, trying to steady her breathing and regain her composure.

Her body was thrumming with panic and wild excitement. 'What do you think you're doing?' She looked up and down the corridor, horrified at what had just taken place in such an open space. What if someone had seen?

'It was just a kiss...'

Just? The way he'd gathered her up and drawn her into his arms, moulding her body so intimately to his, invading her mouth with his tongue like that, could never be described as *just* a kiss. He had given her a taste of what he could offer her if they went ahead with this marriage, and now she knew with absolute certainty she should say no, refuse his proposal and prepare to be banished. Because now, and she hated to admit it, but she could see their potential. She could tell that he was dangerous to her, in every way a man could be dangerous to a woman, because he had left her wanting more.

'Don't ever do that again!' she bit out, more afraid now than ever, pulling open her door and storming through it.

'Never?' Njal grinned, his glittering eyes mocking her, his hand resting on the door-frame. 'What a great torture that would be for the both of us.'

She slammed the door in the dark warrior's face and rested her forehead against the cool wood—the man who in just one day had turned her life upside down, and with just one kiss, had her wanting things she had never desired from anyone, ever. Things she knew she could never have.

Helvete!

Njal was desperately trying to get his breathing in check; trying to cover up the shock he felt at the way his body had reacted to the princess being in his arms.

The first touch of their lips had been potent; the gentle, experimental flick of her silky tongue sending a shiver down his spine and heat to his groin. Her whole body had trembled in his embrace and he was damn sure it had more to do with desire than her being afraid of him. It had been everything he knew it would be and more.

He'd had to break away before he'd totally lost control and done more than just kiss her. He'd wanted to pick her up, carry her over the threshold, throw her down on the bed and make her his.

But he would just have to wait. He would do this right.

He leaned against the wall outside her door and lowered his body down to the floor. Thoughts about everything that had happened throughout the day kept running through his mind. It had been a great battle, and his men had fought well. His muscles were weary from the fighting, but he'd been lucky to escape unscathed. And he thought the battle had helped to rid him of some of his rage, knowing he had reciprocated a little of the pain the Saxons had caused him.

He couldn't believe his brother had taken on the king... He was still furious with Ove for his behaviour today—and yet, at the same time, he missed him. Their banter, their camaraderie. They should have celebrated their victory together tonight, yet he didn't even know where Ove was, or what he was up to.

It was strange to think the king—his enemy—was lying unconscious in a room just down the hall; that he would be sleeping under the same roof as that man. It was an unsettling thought. But at least it was a roof he now had control over. *He* was in charge. And he would turn things around for the better. Yet he couldn't deny the responsibility weighed heavy on his shoulders. The lives of all those who lived in Jorvik, and all those who had fought alongside him, were now in his hands.

He kept second-guessing his decisions about today—about letting the king and the Saxon prisoners live, his negotiations with Cwen and his proposal. Ove had made him question his judgement, but he'd been ruled by his animosity for so long, and he could now see what damage that was doing to his brother. Ove was losing himself, drowning in his hate. It was sucking him in, pulling him under, and Njal knew he didn't want to be like that. He had to swim to the surface and break free of it. He wanted a life. He wanted to find contentment and happiness again. A family of his own. Could he have all that with Cwen? If that kiss was anything to go by, it was a definite possibility.

And yet, he wasn't entirely sure he was cut out for being a father. When he'd watched Cwen tuck in her son, and gently place a kiss on his forehead, he'd wondered if he'd failed Ove. His own father had been faultless, and he wished he could live up to that. But perhaps many men couldn't. It sounded as if Cwen had suffered at her father's hands too—that she'd paid a heavy price for being his daughter. So Ælfweard had been a terrible father, as well as king.

He knew now, Cwen hadn't known the extent of her father's atrocities. It was his sin and his alone. It wasn't her fault—and yet she had apologised for the king's misdeeds anyway. She hadn't needed to do that—it had shocked him; helped to further temper his anger and resentment towards her. He had appreciated it.

He would never be able to forget what her father and some of her people had done, but might it be possible he could separate the past from his future with Cwen now?

He rested his head back against the wall, closing his tired eyes, her pale grey gaze, her soft, pliable lips at the forefront of his mind.

Despite what Ove had said, he couldn't bring himself to regret asking her to marry him, to form an alliance—something in his gut was telling him it was the right course of action, carrying him forwards. That it was what was needed to bring their people peace and prosperity. Besides, it would hardly be a hardship to escort her to bed every night—and that incredible kiss had just sealed the deal.

Chapter Five

Sleep well? Njal had wished her the impossible. Cwen couldn't sleep at all, knowing there were Danes in the fortress—Danes who were now running her father's stronghold and Northumbria. Danes who up until today had been their enemy. And a Dane who had said she must marry him.

And it was thoughts of that one Dane who was keeping her awake, his mocking, startling blue eyes racing through her mind, as well as that burning kiss. It made her feel hot and feverish, and she tossed and turned in frustration. She was now even more wary of him than she had been, and before she slipped under the furs, she pushed her table across the floor, moving it up against the door, blocking it. She wasn't prepared to take any risks.

But it was the screams in the middle of the night that had her sitting bolt upright in bed. She listened closely, and she realised with dread pounding in her chest that the wailing was coming from her father's chamber. It was her mother's cries.

She raced to the connecting door between hers and Leof's room, and checked that he and Eadhild were still asleep, before attempting to push the table away from her door. She had just created a bit of space when the door burst open as far as it could.

Njal.

Njal was knocking down her door in the middle of the night.

'What are you doing here?' she gasped, standing there in her nightgown, panic erupting in her chest. She was not ready to see him again yet—or prepared for the impact he instantly had on her already restless body.

'I was guarding your door, making sure you're safe,' he said, his eyes raking over her, before looking down to notice the table blocking the door.

'I thought your man was going to do that,' she said.

'Perhaps I don't trust anyone but myself in this instance,' he said, his intense gaze back on her. 'I heard screams.'

'So did I. It wasn't me,' she said, shaking her head. 'It's coming from my mother's rooms.'

'Let's go,' he said, taking her arm, pulling her through the door, but not before he gave the table one last look. 'I noticed you locked your door last night. Did you barricade it too?' he said, as he began to stride quickly down the corridor, his hand wrapped round his sword, and she tried to keep up.

Her footsteps faltered. 'Were you out here all night?' she asked. The very thought was disturbing—that he'd been just feet away as she lay in her bed. What had happened to his man?

'Considering we've slept under canvas most nights for the past two winters, anything was going to be better than that. Come on.'

'How did you know my door was locked?' she said,

unwilling to move any further until he'd answered the question.

He flashed her a look, and her heart began to pound. Had he just assumed, or had he tried to get in?

'I was afraid someone was going to break down my door and attack me while I slept. It seems it was a fair assumption.'

He smiled. 'I was just checking on you.'

'If you were hoping for a repeat of what happened earlier, that will never happen.'

'You didn't enjoy my kissing?'

'No!'

He grinned wider. 'You're a bad liar.'

The thought was disturbing—that he'd tried her door. And a thrill chased through her blood, but she told herself it was burning anger, *fear* she was feeling, not heated excitement. She was troubled by the interest he sparked in her.

Damn him, how could he look so good on no sleep? And how could she be so aware of his nearness at a time like this, when her mother was clearly crying out for help.

They raced the rest of the way, and when they arrived at her parents' door it was already open, a commotion going on inside. They pushed themselves to the front of the crowd and she sidled up next to her mother. Everyone was watching her father, who was awake— and furious. He was staggering around in his tunic, his eyes wild, wielding his sword at anyone who came near, even her mother.

'This is my fortress. My kingdom! No one shall take it from me!'

'It's the wound,' whispered the healer, turning to face

her. 'It has given him a fever, making him irrational, causing him to lash out.'

'The crown belongs to me or my daughter. My grandson... If you take it, there will never be peace, there will be another great war over my succession. I'd rather die than see my bloodline removed from the throne of Northumbria.'

Cwen could see he had already hurt two of Njal's men, who had perhaps tried to seize control of him, and seeing the instant tension in Njal, the hard set of his jaw, she knew he wouldn't stand for much more. He'd already been lenient, letting her father live, given what he had done to Njal's settlement.

Her father was surrounded—he had nowhere to go—and if he didn't calm down, she was concerned they might make his greatest fears come true.

Her mother was a mess, crying hysterical tears. Cwen had never seen them both so broken; so at a loss. How the mighty have fallen, she thought, thinking of the words from the Bible.

But she did not want to witness the demise of their family's seat here in Northumbria. She didn't want to be accountable for that. She knew she had to do all she could to secure her status as heir. Everything she had gone through, all the lies she had told, she'd done so to ensure her family's survival—she couldn't let it all be for nothing.

Her father waved his sword again, more ferociously, and Njal's men seemed to close in on him, raising their weapons. Her heart was in her mouth. She felt as if everyone was talking, trying to calm him, or threaten him, but she was in a tunnel and she could hear voices but not what they were saying. It was muffled, as if there was a rushing in her ears.

'Please, don't hurt him,' she said, turning to Njal.

'I cannot have him attacking my men.'

She could see the anger inside him, rippling off him, now he had come face-to-face with the man who had murdered his family again, and she was terrified about what he was going to do. And then she realised—she had the power to end all this, by giving both men what they wanted. By sacrificing her own happiness, her freedom, again, she could free her father and appease Njal. Yes, she would be forced to live a lie once more, but she could see no other option. She would endure the heartache so others didn't have to.

As her father slashed the air, the Danes let out a roar, and she rushed forwards. 'Father, stop. Please. Everything is going to be all right. An alliance has been made, between us and the Norsemen.'

Her father's wild, frantic eyes sought out hers and as he focused on her, recognition dawning, she gripped his arm that was holding his sword.

'I am to be married...'

The king stilled, lowering his sword a little, and Cwen took a hesitant look back at Njal. He was staring at her intently.

'Married?' her father asked.

Njal stepped forwards. 'You have lost your throne, but I see no reason why your daughter must suffer as well.' His intense gaze didn't move from hers. 'So is that a yes, you are accepting my terms?'

'You are to be queen?' her father asked.

'Yes,' she said with a sigh, answering both of them

at once. She didn't have a choice. She had been born a royal, with a duty to fulfil, to her kingdom and her people. And if she had the chance to save the lives of those she loved, she knew she had to do whatever it took to do so. She must go along with this and wed the Norseman. 'Although the finer details need to be discussed,' she bit, aiming a look at Njal, warning him this conversation wasn't over.

She might have agreed to be his wife, but she would not lie with him. She couldn't. That was non-negotiable.

The moment Ælfweard's weapon dropped, Njal's men descended, swooping in, restraining him.

'You and Mother will retire to the country, Father. You will be safe there.'

He nodded. And for the first time, she noticed the strain on his face; and realised he was tired—ageing fast. 'I am proud of you, Cwen,' he said, as he sat down, allowing her mother to fuss over him, to reinspect his wound. 'I would not be content to hand my crown over to anyone else.'

It was probably the nicest thing he'd ever said to her and she swallowed down a lump in her throat. 'Thank you, Father.'

It meant a lot. Her father had overlooked her these past few years, hoping he would live long enough to see Leof come of age, preferring a male heir for the crown and willing to bypass his daughter. She had felt it unfair, and had resented her mother further for jeopardising her position. If only the king had known the truth about her son...

'Come, let us leave them,' Njal said, putting an arm round her shoulder, pulling her away. She could tell he didn't want to be in her father's company for a moment longer than he had to be. 'Your father needs his rest, and we have much to discuss.'

'When will this happen?' the king asked, as they began their retreat to the door.

'I would like it dealt with as soon as possible,' Njal said.
Dealt with? Cwen thought.

'As soon as you are able to travel, we will arrange transport for you to leave Jorvik.'

Her father nodded, and Njal wasted no more time in getting them out of there.

'You've made the right decision,' he said, as he walked her back down the silent, candlelit corridor. 'You won't regret it.'

But she already was, her skin burning where he was holding her round the shoulder, and she shrugged him off. She had agreed to his proposal, but she knew she had to tell him in no uncertain terms what that meant. He needed to have all the facts at his disposal. It was now or never. And better now than on their wedding night.

She knew it was wrong of her to agree to the marriage and then tell him that she would never sleep with him—that she wouldn't be taking their marriage any further than this convenient arrangement. That she would never consummate their vows. It was unfair. But she could see no other way around it.

She rounded on him in the corridor, halting his progress. She poked a finger into his chest. 'I may have agreed to marry you, but there's something you must know about me before *you* decide to go ahead with this.'

He stared down at the finger prodding him and looked bemused. 'All right.'

She lowered her hand and twisted her ring on her finger. She couldn't bring herself to look him in the eye, so instead, focused on her feet. 'I can't give you children.'

It had been a truth she'd been made aware of five years ago, since Leof had come into her life, and she had taken a long time to come to terms with it. That day, that moment, had changed her life, her future, in more ways than one. It had been bittersweet. A heartbreaking realisation, and yet there had also been joy when she had held Leof for the first time. She knew this revelation would come as just as much a shock to Njal too, if he wanted to be a father. His hopes would be dashed.

He cupped her chin in his hand and raised her face to look at him. 'Can't, or won't?'

She took a deep breath, as a pang of guilt hit her. 'Can't. There was a complication before. With Leof.' She swallowed and shook her head. It wasn't completely a lie. 'I do not wish to discuss the details. It's personal, private. But please, you must believe me when I say we cannot have heirs.'

His eyes narrowed. 'That's very convenient.'

'Nevertheless, it's the truth. I thought you should know…'

He stared at her for a long moment and then released her. He propelled himself away from her, pacing. 'You're saying if I marry you, I won't ever have children of my own? That I will never be a father?'

'That's right.'

He swore, raking his hand through his hair.

'And you're only just telling me this vital piece of information, now?' he said, still pacing.

Hurt, she reared back. 'We only met last night! When was I supposed to tell you?'

She watched as he dragged a hand over his beard, the enormity of what she was saying sinking in. 'I always thought I would be a father, one day.' He looked downcast, as if it was a great disappointment. He seemed torn, as if he was deliberating, now, what he should do.

And she knew his pain. She had suffered it every day these past years, grieving for a child that she didn't know, and would never meet.

Pausing, he turned back to face her. 'I'm sorry. I didn't mean to sound cruel. This must be a great torment to you too. Although you must take great comfort in the fact you've had a son already.'

His apology made her reel. It was so unexpected—that this fierce warrior was acknowledging her pain; that she might be suffering—and it made her feel even worse. It threw her, and a anguish tore through her chest. Because it was still a great heartache, even though she wasn't being completely truthful with him.

She shook her head a little and tried to focus on the present. Did this change things—had it put him off?

She began to panic, as she realised what he had offered her could now be snatched away. If he no longer wanted to marry her, would he still spare her and her family, and her people? But shouldn't she be pleased she might have a reprieve?

He stalked back over to her, his face dark, and she realised she was holding her breath. He looked down into her eyes and took her hand in his. He seemed to be searching her soul, trying to make his decision. 'Disappointed as I am, we will marry anyway,' he said slowly, his words at odds with the strain on his face; the reluctance in his voice.

Her heart began to pound. She didn't know what she'd been expecting him to say, but it wasn't that. 'You still want to go ahead?' she whispered, feeling worse than ever. She couldn't believe it. He was prioritising marrying her over having a child in the future. Why?

'Yes. And soon.'

She bit down on her lip, deep in thought. It was such a huge thing to give up—and she felt wretched. A terrible person. Could she really ask that of him? Or was he simply willing to give up the chance to be a father to secure his place here on the throne? Because that was what was truly important to him. She was desperate to understand his motives; why he was so set on this.

Did he understand hers?

She stared down at her hand in his and gently retrieved it.

Did he understand she was telling him that if they weren't going to have children, there was no need for him to touch her, to lie with her?

When they reached her door, she turned to look at him, suddenly more nervous than ever before. 'So we're still doing this?'

'Yes.'

'And you will free my people. My parents?'

'Yes.'

'Well then, I hope you're satisfied,' Cwen said, her brow furrowing. 'It appears you've claimed a kingdom, a throne and a queen all in the space of one day,' she said.

The sensual curve of his lips rose. 'I'm pleased.' He raised his hand to her cheek and she had to fight against her peculiar desire to lean into it. 'As for feeling satisfied, I'm feeling anything but.'

She stepped away from him, her back hitting the wall, her traitorous thoughts returning to that kiss earlier. It had left her breathless. She hadn't known it was possible to feel like that. Her body had literally come to life. It was absurd! He was a Dane! The man who, just the day before, had captured her throne, her home, her family and her people! Who for two years had been on the rampage, destroying their villages, hunting them down. She must never forget it—what he was capable of. She must resist him—she couldn't allow him to kiss her again. Weaken her.

She had never had this reaction to anyone before; never had these heated thoughts. So why did she have to have them for this man, now, who was dangerous, who could never be gentle, who would do anything to protect his people and his position here—and who she could never share her secret with, for he would almost certainly use it against her?

Now that she had agreed to be Njal's wife, she would need to keep her guard up at all times; continue living a lie. She would need to make this Norseman warrior see reason—that there was no need for them to consummate this union, to make sure he didn't discover the truth. That she had never slept with any man and had never given birth to a child.

For how could she tell him—her father's enemy—that Leof, the heir to her throne, was in fact not her son, but her brother?

No, she could never. If word got out about Leof's heritage, it would destroy her family's reputation. It would undermine her position here and the trust of the people. It would devastate her father and ruin her mother. And it would break Leof's heart.

Njal's bride-to-be moved quickly, out of his reach, and frustration roared inside him. He stepped back, glancing up and down the corridor, running a hand around the back of his neck. But there was only so long she could avoid his touch.

'What are you doing now? It's almost daybreak. How about that tour of the city? It would be good to know my way around the place.'

'I need to get back to Leof.'

'Bring him too. It might help if he got to know me a little.'

She thought about it for a moment and then nodded. 'All right. We'll meet you outside?'

'I'll wait until you're ready.'

He was still reeling from what she had told him, so he was glad to have a moment to himself. Cwen telling him she couldn't have children was a devastating blow, for the both of them. It had crushed him, more than he hoped he'd let on, and yet he had momentarily considered if she was telling the truth, or if it was an excuse, hoping it would mean that she wouldn't have to share his bed. And he wondered if he would always doubt her, whether he would always be wary, waiting for her to betray him, after what happened with Synnove.

But then he had felt like a brute for thinking that way. If she couldn't have another child and wanted one, it was a huge misfortune. He wondered what had happened—

had it been a difficult birth? But at least she had Leof. He had sired no children. And now he never would.

He was still trying to come to terms with it, his heart trying to catch up with his head. He felt as if he was in a state of shock.

Was it possible the healers had got it wrong, and there was still a chance? And yet she seemed adamant.

Being a father was something he had looked forward to. He had just taken it for granted that it would happen one day. This was a massive setback—that the woman he'd proposed to couldn't have any more children. When she'd told him, it had overwhelmed him completely—it had come as such a surprise, he'd had to fight for composure, to rein in his own disappointment as he didn't want to hurt her feelings further on the matter. But it was a great loss.

Yet he'd known he had to make a choice—put aside his plans to marry her and form a union between the Saxons and Danes or stick to the course. He could rule this kingdom alone, wait to marry someone else, but how could he be sure he'd be able to have children anyway? And looking back at her, standing in the corridor, in her floor-length white tunic, his mouth had dried. He'd wondered if he would ever find someone he desired as much as he did her?

She had told him yesterday, in her father's state room, that she had no intention of sleeping with him, and yet she'd also said she had no intention of agreeing to marry him, and she had changed her mind on that. And did she not know by now how persuasive he could be? She'd succumbed to his kiss and it had given them both a taste of what was to come...

So, he'd made his decision. He would still take her as his wife.

Cwen and Leof had dressed quickly, and they had led Njal down a labyrinth of corridors, showing him various rooms off the great hall—more state rooms, the kitchens—before heading out into the courtyard and up onto the ramparts. Cwen told him the stronghold was built on the site of an old Roman fortress, and looking out over the meadows where yesterday they had been at arms, he realised it stood in a commanding position that dominated the rivers Ouse and Foss. He could use them for defensive purposes, but also for trade, as his eyeline followed the waterways that headed out to the sea.

Assessing the damage that had been done to the fortress during the battle, he knew he'd need to start repairing the walls and gates, and soon, if the rumours were true about Ælfweard's allies rallying an army. He hoped they were just that—rumours. He was looking forward to having some stability, some peace—he'd like to walk around without having to carry his sword on him for a while; to not have to think about battle tactics or burying the dead.

The city was starting to wake up, the Saxons going about their morning routine with caution, aware of the Norse warriors watching on from the battlements. As they walked down narrow streets, Njal inspected the various market stalls selling spices, wool and weapons, and he took an interest in the craftsmen in the workshops, and seeing the armoury and the stables. It didn't take him long to get his bearings.

When the people heard the princess had left the royal buildings and was walking through the streets, many came out of their farmsteads to greet them, bowing to Cwen or offering her flowers. But when they saw she was accompanied by the leader of the heathen army, many cowered in fear, or stared on in awe. When they realised the princess was safe, they began pushing forwards, begging for food or asking for her help with injured loved ones. Njal was struck by the scenes of adulation, and the people's need for contact, and he turned to Bjorn, asking him to get some cauldrons of hot food brought out to feed the masses.

'And the prisoners?' Bjorn asked him.

'Make sure they're fed too—and release them. Inform them of our impending nuptials and tell them they can leave or stay, it's their choice.' Now that their union was set, and having seen the people's support for Cwen, Njal felt confident the ealdormen and their wives would be loyal to their rule, and want to keep their homes, rather than leave. And as for the prisoners from the battlefield, they'd demonstrated their support of the princess when they'd lowered their swords and yielded, so he felt they would bend to their will once released.

'It's done,' Bjorn said.

'Thank you,' Cwen whispered.

The more Cwen showed him around, the more Njal thought he was going to like it here, but he wondered if that was more to do with his impressive new home, his newfound power or the woman at his side.

'You grew up here?' he asked, as they strolled back towards the hall. You must have a lot of memories.'

'Yes, it was my first home. I know it well. But I do miss Bamburgh. I made a lot of friends there. It was my dominion—where I could please myself. I wanted to stay there, when Feran died, but my father insisted we move back here.'

'As queen of Northumbria, you will rule over both fortresses, although I cannot imagine a place grander than this.'

'Worried you'll feel out of place?' she asked, wryly.

'Not at all,' he smiled.

He had never thought this would be his destiny, he had never desired riches and power. He had been an ordinary boy and lived a simple life. He'd had everything he needed, he and his brother swimming in the sea, carefree—none of the strict upbringing and formalities that Cwen must have had to endure. And he turned to the boy at his side. He thought it must be lonely being an only child, and after what Cwen had told him this morning, he knew that wasn't about to change any time soon.

'What's up there?' he asked, pointing to the tallest structure of the fortress.

'The lookout tower,' Leof said.

'Show me?'

'It's a long way up. Three hundred steps,' Cwen said.

'Reckon we can make it?' he asked Leof, and held out his hand for him, and his heart lifted a little when the boy took it.

Did he get to climb trees and wrestle in the mud with other boys his age? He hoped so. He had been playing with a sword when Njal had met him yesterday, but he didn't want the children of Jorvik growing up having to fight. And then he realised, he was in charge now. Whatever rules or traditions he didn't approve of, he could change for the better.

Struggling for breath, they finally reached the top of the steps.

'Beat you.' The boy grinned.

'So you did. Well done,' he said, ruffling his hair.

Njal was still trying to deal with the emotions he was feeling about knowing he would never have a child of his own. But he had to wonder if perhaps it was a good thing—raising Ove these past two winters had been hard enough, and he hadn't been too successful given the events of late. He would have to try to turn that situation around.

Meanwhile, looking down at the boy smiling up at him, he realised there was a child here who had lost his father and needed someone to look up to. And gazing out over the city, he recognised, so did the people.

'You can see all across Jorvik towards the sea in the east,' Leof said, excited to be showing off his home to a warrior.

And yet, from up here, Njal could also see the devastation the fighting had caused to the lands around the city—lasting scars on the landscape as well as their lives. Where grass and wildflowers had blossomed, and animals had roamed, the ground was now nothing but barren mud, and he vowed there and then he would make the kingdom thrive again. He would do his best to protect these lands and nurture them, not fight on and over them. It was hard to believe he was the ruler of it all—

and soon to be the ruler, the husband and king, of the woman at his side.

He was glad he was going ahead with the wedding anyway. After all, there was fulfilment to be found in other areas of a marriage beyond parenthood.

'The view is incredible, isn't it?' she said, forgetting herself and smiling at him for the first time.

And he stared down at her and agreed. 'It really is.'

Chapter Six

Cwen knew it was natural for every bride to feel nervous, but enough to make them feel feint?

The past few days had been a blur. Njal had been consolidating his power in Jorvik—he and his men had been digging new defences and repairing parts of the fortress. There had been meetings with the ealdormen, given most of them had decided to stay, where they had formed a tentative truce, and since they had heard King Caedwalla in Mercia had mobilised his forces, there had been tactics to discuss. But whether Caedwalla planned to come to Ælfweard's aid and attempt to reinstate him on the throne, or intended to claim Northumbria as his own remained to be seen.

The people were restless, fearful about another battle coming to their door, but Cwen had more immediate concerns to contend with.

Njal had decided he and Cwen must marry immediately, so amid spending the past days looking after her parents and the people, making sure their wounds were seen to and families had enough food and water, while also making room and finding accommodation for the new Danish inhabitants of their settlement, she'd had a wedding to plan.

Thankfully they had decided on a small ceremony, with just a few essential witnesses, and it felt surreal now, as her maids fussed over her, braiding her hair, decorating it with flowers. She couldn't believe it was actually happening; that she was really going ahead with this. And when she began to walk up the aisle of the church and saw Njal standing at the altar, waiting for her, her legs started trembling. When he turned, and his piercing blue gaze locked with hers, her steps faltered.

She could barely catch her breath in her tight blue bridal tunic, but she knew it was less to do with the material and all to do with the man she was walking towards. The man she was about to promise herself to. How did he have the ability to affect her ability to breathe and to walk?

It was just fear, she told herself.

And yet she realised, deep down, she was no longer afraid of him, not as a heathen warrior. She knew he was strong, and determined, but she no longer thought he was cruel. He had been true to his word and released his Saxon prisoners. He'd been reasonable in his treatment of her father, and he had even been kind to her boy. He had been generous in his distribution of food and ale around the city. So far, his rule here had been peaceful and fair.

But she was afraid of him as a man—a man who made her feel things, who made her want things she knew she shouldn't. She felt torn between her unexpected longing for him, and feeling like a pawn in his and her father's game. She wondered if she was just being used as a political tool, to secure his crown. And once he'd got a ring on her finger, how he would treat her.

Today was the first time she'd seen him out of his armour—and without his sword. He had bathed and his long dark hair had been combed and was neatly fastened, his beard trimmed. He was the most attractive man she had ever seen, she admitted to herself, but that did nothing to calm her nerves—if anything, it just made everything worse.

She felt the need for some kind of armour, and wished she could have worn the chain-mail she'd been wearing the day she'd met him on the battlefield. She wasn't sure she could move another step, but then Leof took her hand and it gave her the strength to keep going.

The church looked beautiful, bedecked in flowers, and was only half filled, with just the few faces of those they both trusted. She tried to smile at the members of her father's witan and their wives that she'd known since childhood, and Eadhild, hoping to reassure them everything was going to fine, even if it felt like anything but.

Njal's right-hand man, Bjorn, was stood next to him, but she noticed his brother, Ove, was absent, as well as her parents. Ove had spent the last few days stomping around the fortress, making his presence known, but she'd tried to stay out of his way and was pleased Njal seemed to have got him under control—yet he obviously hadn't wanted to witness their union today.

'You look beautiful,' Njal whispered, as she reached him at the altar, and a ripple of pleasure washed over her.

It felt strange going ahead with the wedding without her father there to give her away. He had been overbearing at her first wedding, not letting her out of his sight until she'd said her vows, perhaps worried she might go against his wishes. He was recovering well, but she had known Njal wouldn't want him here. She wondered how many days it would be until he was well enough to travel and Njal would send him and her mother away. Would she ever see them again?

Her mother had been a dutiful wife, barely leaving her father's side since his injury. She had helped Cwen dress today, gently dabbing at her eyes. And Cwen had felt burning resentment in her stomach that once again, she was having to sacrifice her freedom to keep everyone else happy. Her father, her mother—and she must not forget Njal—had demanded this happen; had forced her into this. She was surrendering her own happiness, marrying a man who didn't love her, and she would do well to remember that; to keep her anger towards him in the hours that were to come.

The priest was speaking, but Cwen could barely concentrate on his words. Even though this was the second time she was going through this service, it felt wholly different. She felt so out of her depth.

For a start, she wasn't marrying a friend, but a stranger. A Dane, who just days ago had been her enemy. She hadn't had any concerns about her wedding night with Feran, but with Njal…he had professed his desire for her. He had kissed her with a passion she had never before experienced. Would she be able to keep him at bay?

'Assist with thy blessing these two persons, that they may both be fruitful in procreation of children, and also live together so long in Godly love and honesty. Amen.'

'Amen,' the congregation repeated.

She looked up into Njal's face and she couldn't understand why he had agreed to this, giving up his chance of children. It was a huge sacrifice. It was one thing her making it for her mother, but he didn't need to do this. Did her title really mean that much to him? And would he come to regret it, and resent her later?

And then another thought struck her. She knew it was the king's right to take a mistress if he should wish—would Njal? If she couldn't give him what he wanted, in the bedroom, and in terms of children, might he look for it elsewhere? And the very thought was sickening—it had jealous heat searing her stomach. Yet surely it wasn't fair for her to demand celibacy?

Cwen looked up into Njal's eyes as they were pronounced man and wife.

'You may now kiss the bride,' the priest said.

Her heart hammered as panic flared. How had she forgotten about this part? She didn't want him to come any closer—she didn't want the congregation to see her instinctive reaction to him. But there was nothing she could do to stop it as Njal stepped forwards, his hands coming up to hold her face, capturing her between his hands as if he knew she was about to step away. And he lowered his head to press his lips gently against hers. His face swam before hers and she closed her eyes, trying to fight the incredible sensations fluttering through her as she drew in the familiar scent of his skin and felt the warm pressure of his mouth. His lips lingered, too long, making her breathless, and her body quivered in dreadful excitement at his disturbing touch.

When he pulled away, he smiled down at her, as if he knew the effect he had on her. And she realised she'd made a huge mistake. She didn't have the skills, or experience, to deal with him. But there was no going back now. It was too late. She was his.

To have and to hold...

Yet she had no intention of letting him have her.

Njal wrapped his fingers around hers and they began to walk hand in hand down the aisle, the heat searing up her skin offering her no reassurance for the evening ahead.

There was, of course, the chance the ealdormen would demand to witness their consummation, but she had to hope Njal wouldn't approve of that; that he would want to keep their time together private.

The feast passed in a daze of people congratulating them, offering them food and ale, telling them they would have fine children together, that they would make a wonderful family, and Njal had accepted all their comments with gracious thanks, but Cwen felt wrung out. Each one was like they were scraping back the scab on a wound, picking at it, and she felt miserable. She just wanted to get far, far away from here.

By the time her mother came to fetch her for the bedding ceremony, she was beside herself. She couldn't bring herself to look at Njal as she was led away on trembling legs to her chamber, to be undressed by her maids. Her stomach churned.

There was, of course, the chance he would force her—and if he tried, she would be no match for his strength—but she knew deep down he wasn't that kind of man. She could never have gone through with this ceremony otherwise. So she would just have to stand firm. Say no. Not give in.

It had never been like this with Feran. She remembered the door closing and them both dissolving into fits of giggles, pleased with themselves that they had fooled everyone. But she didn't imagine Njal would find the situation funny.

The maids let down her hair, brushing it through until it shined, before escorting her to Njal's room. Her heart was in her mouth as she walked down the corridor in her bridal tunic, and she hoped to God there would be no ealdormen waiting—no audience.

Fortunately, there was none.

But her relief was short-lived, because when the women knocked on the door, blushing, their faces full of worry for her that she must lie with a heathen, her mother asking her if she was all right, Cwen felt her legs might give way beneath her. She wasn't sure she could bring herself to step over the threshold.

'Come in.'

Even his deep, velvety voice sent tremors through her body.

They pushed open the door and ushered her through, not giving her a choice.

Inside, he was waiting, standing in the middle of the room, and she stared up at him as she waited for the door to thud shut behind her, leaving them alone.

The silence stretched. Njal had removed his leather vest and loosened his tunic, and he looked darkly attractive. Relaxed. And she silently cursed him for seeming so in control. She tried to feign the same nonchalant look on her face, yet she felt as if she was having palpitations. Maybe she would pass out so she wouldn't have to deal with this.

'Wine?' he asked.

She nodded. 'Please.' She hated that she could hear a quiver in her voice. Why was she so nervous, when she'd already told him nothing was going to happen between them? Was it because he'd offered her no reassurance on the matter—that he hadn't agreed?

He poured the liquid into a tumbler and handed it to her, their fingers brushing, causing a ripple of heat to shoot up her arm, and she took a large gulp to try to calm her nerves. It tasted spicy and sweet on her parched tongue.

'So,' he said, looking at her. 'It is done. We are married. Did you enjoy today?'

She was excruciatingly aware of his proximity, and she crossed her arms over her chest, trying to create a barrier between them.

'As much as to be expected.'

He frowned. 'You did not?'

'Was I meant to?'

'It was your wedding day. I know you have done this before, but it should still be one of the best days of your life.'

'If you are marrying for love. We are not.' And then she relented. 'It was long and I am tired.'

He nodded as if he understood. 'You can relax now.'

Relax? How could she possibly? They were alone, he was a stranger and she had never felt so vulnerable.

She placed her tumbler down and looked around the room, rubbing her arms. 'I have not been in here before.'

It was a beautiful room. There was a central hearth and a table and chair, but the enormous bed dominated the space. She tried to look everywhere and anywhere apart from at him and the bed, which seemed to be covered with the finest silk and a mountain of cushions. A bed she was meant to...

'Your father currently occupies the royal bed chamber. But I rather like this one,' he said. 'It is private. Quiet. We shall not be disturbed.'

She shivered. That did not sound good.

'Are you cold?'

'A little.'

He stalked over to the hearth and crouched down, stoking the fire.

'There's fruit over there, if you're hungry,' he said, gesturing to a platter on the table. 'You barely ate anything at the feast.'

She was surprised he'd noticed. But it was true. She had been too nervous. 'There was too much going on.'

She still didn't think she could eat anything now, but she picked up an orange and peeled it anyway, to give her fingers something to do.

'You looked beautiful today,' he said. 'You look beautiful now.'

'Thank you,' she said, swallowing hard. But she didn't want his compliments. She didn't want him to think she was beautiful. Right now, she didn't want him thinking about her like that at all.

He came back towards her. 'Are you all right?' he said, peering at her. 'Apart from being thirsty, hungry, cold, tired... You look pale.'

'I'm always pale.'

'That's true. But more so than usual.'

'If you must know, I'm concerned about Leof.' She

shrugged. 'I'm unsure about leaving him on his own at the feast.'

'He's with Eadhild?'

'Yes.'

'Then he's not on his own. And I asked my man, Bjorn, to keep watch over him.'

'You did? Thank you.'

But still she wrung her hands.

'Are you sure that's all you're worried about?' he asked.

'Actually,' she said, pacing, before coming back to him, taking a deep breath. 'I think I might have made a mistake. I can't do this,' she whispered. She felt as if she was speaking in fractured sentences.

'It's natural to feel nervous...' he said, lifting his hand, drawing his knuckles down her cheek, and disturbing tingles rippled across her skin. She felt as if she couldn't breathe.

'Nervous?' Panic flared. 'About what?' She turned her head away, forcing him to drop his hand. 'You agreed this would be a marriage in name only.'

He stilled. 'I said no such thing.'

'You did! We agreed, no children.'

He looked perplexed, as if his mind was trying to catch up with her thinking.

'The only need to be intimate is to have children, is it not?' she said, explaining, wringing her hands. 'And as we cannot, there is no need to do this.'

'Is that what your late husband told you?' he asked, frowning. 'That you only need to lie with someone to make a child? Children are an *additional* benefit—did he not show you this is also about pleasure?' He came towards her. 'Yours and mine. The only *need* to be intimate is to fulfil your desires. Because you want to touch someone, get close to someone. And I want to touch you, Cwen, and make you mine.'

'But I thought we'd agreed,' she said, panicked, his words making her feel flustered. 'A marriage without the obligations that come with it.'

He raised his eyebrows. 'By obligations, you mean sex?'

She cringed at the word; his outspokenness.

'You can't be serious,' he said, staring at her, his eyes wide. It was as if he didn't know whether to laugh, or get angry. 'That's not a marriage.'

She backed away, as far away from him and his touch as she could. 'But I don't *want* to do *this*,' she said.

She'd told him she couldn't have children, using it as justification not to be intimate. He had wanted to go ahead with the union anyway but she had hoped he would not still try to touch her, to lie with her—as there was no reason to. But who was she kidding? Did she really think he would agree to it? No. What man would? And now they were married, he had rights over her, over her body. But she couldn't let it happen. She had made a pledge to herself and her mother.

She had to keep him at arm's bay, to protect the fact that she had never slept with any man. That her virginity was still intact. That Leof was not her heir.

He frowned. 'Let's be clear. You don't want to lie with me?'

'No.'

'Tonight, or...?'

'Ever.'

His eyes darkened and he shook his head. 'What the hell?' He raked his hand through his hair.

'Don't shout at me!'

He let out a long, slow breath, and she could tell he was trying to keep his anger in check. 'So you're refusing to do your marital duty, for the rest of our lives?' he said, putting his hands on his hips, looking as if he was still unable to comprehend it.

'Yes, because that is what it would be. A duty.'

He took a step towards her. 'Not a pleasure?' It was as if he didn't believe her.

'No.' The heat rose in her cheeks.

'Are you quite sure about that?'

'Yes,' she said, bringing her hands up to her hot cheeks. 'I don't know what you expected. You forced me—manipulated me into this union. You gave me an ultimatum, marry you or leave everything I hold dear. Why did you think I would want to do this, given the circumstances?'

A muscle flickered in his cheek. 'I gave you a proposition. A choice,' he said sternly. 'You *chose* this—to be mine, just like I am yours...'

Hers? She was shocked by the responsive heat that rippled through her body at the word.

'My options were limited—marry you or put my family, my kingdom, my throne in danger. What kind of choice is that?' she said, wringing her hands, rounding on him. 'And if we'd have gone, if you'd banished us from here, what kind of life would that have been for my son, waiting around to be murdered in our sleep by one of your men?'

'Only your father does things like that,' he said, his

voice like ice. 'You could have just said no.' He stalked over to the table and poured himself more wine.

Could she have? She didn't think so...

'Besides, I thought it was my crown that was important, not my body.'

He swung his gaze back to look at her. 'It was both.'

Her blood soared and she paced away, before coming back. She sighed, trying to regain her composure. 'Look, I would do anything to protect those I care about. I'm not saying the marriage, this alliance, is a bad idea. But it doesn't mean I want to...do this...' she said, gesturing to the bed, her face burning.

'Sex.' He said the word again, as if mocking her that she couldn't say it herself.

'Whatever!' she said, throwing her hands up, exasperated. 'I thought you had accepted my terms.'

'Never!'

'Can't you understand?' she said, twisting Feran's wedding ring that she'd moved onto a chain around her neck. 'You are a Dane.'

'So?'

'A stranger. I cannot lie with a stranger. I cannot lie with a man I do not care for...' A man who did not love her or trust her. A man who gave her ultimatums.

And a man who made her want to know what sex felt like, a little voice in her head mocked her.

'Most men in my position would have taken you already whether you liked it or not.'

She reeled, and he ran a hand over his beard.

'I can tell you are angry, and I'm sorry,' she said. 'I married you because I could see the rationale behind it.

You are right, it helps us both. It helps our people. But I was thinking perhaps we could live as...as...'

He came back towards her and took her chin between his thumb and forefinger, forcing her to look up into his eyes.

'As what?' His voice was deadly.

'As friends,' she offered weakly.

'Friends?' His warm breath whispered across her face and her heart skittered at the invasion of her body space, his spicy, musky scent wrapping around her.

'Yes.'

He dropped his hand in disgust—with himself or her, she wasn't too sure—and he stalked away. He picked up his wine and downed it in one. 'I don't think so. Friends don't kiss the way we kissed the other day.'

She tried to block out the instant images that flooded her mind, forcing her to remember the kiss, and the way his lips had brushed against hers in the church earlier today. Her gaze lowered to his full lips, his generous mouth.

'Friends don't tremble the way you do when I come near you,' he said, his eyes narrowing. 'Or hold their breath.'

She tipped her chin up. 'That's because I'm afraid of you.'

'You said you weren't.' And she remembered, she had said that, and she felt bad for being caught in a lie.

'I told an untruth.'

'So it seems, when all I asked for was honesty.'

And she couldn't believe it—how was he making her feel like the bad person, when he had come here, attacked their fortress and turned her world upside down? But he was right. He had been honest about his intentions—and his desire—from the start. He had never given her false promises of love, but she had said yes to his offer, giving him unfair hope. She should have made it clear that she would never be able to share his bed.

He set his cup down on the side, sighing loudly. 'You have no need to be afraid of me. If I was going to force myself upon you, Cwen, I would have done it already.'

And deep down, she knew that. He turned back towards her and his eyes seemed to penetrate her, holding her gaze for a long moment. 'So here's what's going to happen... I am prepared to wait until we are no longer strangers. Until you are ready.'

'No!' she said, disturbing excitement fluttering in her stomach. She wanted this to be agreed on, set in stone, tonight, so she didn't have to worry about it, think about it, every moment she was with him. 'I told you. That will be never.'

A muscle flickered in his cheek. 'So you keep saying.' She could tell he was barely containing his anger. 'Why don't I believe you?'

She shrugged. 'That's your problem.' She wasn't handling any of this well at all. She felt she was spiralling out of control.

'You don't feel this raging, burning attraction between us?'

'No,' she said, sitting down on the edge of the bed before her legs gave way.

'All right. I'm just trying to work out why you're lying to me and yourself...'

You fool! Njal told himself. He was a fool for trusting her. He had paid a high price to bed her—he had tied himself to her, even knowing she couldn't bear him a child. Yet now she was denying him even more.

Standing there, in a beautiful tunic meant only for her husband to see, Njal felt a flicker of frustration at his temple. He was finding it difficult to have a conversation with her—the soft material clinging to her gentle curves, her long dark hair tumbling over her shoulders—let alone keep his hands off her. His fingers were itching to reach out and touch what was his. She was temptation itself, and he felt angry with her for denying him, but also furious with himself for getting himself into this situation.

Was this his comeuppance for wanting to sleep with the enemy?

He had wanted her from the moment he'd seen her, and he was certain she felt the same. Had he got it wrong? Had he been duped once again? It was possible... and yet, he didn't think so. He couldn't have imagined the passion behind that kiss, or the explosive reactions every time they touched. It was much too powerful to be one-sided. And yet, she was adamant.

It was destroying his trust, causing him to be cautious. To harden his heart against her.

He had wanted a marriage like his parents had had—passionate and all-consuming. It was why there was such an age gap between him and Ove. His parents had tried and tried to have children, when eventually, Njal had come along. But afterwards, nothing. And then, years later, their passion still burning as bright as ever, they'd conceived again. It had been a shock, but Ove had been much wanted by all.

Perhaps that's why he'd been willing to overlook Cwen's

inability to have children, knowing sometimes, healers got it wrong. But had it been a fool's hope?

His gaze raked over her stunning face. Was this really just about her not feeling like she knew him? He could understand that. They were strangers. She had probably lived in fear of him for months, even years, as he'd travelled across country, fighting and conquering, drawing ever closer like a dark wave, set on destroying her father's life. Her father had been hurt at the hands of his men. Many Saxons had died. But he didn't think she was as afraid of him as she had declared.

Perhaps she had just used him, double-crossed him, to keep her position here, because she wanted to be queen. People had done worse in the pursuit of power. But it took a lot of guts to marry him and then deny him—on their wedding night. How was she to know he wasn't the type of man to force a woman? If she thought he could be, she was playing a risky game.

But he wasn't, so what could he do? His only option was to be patient. To try to persuade her and win her round. Perhaps he had gone about this the wrong way by giving her an ultimatum, telling her to marry him or leave behind everything she knew and loved. Given what she'd told him about her father ruling her life, he could understand that his demands wouldn't have gone down well.

He sighed, dragging his hand over his face. The situation was less than ideal. He couldn't leave the room as then his men, and the Saxon ealdorman, would know they hadn't consummated their relationship, and his pride would not suffer that. He also needed them to think this union was real—that the alliance was secure. He could hear the faint sound of laughter coming from the hall even now, the celebrations for their wedding going on late into the night. He could not reappear. It would be humiliating. But it would be unbearable being stuck in this room with her tonight, and every night, and not being allowed to touch her. It would surely drive him mad.

Realising this wasn't going to be the wedding night he'd had in mind, he thought the sooner he accepted it, the sooner he could cool the lust burning in his veins, and perhaps get some sleep. And for once, at least, he would not be sleeping on the floor.

He began to lift the cushions off the bed and throw them onto the chair. 'You have married me now and as the priest said, what God hath joined together let not man put asunder. We will share this room tonight and every night anyway, until you change your mind.'

'I—' She went to protest, standing up.

He stopped what he was doing and held up a finger and placed it over her lips to halt her from speaking.

'I won't touch you until you ask me to, but in return, you will do me this courtesy. I don't want any questions over whether we have done our duty and consummated this relationship. The people, the country, need to see us united. They need to believe what we have is real. I don't want anyone questioning the validity of our marriage. Is that understood?'

She swallowed and nodded her head.

Then he returned his attention to the bed and lifted the furs, drawing them back, ready to clamber in.

'What are you doing?' she shrieked.

He looked up at her, bemused. 'I'm tired. It's been an

exhausting few days. If we're not going to *do this*, I'm going to get some sleep.'

She looked around, raising her arms. 'And just where do you expect me to sleep?'

He sighed. 'Look, Cwen, I will respect your wishes. I will keep my hands to myself and I won't touch you. But if you think I'm going to spend the night on the floor because you don't think you can trust me, you're sorely mistaken. That is your problem.'

He pulled off his tunic and threw it on top of the pile of cushions, and when he looked back over at her, he realised her mouth was hanging open as she stared at him, her eyes wide. If he hadn't been so frustrated he might have been amused.

'Good grief, woman, what is it now?' he said.

'That,' she said, gesturing to his chest, and then she looked away, beautiful pink stains appearing on her cheeks. She baffled him. It wasn't like she had never seen a naked man before so why was she acting like an innocent virgin who had never watched a male take his tunic off? He could not work her out.

He looked down, as if he didn't know what she was talking about. And then he realised.

'You haven't seen a man with ink on his skin before?'

She shook her head.

'It is custom where we're from.'

'Why?' Her voice sounded strangled.

He sighed. 'We paint ourselves with totems or markings of our clans. It's just dye. Wood ash. Nothing to be afraid of.'

She stood on the other side of the bed, chewing her lip.

'Are you going to get in?' he asked.

She shook her head. *Skit!* She was so stubborn!

He sighed and suddenly feeling like a brute for making her feel uncomfortable, he walked around the bed towards her. Without warning, he picked her up and she yelped, kicking her legs in protest, before he lay her down on the furs.

'You said you weren't going to touch me again,' she squealed.

To be honest, he wished he hadn't. The feeling of her breasts crushed against his chest, the weight of her thighs under his arms, even for just a moment, had made him instantly hard.

'This is not touching you—not properly! When I touch you, I will make you scream not yelp.'

'That will never happen!'

'We'll see,' he said, coming back round the bed and lowering his body down onto the furs next to her. He blew out the candles, descending them into darkness, and he stretched out, trying to relax his muscles. 'Now go to sleep.'

He really was tired. He hadn't slept properly in months, and now he finally had the comfort of a bed to rest in, he would be having another restless night with Cwen lying beside him, out of bounds. He felt tense, and irritable, her delicate floral scent wrapping around him.

He could hear the rain pelting down onto the stone walls outside, and he told himself to be grateful he wasn't out in it, under leather and canvas, feeling chilled to the bone, lying on the cold ground.

She rolled over onto her side on the very edge of the bed, turning her back on him and putting herself as far away from him as possible, as if she couldn't bear to look at him; be near him, and he felt a pang in his chest. Perhaps he'd rather brave the elements outside than deal with her icy treatment. Maybe Cwen really didn't like him and foolishly, he felt hurt by her rejection. He warned himself to be cautious. He could not allow himself to develop feelings for her—this was meant to be about quelling his lust. She was being guarded, and he knew he must be too.

But he was so damn frustrated. Every time she moved, his body tensed. Talk about torture. How was he going to survive the night, being so close to her, cooped up in here? At least if he was camping out, the ferocious rain would help to cool his desire.

'Stop fidgeting!' he bit out, when she moved for the hundredth time.

'Stop breathing!' she retorted.

And he grinned into the darkness. He did like her spirit. He had never met anyone like her. And suddenly he wondered, was there something she wasn't telling him? Something that was preventing her from allowing her to take her own pleasure, to be intimate with him?

'Did your late husband hurt you, Cwen?'

'What? No!' she said. 'He would never...'

He'd had to ask. His mind was racing. He still couldn't believe he'd got it so wrong—again. He was trying to think of another reason why she wouldn't want to do this, when her pulse seemed to race whenever he came near her. He had thought, maybe, she hadn't enjoyed her intimate experiences before. After all, she'd called them an obligation. A duty.

But he was reaching... He had known she cared for Feran. She had been wearing his wedding ring when

Njal had arrived here, and he'd noticed today she was still wearing it, only now she wore it round her neck as a pendant. He wasn't sure it was wholly appropriate, but he hadn't said anything about it. Yet. He hated the way her face brightened when she spoke of Feran. It made him want to tug her back, pull her into his body and start laying claim to her, if only to rid her of her thoughts of that man. It was taking all his restraint not to do so—after all, she was his now. But he was no brute. Was it possible she was still grieving; that she felt guilty lying with another man?

He sighed. 'Why don't you tell me about him?' he said.

He could just make out her silhouette in the dark, and she turned to look in his direction, over her shoulder. 'You want to hear about Feran?'

Not really, he thought, but it was the only topic he could think of that might dampen his desire. 'We may as well talk if we're not going to touch. It might help the dark hours pass quicker.'

He felt her roll over onto her back and sigh. Their arms brushed, but he didn't move away—she did that for them.

'You loved him?'

'In a way,' she said slowly. 'It was an arranged marriage, I didn't have a say in the matter, but we understood each other's needs.'

'Could happen to us,' he offered, gently teasing her.

'Doubtful.'

But it was interesting. He had thought she'd married for love. Was that why she was so angry about their union today—that once again she'd felt she was marrying out of duty?

'I wonder if he was still here, what would have happened now, when all this was going on.'

'Well, I don't think he would have taken too kindly to us lying here like this, do you?' he said. 'I think he might have had something to say...'

Suddenly she giggled, and the noise took him by surprise, but once she'd let it out, it was if she couldn't help herself, and she did it again. It was an incredible sound—infectious, and he chuckled as well. The situation was pretty absurd, and it felt good to release some of the tension of the past few days—hell, the past few years.

'Sorry,' she said, trying to stop.

'Don't be.'

And he determined he would try to make her laugh again, and often.

Her giggles turned into hiccups and finally she sobered, and there was such a long pause, he wondered if she'd fallen asleep. But then she moved, turning her face towards him.

'Do you think the rumours are true—that Caedwalla will come?'

'I don't know. You and your father know him better than I. Why, are you hoping to be rescued?'

'Not by him!' she bit back. 'He is ruthless. I wouldn't be surprised if he was coming here to take Jorvik for himself, rather than help my father.'

Njal wasn't sure how Jorvik would cope with another battle or siege. And as they lay there, he wondered how to make sense of all the lives that had been lost in the war between their two peoples, which had brought them to this point. It was a huge gulf between them. Was it too great to ever truly be bridged?

'If he does come, we will be ready,' Njal said, determined.

'After Feran died, my father was considering marrying me off to Caedwalla to forge a new alliance.'

Njal drew in a breath. 'Isn't he twice your age?'

'Yes. I have been protesting for months.'

'So, you're saying I saved you then?'

She seemed to ignore his comment and there was another long pause. Perhaps he shouldn't jest about such things.

'Njal, why weren't you there, at the settlement that night, when your parents were attacked?' she asked.

He frowned into the darkness at her change in subject. If she intended to completely cool his desire, she'd picked another perfect topic. Did the attack on his people bother her? He hoped so. He didn't want to think she was capable of the things her father had done. 'I was in a neighbouring burgh.'

'Why?'

He wondered if he should tell her, but he didn't see why not. It was a long while ago. 'I spent the night with a woman.'

'Oh.'

'Jealous?' he suggested.

'No!' she exploded.

He grinned. 'She was a Saxon, like you,' he added.

He felt her face turn to look at him in surprise. 'Did you love her?'

'I thought it was love at the time.'

'What happened?'

'Never mind what happened,' he said.

'And your brother—was he not there either?' she asked.

'Yes, he was there,' he said, shifting uncomfortably. 'He saw it all. I don't think I realised the extent of the damage it caused until recently...' Njal was disappointed his brother hadn't been present at his wedding today, but given his volatile mood, he'd thought it was perhaps for the best. 'I'm hoping, now we're here, he will be able to settle. Find happiness.' He turned his head to look at her. 'Just like me...' he added wryly.

She sighed. 'Thank you. For being so good about tonight,' she whispered.

And he bit his tongue to stop him saying anything that would reveal his true frustration.

'Why *are* you being so good about it?' she asked.

'Because I haven't given up on you yet,' he said. 'In case you hadn't noticed, I'm familiar with investing days, weeks—even years—in the ruthless pursuit of what I want, Cwen. And I feel confident that with time and patience I'll be able to win you round.'

Chapter Seven

When Cwen next opened her eyes, Njal was no longer in the bed. She sat up, looking around, instantly awake. She couldn't believe she'd managed to fall asleep with him lying there beside her; she had thought it would be impossible.

Where was he now?

He had been disturbingly close all night, heat radiating from his large body, and she had been both terrified and excited.

When he'd tugged up his tunic, bringing it up and over his head and discarding it, revealing his taut stomach muscles, she had felt panic—and what could only be likened to the onset of a fever lashing through her. His broad chest was magnificent, and covered in fascinating ink markings and scars.

She should have been repulsed, but she hadn't been. Far from it. He was the most incredible man she had ever seen and she had stared at him in wonder. She had wanted to look at the ink designs properly, to study them, and ask what each one meant. And the scars—where had he got each one from? Had he suffered much pain?

When he'd blown out the candle and they had lain

there in the dark, it had been frightening. Disturbing. She was afraid of her own feelings, as she was beginning to want things she had no experience of—and knew she could never have. She felt like a volcano was beginning to erupt inside her and she willed her blood to stay still, to remain dormant.

A part of her had wanted to reach out in the dark and touch his skin—to see if it was as solid and as smooth as it looked, but of course she hadn't dared. Not after telling him that she wanted them to behave as friends. But she had never been so intimate with a man before—to have shared the same bed. She and Feran had always had separate rooms.

She felt incredibly guilty, as she knew it was a wife's duty to consummate the marriage on their wedding night, but she hadn't been able to bring herself to do it—or to tell Njal the real reason why. She had misled him—he had thought he was getting a wife who would satisfy his needs, even if she couldn't provide him with children, but she had denied him both. He should surely hate her, be angry with her, and yet, he hadn't been cruel. He hadn't used force. Instead, he had been kind. He had asked her questions, seemingly out of genuine curiosity and interest, even going so far as to talk about Feran to try to put her at ease. He had asked her if she'd loved him, and she'd said yes. And it was true. She had. But not in the way Njal thought.

At one point, she had even laughed—perhaps from the hysteria, the absurdness of the situation, but it had felt good to have that release. She couldn't remember the last time she'd laughed.

Eventually, he had fallen asleep, and she had felt restless, irritable, at being so close to him. She'd listened to the sound of his steady breathing and had found it strangely comforting. Until, after a while, his impressive chest began to rise and fall erratically, and he had begun muttering in his sleep. She'd raised herself up on her elbow to look at him.

'Njal?' she'd asked.

But he didn't hear her. He was still asleep.

He must have been having some kind of nightmare and she wondered what was haunting him.

When his head had begun to thrash from side to side, she'd bravely reached out and touched him, placing her hand on his shoulder, offering him some small comfort in his sleep. She was not prepared for him to sit, bolt upright, and cry out a name. A woman's name.

'Synnove!'

His eyes had flown open and he'd turned to see her propped up on her elbow, looking up at him in the darkness.

'Are you all right?' she'd asked.

And he'd dragged a hand over his face.

'This is why I don't sleep. The nightmares are worse than being awake. Did I wake you?'

'No.'

He'd lain back down on the furs.

He was a decent man, she realised now. And he was clearly suffering from all the trauma he and his brother had gone through. At the hand of her father. And she wondered how he could have shaken up her beliefs about who he was in just a matter of days. He was like a different person entirely to the one she'd invented in her mind. And she felt bad for adding to his trauma.

She wondered what had happened between him and his lover, the woman who she now knew was called Synnove?

It was not pleasant—thinking of him lying with other women. Had he had many lovers? But his arrogant confidence, asserting that she would change her mind about him, made her think he had. But why did she care? He was infuriating! And the thought of spending another night in his company was unbearable, she thought, as she made the bed, running her hands over the soft furs. Awful, she decided, placing the cushions back neatly, spending too long on their arrangement. What would he say about them having to spend a second night of frustration together? A tingle of traitorous excitement rippled through her.

If she was ever intimate with him, would he even know that she was innocent, that she hadn't been close with a man before—that she'd lied about Leof?

The direction of her thoughts scared her. She should not be thinking like this. And suddenly, she felt an overwhelming sense of anger towards her mother that she had behaved so recklessly five years ago, and had selfishly expected Cwen to pick up the pieces, forcing her to live a lie ever since. Because her mother had been so irresponsible, she'd put Cwen in a position where she had to sacrifice her desire for love—a real marriage. If she hadn't had to do that, might she have been able to be honest with Njal now? Instead, she was risking their fragile alliance to keep this secret for her mother's sake—and her son's.

But who was she kidding? Even if she was able to tell him, she knew she should never trust Njal—not fully. He was the man who had attacked her home and toppled her father from power. He didn't really care for her. He only wanted her for what she could offer him—her title, her body. He'd even said so himself. And she knew she could never lie with someone without trust and love involved. But likewise, would he ever trust her now, after discovering that she'd married him under false pretences?

She fixed her hair and padded down the corridor to her old room and dressed quickly, wanting to go and find Leof and check he was all right, but she couldn't help wondering where Njal was and when had he left her. She could hear the rain still clattering outside—it had been going on all night, the wind whipping up against the walls, and she knew Leof would be unsettled. He didn't like the thunder.

When she walked into the hall, there was a flurry of activity. Her gaze was instantly drawn to Njal, over at a table, looking serious, directing his men, briefing them on something, and her heart started beating at a faster rate. She realised he was breathing new life into the fortress—and her.

He looked up and their eyes clashed across the hall, and it took her a moment to realise they weren't discussing rebuilding their defences, or Caedwalla's advancing forces, but the inches deep of water she had absent-mindedly waded into. She picked up her skirts, gasping in horror. She had been so focussed on Njal, so excruciatingly aware of him, that she'd failed to notice the hall had flooded overnight.

She glanced all around and realised people were bailing out buckets of water. She couldn't believe it. It had never happened before.

Njal began to wade over to her, grimacing, the water halfway up his boots.

'Morning,' he said.

'Why didn't you wake me?' she said, horrified. She felt bad she hadn't been up, helping. That he hadn't woken her. That he'd left her.

'I thought you might need the sleep since I kept you up all night.' He winked, and she was aware those around her could hear, some of the women giving each other knowing glances, and she flushed.

'You said we would rule here together,' she spat, suddenly frustrated, embarrassed that she hadn't been around all morning. 'Are you trying to push me aside?'

'And why would I do that?' he said, lowering his voice. 'When I think you're the most intelligent person in the room?'

Her breath left her.

'I would be glad of your suggestions, you know the place better than I. It seems we had a flash flood due to the storm last night—the rivers burst their banks. Unfortunately, with the settlement being low-lying, most buildings have some kind of water damage—some more than most. Has this happened before?'

She shook her head. 'No. Not like this. Leof—?'

'He's been helping us. Look.'

And she glanced over to where he was pointing, to Leof sat on the table in the middle of his men, holding a bucket.

'And my parents?'

'Also fine,' he said, although any amusement in his eyes fled. 'I checked with the guard on their door this morning. Your father is almost ready to travel, but he may have to do so by boat now, unless he waits until the water recedes.'

'You don't seem concerned about this,' she said.

'About your father leaving, or the floods?'

'Both.'

'If your father needs to stay a few more days, it won't hurt. And as for the floods, I'm trying to see the positive side. At least they will keep Caedwalla at bay. It will help our defences, as if an enemy wants to approach, they'll have to come through the water. It will make their task far more difficult. But I do feel sorry for the people whose homes have been destroyed. And my men who have been sleeping in the barn—they're not happy they woke up soaked to the bone. But I'm just grateful no lives have been lost.'

She nodded, then glanced around, feeling uncomfortable for biting his head off. 'What can I do to help?'

'We'll need to bring anyone who needs help or shelter inside the settlement, offer them what they need.'

She nodded, glad to have something to do to keep her occupied.

The scene outside of the hall was spectacular, with ducks swimming on the burst banks, glistening, tranquil water as far as the eye could see. It was beautiful—until she realised the devastation the water had caused. Fields and their crops were totally submerged—decimated. Animals were floating, struggling to swim, fighting for their lives, and farmers were attempting to rescue them, waist-deep in water. Buildings were waterlogged, crumbling under the pressure. She couldn't believe all this had happened overnight, while she had been dealing with her own turbulent storm of emotions.

She and Leof began assisting people with their belongings, bringing them inside the fortress and handing out blankets to keep them warm. Some of Njal's men came in with injuries, from buildings collapsing on top of them, or getting trapped by beams under water as they'd tried to help people, and she ensured she or the other women stitched up their wounds.

She was relieved to be out of Njal's proximity for a while. She couldn't think straight when he was around. But if she'd thought she could marry him, then ignore him, she'd thought wrong. She couldn't stop thinking about him. It had crept up on her, engulfing her, just like these floods on their lands.

When he talked to her, she couldn't take her eyes off him, fascinated by the sound of his voice, and when they touched, she burned. She didn't want to feel like this, and yet today, it was worse. When she'd seen him in the hall and he'd looked up, their eyes connecting, she hadn't been able to breathe.

It was a long, tiring day, but the people pulled together, showing their strength, and the next time she saw Njal it was getting dark outside. The hall was heaving with people lining up for food, and she was helping to serve up the cauldrons of pottage. When Njal took his place in line, among all the other men, it threw her. He was their new leader. Her father would always have demanded to be served first—he would never have waited in line for the more needy to eat before him. But then, she couldn't imagine her mother serving up stew either. Yet Cwen thought it was important she was seen to be helping, to be among the people, as one of them—perhaps Njal did too.

When he got to the front of the line and held out his bowl for her, she gingerly took it, their eyes meeting, fingers brushing, and she tried to concentrate on piling it high with meat and vegetables.

'How has your day been?'

'Wet.' She grimaced.

'You're soaked through,' he said, acknowledging her sodden hair and drenched clothes.

'I think we all are.' She handed him his bowl back and hoped he would move on to find a seat, but instead, he lingered.

'I've barely seen you today. Anyone would think you were avoiding me.'

'Of course not,' she lied. 'I've just been busy. There was so much to do.'

He nodded. 'Thanks for your help out there,' he said, motioning with his head to the door. 'The men said you were good with their injuries. I appreciate it.'

She didn't know how to act around him. She was nervous. Her palms felt sweaty and her stomach was fluttering fast.

'What's the matter with you?' he asked, peering closer at her.

'I'm fine,' she said. She didn't want his intense gaze on her, it made her skin tingle.

'No…there's definitely something wrong. You're not snapping at me, arguing with me, or putting me down. You're on edge.'

She sighed. 'How would you know what I'm like when I'm on edge?' she bit out. And yet he was right. She felt tense, her body rigid. She was disturbingly aware of his virile, powerful body standing so close to her, his wet tunic clinging to his muscles, and she was breathing hard.

How could he be having this effect on her? How could he have her wanting things she had never wanted before—things she could not have?

'I already know you better than you think.'

Bjorn came up behind Njal and jested, telling him to hurry and stop holding up the line. The men had been goading him about his wedding night all day long, asking how it had been, and he'd laughed it off, telling them it was good. But damn, he felt cheated.

Njal had lain there awake most of the night, feeling confused and hurt about her rejection—and frustrated, trying to get his desire in check. When he'd finally fallen asleep, he'd had a nightmare, and then not too long afterwards, he'd been woken by the shouts coming from the hall. He had been disturbed to see the damage the floods had caused without any warning. But he'd been glad to have a distraction from Cwen. He had spent the day outside, rescuing people and animals, and trying to save waterlogged buildings.

He wondered why this had to happen now. It wasn't a good start to his rule. How much more could this city take?

It had been raining non-stop all day long and he was hoping the cool water would at least dampen his irritation and desire, because despite what Cwen had said about never wanting to lie with him, he was still feeling the heavy throb of attraction in his groin.

When she'd walked into the hall this morning, she'd looked so beautiful, he'd wanted her, more than ever. He was surprised she'd offered to help and he'd been grateful, but looking at her now—her pinafore was soaked through, the wet material clinging to the generous swells of her breasts, her hips—he felt bad she was so cold. And yet, she looked breathtaking. He could see the dark shadows of her nipples beneath the material, and the shape of her flat stomach; her slender legs. She didn't look like she'd carried a child in her belly—she was perfect. He swallowed down another rush of desire, the hardness in his groin increasing.

He lifted his hand and peeled away a piece of hair that was stuck to her face and chastised himself. Her eyes widened, and he felt bad he was lusting over her while she was stood here dithering.

'You need to warm yourself up by the fire. Can't someone else do this?' he said, about serving the food.

'I want to do it.' It was admirable, but she was to be queen. Surely someone else could do it?

He frowned. She looked pale. He was actually pretty worried about her. 'Well, don't catch your death, will you?'

'I'll try not to.'

Sitting down to a table, he wasn't sure how he was going to get through another night of this torture. Did she not feel the searing heat when their hands brushed? Or the tension in the air when they talked? Could he really be imagining it? And was she dreading tonight as much as he was?

He looked up at her, still serving the long line of people, offering a smile to each person, Saxon or Dane, and he liked her just that little bit more. *Helvete!* After that nightmare about Synnove last night, he should be seeing it as a warning, steeling his heart against her.

Still, he wondered, perhaps he should do a good deed. Offer up a sweetener, of sorts, to try to ease the friction between them, so after he'd wolfed down his meal, he went to find her maid. When he returned to the hall a while later, he was pleased to see most people had eaten and were settling down, creating little camps on the tables, and Cwen was doing the rounds, making sure everyone was all right.

He approached her and took her arm. She looked up at him, startled.

'Have you eaten?'

'Not yet.'

'You need to,' he said, chastising her. 'Eat, and then I have something for you.'

'What is it?'

'You'll see. Come.' He led her over to the cauldron and used the ladle to scrape up some of the last dregs of the pottage, as she had done for him. 'Here,' he said, placing it down on the table. 'Eat.'

'You're worse than my mother,' she said, as she brought a spoonful up to her mouth.

'Someone's got to look after you while you're taking care of everyone else.'

'I wish it would stop raining. I'm worried about what will happen overnight,' she said. 'If there'll be more damage.'

He nodded. 'We're doing all we can.'

He was eager for her to finish the bowl. He wanted to take her back to their room, show her what he'd prepared. He wanted to stop her shivering.

'Njal.'

He looked up to see Bjorn hovering over them both, his face grave.

'What is it?'

'It's Ove.'

He tensed. 'What about him?'

'He and a few of the men have been drinking. They're causing trouble again.' And then Bjorn leaned down and whispered in his ear.

Njal's blood ran cold and he frowned. Damn Ove, he did not want to be dealing with this right now. They had enough to contend with. He pushed out his chair and stood. 'Where?'

'He's in the alehouse.'

'What's going on?' Cwen asked, reaching out and placing a hand on his arm. He stared down at her fingers curled around his skin.

Should he tell her? He didn't want her to worry. He didn't want her getting involved. And he didn't want her to know what a brute his brother was—more so than she already thought. And yet he didn't see any point in lying—she was going to find out eventually.

'He's got Eadhild. And Leof. He's...'

She shot out of her seat so fast, her eyes wide with naked fear, and her vulnerability struck him right in the middle of his chest.

'I'll go and deal with it. I want you to stay here,' he said.

'No,' she said, shaking her head. 'I'm coming with you.'

'It might make the situation worse,' he said.

'I don't care. He's my child...'

Njal sighed and relented, allowing her to join him and Bjorn. 'Stay behind me. Keep quiet. I don't want to inflame the situation.'

When they got outside, they waded through the water into the tavern across the courtyard. It had a shallow coating of water over the floor, and the place was deserted apart from his brother and his own band of men, and they were pushing Leof around, bandying him about between them. The boy's big grey eyes were wide and vulnerable, just like his mother's, but Njal was impressed he wasn't crying. One of the men, Thurston, held Eadhild in his arms, teasing her, and she looked afraid.

'Leof,' Cwen whispered, tensing behind him.

Njal knew he had to tread carefully. Looking around, he realised these men had all lost their families that day their settlement had been destroyed. Ove had picked his company well. They all had a grudge to bear.

They had all fought with Njal on the battlefield, so he was aware he owed them his loyalty, but didn't they owe him theirs too? What did they think they were doing, behaving like this? They were letting them all down, disrupting the newfound peace. Every day he was watching them with growing unease.

'Brother!' Ove said, slurring. 'We wondered if Bjorn would run along and fetch you. Sorry to interrupt your meal.'

'I didn't see you in the hall. Are none of you hungry, or have you filled your bellies with ale instead? What's going on here?' Njal asked, trying to keep his cool.

'Just trying to pass the dark hours of the evening. We're wanting to get to know this boy here—and Thurston his maid.' Ove grinned.

'Let him go, Ove. He's just a child—and his mother wants to put him to bed.'

'I'm afraid I can't do that, Brother.'

Njal clenched and unclenched his fist round the hilt of his sword. 'Why not?'

'Because some people are saying you're going to name him as your heir. I'm hurt,' he said, pulling a face as if he was wounded, placing a hand over his heart. 'I thought you'd always said that would be me.'

Njal felt Cwen's eyes on him, and he knew she'd be wondering if Ove was speaking the truth—whether he'd agreed to that or not, when he had promised her otherwise. It had been one of the terms of their marriage. He'd said Leof would be their heir, unless they had a child of their own. Now he knew that would never happen, securing the boy's lineage. But if something happened to them now, Leof was too young to rule. But Ove as king could be potentially devastating. It would be disastrous for the kingdom.

'I don't believe I said anything about anyone being next in line to the throne. But now you've just expressed your wish to be heir, it's been noted. Let that be the end of it.'

'I wanted to know if the boy had heard if it was true, if he'll be king one day. And do you know what he said? He said he will be king, that his mother had told him you'd agreed to it—even though he doesn't want to be.'

Njal looked at Leof. He wasn't his son, but now he and Cwen were married, this boy was as close to having a child as he might ever get. And he could understand his desire not to wear the crown. Njal had felt the same burden as he'd grown closer to taking over the fortress.

A strange feeling of responsibility took over him, just as it had that day he had known he would have to raise Ove. Right now, he had to protect Leof.

How had he failed so spectacularly in bringing up his brother these past two winters? Or had the damage already been done, when their parents had been killed? Would Ove have turned out like this however he'd been brought up? But he had to believe there was still hope for him; that he could still turn this around. He couldn't give up on him yet.

'So if he's going to be a rival, I was thinking, why not just kill him now? Why wait until he's old enough to fight back?' Ove said.

Njal's blood iced over. He heard Cwen gasp behind him, and alarm flared in his chest. He didn't want her to do anything foolish. He didn't want to have to worry about the both of them.

The men tussled with the boy some more, and Leof tried to get away. Njal's heart pounded.

Yes, Leof was a threat to Njal's own position here—there might be no end of plots to place the boy on the throne later on. And he was a threat to Ove, if his brother wanted a pathway to power. But he was just five winters old—and Njal liked him a lot. And right now, he was a lot less of a threat than his own wayward brother. He couldn't believe Ove was being like this. While Njal wanted to turn his hand to rebuilding, to peace, Ove seemed to have chosen to focus on violence and destruction.

Njal knew Cwen would never forgive him if something happened to her child. He would never forgive himself. He tried to focus. 'We don't hurt children, remember?'

'*They* did. Don't *you* remember? Or have you forgotten, Brother? I was just a child. Look what they did to me. They took my father, my mother, my friends—they burned down my home in front of my eyes. They stole my life.'

Njal could tell Cwen was becoming more and more agitated beside him, desperate to have her child back in her arms, and he was unsure what she was going to do. He hoped she wouldn't do anything rash. He knew how stubborn she could be.

'I remember. Still, *we* are different. And you have the rest of your life ahead of you to enjoy.' He spread out his hands in explanation, letting go of his sword. 'I don't want to fight you, Brother. But I also can't have you going against my orders, causing turmoil every time my back is turned. We need to instil peace here—lead by example. I need to be able to trust you.'

'That's what *you* want, Brother. Maybe we don't.' And yet Ove's men were looking between each other, uncertain, and it made Njal wonder if they would totally back him up when it came to it. 'Why do we need peace?'

'You want to spend your life fighting?'

Ove shrugged. 'Why stop now—why settle for here, when we could use our power to continue our raids across the country, taking whatever we want? That's what I'd do, if I was in charge.'

'That's what you'd choose to do if you ruled here?' he asked. It was so disappointing.

He must ensure that never happened, Njal thought, a determination solidifying in his stomach. But he wondered if Ove really meant it, or if he was all talk. Was he just trying to deceive his older brother into believing that he might do something, taunting him, like when they were younger? 'Then go ahead, hurt this boy...' Njal said.

Cwen gasped beside him.

'Do this, and I guarantee there will be consequences. Another need for vengeance. It's a vicious cycle, Brother, haven't you realised that yet? You will have a whole country of Saxons, but also Danes, turn against you. The whole of England will know that Ove the great warrior was threatened by a boy of five. Is that what you want as your legacy, Ove?' He could hear the anger vibrating in his own voice.

His brother stared at him.

'Hand him back, Ove, we've had our fun,' Thurston said. 'Besides, I'm starving. Aren't you?

Ove wavered, and then shrugged, uncomfortably. He gave a nervous laugh. 'No need for the dramatics, Njal. I'm prepared to hand him back, unharmed...' And then his smile vanished. 'But I meant what I said about his title. I've fought alongside you, followed you into battle for two winters. I'll hand him back, but you must promise me you will strip him of his inheritance and name me as your heir.'

Njal sighed. 'Is that all you care about?' He felt let down. Since when had Ove become so ambitious? When had he turned against him? He could no longer depend on him. He didn't know why he was surprised; he should know by now the people you cared for often let you down the worst.

'The same goes for you, Njal.'

'No, I care about making sure we have someone to represent our people, to allow them to live here, safely,' Njal said, pushing a hand through his hair. 'You want to be heir? Then go ahead, kill him.' He moved closer, his voice deadly. 'But you'll never step foot inside this fortress again, let alone near the crown.'

The men seemed to falter, the reality of what Njal was saying finally kicking in, and the thought of their own positions here being at risk becoming a real possibility.

'Even now, my men have this building surrounded. You won't get out of here alive. Give him back, and we'll pretend this little episode never happened. No one need know, and I'll consider your request to be my heir—however small that likelihood is now.'

The boy tried to wrestle his way free, and suddenly Ove released him, letting him escape, and Leof raced over to his mother. Njal watched Cwen pick up her son and hold him close. He allowed himself a small sigh of relief.

'That's the first sensible thing you've done all week,' Njal said, and without warning, Ove drew back his fist and punched him right on the jaw.

He heard Cwen gasp beside him, and he instantly tasted blood on his lips.

'No, I think that was,' Ove said, as he and his men, as well as Bjorn, all reached for their swords.

Njal spat the blood onto the floor and looked back at his brother, his eyes turning glacial. 'You shouldn't have done that.'

'I thought you needed reminding, Brother, that king's bleed too…'

Njal was thrumming with anger. He couldn't have Ove go against him like this. He'd had enough.

Long gone were the days of them wrestling on the beach as he'd taught Ove to fight under their father's amused gaze. Njal had always been stronger, but sometimes he'd let Ove win. And sometimes his brother had played dirty, cheating the rules, and their father had paid no mind. But Njal would not be able to let this go.

He signalled to Bjorn, and all at once the men outside burst through the doors.

'Seize them. Put them in a cell for the night without any food and let them sleep off their ale. Give them the night in a cold, damp room to think about what they've done,' Njal said.

His men crowded forwards and a brutal fight ensued. It saddened Njal to see it—men who had fought alongside each other for years, now fighting one another. But Ove's men were so inebriated, they were no match for Njal's sober warriors.

Njal retrieved Eadhild from the back of the room and she reassured him she was fine, muttering her thanks. But he could tell she was shaken. And he was enraged. He didn't want anyone to live in fear here. He couldn't believe his own flesh and blood was the cause of it.

'Come,' he said, turning to the women and the boy. 'You don't want to watch this. Let's get you inside.'

He walked quickly, taking Cwen's arm and leading her back into the hall and through the corridors. He rushed them all forwards, at speed, rage shimmering off him, wanting to get them back to their chambers, safe. He was furious with his brother and his insubordination. He was ashamed of him. He couldn't believe that now they'd achieved all this; set out what they'd hoped to do, they were fighting amongst themselves. It made them look like fools!

He pushed open the door to Leof's room and ushered

them all inside. He ruffled the boy's hair. 'You all right?' His admiration for him had grown tenfold. 'You were very brave out there.'

The boy nodded.

'I didn't mean what I said, about them hurting you. I was trying to work out his true intentions. I didn't think he'd go ahead with it.'

'I know,' the boy said, nodding.

Skit, Njal was so wound up, he couldn't stop pacing. He felt awful that they'd had to suffer that—it had been such a long and terrible day as it was. And he thought they would probably prefer it if he left them alone. He was sure they'd think even more unfavourably of him now.

'I'll leave you all to it,' he said, as he retreated out the door. 'I'll have a man guard the door.'

He pulled the door to and stalked down the corridor to his own chamber. He poured himself a drink, downing it in one, going over everything that had happened, all that was said. He didn't know what he was going to do about his brother. It was as if he was purposely trying to be deviant. Vindictive. When Njal had seen the boy in his grasp, a possessiveness had lashed through him, and for once, his loyalties were divided.

He stared at the barrel of water, which he'd had prepared for Cwen. It had taken a long while to fill up, the maids carrying cauldrons full of boiling water down the corridor. He dipped his finger in and swirled it round. It was still warm, but he cursed—why did Ove have to ruin everything?

A soft knock at the door interrupted his thoughts. He went to open it and was surprised to see Cwen standing there. His pulse instantly kicked up, despite it all.

He hadn't expected to see her again tonight, but to stay with the boy and make sure Leof was all right.

What was she doing here? Had the guard not appeared?

'I didn't think I'd see you again tonight.'

She wrung her hands. 'I can go...'

He shook his head. 'No, that isn't what I meant.'

She stepped inside, brushing past him, her delicate scent drifting under his nose, and he swallowed down a rush of desire. How could he want her, even now?

She glanced past him and saw the barrel full of water, and then looked back at him, wide-eyed.

'I thought you might want to take a bath,' he explained, shrugging his shoulder. 'Warm up a bit.'

She swallowed. 'Thank you. And for what you did out there.'

'Is Leof all right?'

'He fell straight asleep. I think he was exhausted after everything that's happened today,' she said. 'Are *you* all right?'

'Me?' he said, as if he was taken aback that she was asking.

'It must be hard, seeing your brother behave like that. Being caught in the middle. Having to pick sides.'

He took a deep breath, shaking his head. Did she really understand? 'I don't get him. We've always been so close,' he allowed himself to reveal.

She nodded, encouraging him to go on. And he was so worked up, he wanted to share his frustration. 'I don't know what's happened. He seems so angry. Seems to be blaming me, whereas he once looked up to me.'

It felt good to let it out—to tell someone about it and

share how he was feeling. But he wasn't sure he should be telling her, opening up to her. He had determined he wouldn't.

'It seems to me that admiration has turned into something else,' she said.

He frowned. 'What do you mean?'

'He seems jealous. As if he doesn't like being in your shadow.'

'Jealous?' Njal asked, staring at her.

'Perhaps it has something to do with the battle and my father,' she said. 'That he was the one who wounded him. Maybe it made him feel powerful, taking his revenge. Maybe he feels he deserves more.'

He let her words sink in and nodded. 'I think you might be right.'

'He's only young. People that age—they're not great with authority.'

'How do you know?' he asked.

'Because I wasn't. Were you?'

He grimaced, thinking back to how he used to test his father's patience. 'Perhaps not. But he's gone too far lately.'

She nodded.

'I didn't choose to have him—my parents did. Sometimes I begrudge my responsibility. And yet, I also wouldn't have had it any other way.'

'I understand that,' she said. 'More than you know. You have had to step up, you've done everything for him, but he doesn't see your authority—you're his brother. Your lip's still bleeding, by the way.'

He put his fingers to his mouth and brought them down. He couldn't believe his brother had hit him and drawn blood. 'Great.'

'Here,' she said, going over to a chest in the corner and finding a piece of wool. She came back towards him and brought the material up to his lips, pressing it against them.

'Thanks,' he muttered, staring down at her.

'Parenting, especially on your own, is a difficult task. A greater challenge than any you probably faced on the battlefield. You never know if you're getting it right. And you never get to live your own life. Not really. But we do our best.'

How did she understand it so completely? Understand him, and how he was feeling? It felt good to discuss their shared experience of raising a child, even to take a glimpse back at their former selves.

He had seen Cwen in a different light today and he realised she was constantly surprising him. He had known she was strong, and a caring leader to her own people. But today he'd seen her kindness towards his men—and it had made him respect her, like her, all the more.

'Thank you, for looking after my men today. For your help.'

'I'm starting to realise they're not so different to the rest of us,' she said wryly, and he nodded.

'There's hope for me yet.' He smiled. And then he raised his hand to her cheek. 'What are you doing here, Cwen?'

Chapter Eight

Cwen wondered what had possessed her to knock on Njal's door. He had given her a chance to escape him for the night, to sleep in the other room with Eadhild and Leof. But she couldn't go to bed and leave things the way they were—without thanking him for what he'd done. Without checking he was all right. She'd known he must be smarting, angry about his brother's behaviour—because she'd been right that first day they'd met. He and Ove were nothing alike. Now he'd put her son's safety over his own brother's needs and she was extremely grateful.

'Do you have to get back?' he asked.

She shook her head. 'No,' she said, lowering the wool from his perfect lips. 'I think you're right. It wouldn't look good for us to have different rooms. We need to appear united.'

'Even though you have the perfect excuse to get away from me?' he asked, his eyebrow raised.

She shook her head. 'But my feelings on the matter, us, still stand.'

'Can I get you anything?' he asked. 'You look colder than ever. You should get out of those wet clothes. You could still use the bath.'

'Maybe. I am shivering.'

He nodded. 'I'll get a fire going, then leave you alone for a while.'

She sat down on the edge of the bed and watched as he got down on his haunches and lit the wood, and then he sat back on his knees.

'All right. I'll be back in a while.'

'Wait,' she said, biting her lip. 'I need your help.' She cringed. 'I can't get this tunic off by myself. It's knotted.'

He looked at her, incredulous. 'Seriously? You want my help to remove your clothes?'

'No,' she tried to say, but he spoke over her.

'And expect me not to touch you afterwards? Just how good do you think my control is?' he said, and she couldn't help but smile. He cursed softly. 'This will call for some serious restraint.' He stood up and took her hand, lifting her up off the bed. 'Turn around.'

She liked how he put her at ease, making light of the situation. But when he drew her hair away from her neck and began to unfasten the tie that had knotted at the back, her smile faded as goose bumps erupted over her skin.

She stilled.

With every loosening of the cord, she was aware he was exposing a little more of her skin, and his warm breath whispered across it.

'Arms up,' he said.

And she reluctantly did as she was told, raising her arms up in the air so he could draw the material over and off her, leaving her in her floor-length tunic.

He placed his hands on her shoulders and turned her around. He leaned closer, ever so slightly, and she felt sure he was going to cover her mouth with his. When he pulled away, she wasn't sure if she was relieved or disappointed.

'Can you do the rest on your own?' he asked.

She nodded. She didn't think she could speak.

'Then I'll be back shortly,' he said gruffly.

And when the door clicked closed behind him, she sagged back down on the bed. She didn't know what was the matter with her. Was she that weak that she'd fallen for a Norseman in the space of a few short days? She had vowed she wouldn't.

Her mother's words reverberated in her ear: *'You must keep him at arm's bay. You must keep our secret.'*

She threw off the rest of her clothes, placing them by the fire to dry, and climbed into the barrel. She couldn't believe he'd had a bath prepared for her. It was kind of him. Thoughtful. And he hadn't insisted on staying, or getting in with her. He was a good man, she was starting to realise. She thought she was actually beginning to trust him; like him. How could that be?

The water felt glorious. It felt good to wash away the stresses and strains of the day, and she held her breath and dipped her head under the surface, washing her hair. Everything was silent.

A while later she climbed out and looked around for something to dry herself with. She pulled a blanket off the bed and wrapped herself in it, and went over to stand by the fire, trying to warm herself up. The cold had seeped through her bones today, but she also thought the shock of what had happened outside was starting to sink in. Would Njal's brother really have hurt Leof?

The knock on the door made her jump, and she padded over and opened it.

'All done?' Njal said, coming back inside and locking the door behind him. 'You look colder than ever!' he said, taking in her chattering teeth. And his arms came around hers, rubbing them up and down through the material.

'I've realised I don't have any dry clothes,' she said, regretting leaving everything in the other room. 'My things are all down the hall.'

'I can go and get you something. Or I have a spare tunic,' he said, and reached for the one he'd worn to their wedding yesterday, which was still hanging over the back of the chair. 'Put this on.'

She fumbled with the blanket and the tunic, trying to keep her dignity, and managed to pull it on over her head. She could smell his woody scent on the material. It was huge and came to halfway down her thighs, but she still felt exposed, her legs on show.

'Mind if I get in?' he asked, nodding towards the bath. 'I've been soaked through all day too.'

She shook her head and turned around, trying to busy herself with her damp clothes as he undressed. She heard his sodden tunic and breeches descend on the floor, and then his body move in the water as he clambered in. Finally, she thought it might be safe to turn around if she kept her gaze at eye level.

'It's not the warmest, is it?' He grimaced.

And she glanced over at him. 'It was better than nothing.' But the moment she looked, she wished she hadn't. He was washing his face and his arms, scooping the water up over his muscles, and her eyes were drawn to the droplets cascading over his glorious chest. His ink. But this time, she didn't look away. She was mesmerised.

The designs were so detailed. So intricate. It must have taken someone a lot of time to etch them into his skin. She wondered who and her stomach burned.

'What do the markings mean, on your skin?' she said. 'Will you tell me about them?'

He pointed to a strange knot-like design weaving over his left shoulder. 'This is the Knot of the Slain. It represents courage and protection.'

'And that one?' she asked, coming closer, nodding to the one on his right shoulder.

'Gungnir—Odin's spear. It symbolises ambition. Determination.'

But she could also see a large cross in the middle of his chest. She knew that one, and she was intrigued that he should combine his Christian beliefs with Norse myths.

'Why both?' she asked. 'A mixture of Christian and pagan symbols?'

'I am a mixture of both, I suppose. I haven't forgotten where I've come from, even though I now see England as home. And the gods follow you everywhere.'

Yes, he was definitely a man of two halves, she thought. A Norseman, but also an Englishman. He'd be a king when he was coronated, but he was also a farmer. A fierce warrior, but also surprisingly gentle.

'And the scars? Were they all inflicted by my father's men?'

'I think I came better off than they,' he said.

She shook her head. 'It must have been a shock, going from brother to parent, farmer to fighter, overnight?'

'Yes. But we were always taught how to defend ourselves, from a young age. Like you. It's sensible. My mother never had a stomach for violence though. She hated me and Ove fighting with each other or anyone else. But my father said it was good for us—to build up our strength; to know what we were capable of.'

Suddenly she realised she'd stepped too close to the tub, spellbound by his incredible body, her eyes dipping lower, and she gasped, spinning around.

'What's the matter, don't like what you see?'

'No, I do not,' she said.

'You keep telling yourself that,' he said, chuckling, and she rolled her eyes.

She couldn't believe he was naked, just inches away from her. He was sharing her bath water. And she was dressed in his clothes. It was all too intimate, and she wondered how things had progressed so quickly.

She stole round the bed and got in on her side.

Her side?

'Time for bed, then?' he said, grimacing, looking at her across the distance.

'I barely slept last night,' she said.

'No? You seemed to be snoring pretty loud,' he teased.

'I was not!' she fumed.

He grinned, and then hauled himself out of the water in one swift move.

The breath left her body. Her mouth fell open. 'Do you mind?' she said, pulling the blanket over her face, covering her eyes, while her cheeks—in fact her whole body—went up in flames.

'You didn't have to look!' he goaded her.

'I didn't have any choice. You didn't give me any warning,' she bit back. She had never seen a naked man before—and he was extraordinary. Every part of him.

She could hear him rummaging about, pulling on clothes.

'Well while I was snoring,' she said, returning to their safer conversation. 'You were having a nightmare last night.'

She heard him stop moving, but she didn't dare look up from under the furs.

'Tell me when you have some clothes on,' she said. 'I don't want another shock.'

And then she felt his hand on hers, pulling the blanket away from her eyes. 'I'm decent,' he said. 'Ready for bed. Although I'm going to be honest, sleep is the last thing on my mind.'

She stared up at him and saw he at least had his wedding breeches on, even if his chest was bare.

'Tell me about your nightmare,' she said.

He ran a hand around the back of his neck. 'I don't remember it.'

'Liar,' she said. 'You called out a woman's name.'

His jaw clenched. 'Did I?'

'Synnove.'

'Cwen,' he warned.

'Was she the woman you were telling me about? The one you were with that night?'

'Yes,' he said, moving round to his side, busying himself with moving the cushions.

'Won't you tell me what happened?'

He sighed and reluctantly sat down on the edge of the bed. She could tell he was deliberating whether to share it with her. 'She was a Saxon, as I said. I liked her. But her father didn't approve of me,' Njal said. 'So our unions were often in secret, and late at night. My father said if we couldn't be seen together, if the relationship wasn't honest, it had no future. He was right, of course. He always was.'

Cwen swallowed.

'Not that I listened.'

'What happened?'

'I discovered she knew about the attack—that it was going to happen. Her father was even one of the commanders in charge of the massacre that night,' he said bitterly.

The revelation sent shivers down Cwen's spine and her heart went out to him.

'She had protected me, but not warned me, not told me about it, so I couldn't help my family. I refused to forgive her,' he said, getting back up and walking over to the table. He poured them both some wine. 'Afterwards, I never saw her again. We went to war. But I struggled to trust people after that. After it all.'

The betrayal had cut deep, she could tell. It explained why he was suspicious, assuming the worst of people, assuming the worst of her, constantly preparing himself for the next betrayal.

No wonder he was guarded.

'And I struggled to forgive myself.'

'Why?'

'I should have seen the signs. I should have been there, with my family, not with her.'

It had changed him, made him doubt himself and his judgement, she realised.

'It wasn't your fault, Njal,' Cwen said. 'What happened would have happened whether you had been there or not. I'm sure your parents were pleased you weren't.

And Synnove would have had to live with her decision since, knowing she lost you, like you lost your parents. There was no winner that day.'

He looked at her, nodding.

She could tell it had made him reluctant to get close to anyone; to trust them. He needed honesty, and yet she realised with a pang of remorse that was ironic—as it was the very thing she couldn't give him. A prickling feeling of compunction assailed her for lying to him. She felt awful.

He came back towards her and handed her a cup. 'You're sure you don't want to...*you know*?'

'Yes!' she said, a little too forcefully. 'I'm sure.'

'Not even a goodnight kiss?' he asked, raising his eyebrow.

'No!' she said, sitting back and pulling the furs over her. 'Do all men want the same—*this* and nothing else?'

He reared backwards, as if surprised by her comment. 'Is that what you think? If that's all I want, I've paid a heavy price to get it,' he said. He stalked round the bed and got in beside her.

'You told me you have chosen me for my looks. My bloodline. Because you want children.'

'I married you in spite of that, or have you forgotten?'

Of course she hadn't!

'I want you—what's so bad about that?'

She blushed, and felt a fizz of excitement in her stomach, and lower. She wondered at how he could speak so freely about his desires. 'And to think I questioned your motives,' she bit out.

He reached out to take her chin in his hand, turning her to face him. 'I like you. I have since the moment I met you. You might be annoying, stubborn, and very grumpy, but I still like you. I'm just hoping you change your mind about me and start to feel the same.'

She swallowed. Did he really like her? She thought he desired her; she didn't think he actually liked her. His words sent a rush of pleasure through her, and yet she also felt bad. Had she been grumpy and annoying? And why couldn't she tell him she was starting to like him too?

Because she mustn't. She knew it was against the rules.

'You're not anything like the man I was told you were,' she whispered. He was unlike anyone else she'd ever met.

'Is that a good thing?' he asked, quirking an eyebrow.

'I am grateful you have not been cruel.'

'I told you, I'm not like that,' he said, frowning. 'Have you not realised that by now?

'Many think you are. The men fear you—I could see it in their eyes out in the courtyard.'

'Good. I can't have my enemies, or my men, thinking I'm soft, can I?'

'You are hardly that!'

'I don't know—I'm starting to think maybe I am.' He drew his knuckles down her cheek and her breathing halted.

She liked the fact he was willing to show her a side of himself he didn't show others. That he saved it just for her. But she forced herself to turn her cheek away, making him drop his hand. 'Can you read?' she asked.

His brow furrowed. 'Is that important?'

'I thought it was something we could do, to pass

the time. There are books and games in that chest over there.'

'Great,' he said sardonically, leaning back against the furs, raking a hand through his hair. 'The answer is no, but I like games. We could play one. Anything is better than lying here all night wanting to kiss you and knowing that I can't.'

She licked her dry lips, her mouth feeling parched. She wished he'd stop talking like that. 'What do you want to play?' she said, ignoring his comment, throwing the furs off again and moving over to the chest. 'There's Hnefatafl—do you know it?'

'Yes.'

She brought the board over to the bed and placed it between them, and he turned onto his side, resting his head on his hand, and she sat cross-legged, and set up the board.

She should have known he'd be good at it—it was all about strategy, and she knew that was what had given him an edge in the conflict with her father, because he'd secured victory despite the Saxon's superior numbers. But she wasn't that bad at the game—she managed to hold her own up until the very last moment.

'Yes!' he said, punching the air, when he won with his final move.

She shook her head. 'Have you always got everything you wanted by fighting?' she said.

He pretended to be wounded. 'That's not fair! I believe in reasoning and negotiation over fighting. It's just when men are unreasonable, sometimes there's no other way.'

She thought back to his quick thinking and reasoning about why they should wed, and how easily he'd won her round. He had cut her legs out from under her with that kiss…quite literally.

'How about a little negotiation now?' he said, his eyes glittering up at her.

'What do you mean?'

'I don't think either of us is looking forward to sharing this bed again. What do you say about us finding a compromise?'

She frowned, trying to tug her tunic down over her thighs a little further, to cover her bare skin. 'You want me to sleep in the chair?'

'No. I will.' He pushed himself up so he was sitting opposite her, looking into her eyes. 'I'll let you get a good night's rest and I'll sleep in that chair over there, but first, you have to kiss me goodnight.'

'No!' she said, putting the game away, throwing the pieces into the wooden box, outraged. 'Absolutely not! I'd rather take the chair myself.' She got out of bed and went to put the game back in the cupboard.

'That's a shame. But all right then.' He lay back on the bed, stretching his arms and legs out wide, taking up as much room as possible, and she couldn't help but let out a laugh.

'You are so annoying,' she said, coming back to stand by the bed.

He grinned. 'My brother used to tell me that.' And then he sobered, and she knew he was thinking of Ove. 'I knew you'd cowardly take the easy way out,' he said, suddenly serious.

It got her back up—she didn't like being called a coward. And she also felt guilty. She knew she was behaving badly—after all, she was his wife, and he'd been good to her today.

'Just a kiss?' She sighed.

And she couldn't believe she'd said it, her stomach flipping.

He lifted himself up onto his elbows. He gave a single nod of his head. 'Just a kiss.'

'Like the other day. Nothing more?'

'Nothing else. I promise,' he said.

'Isn't your lip sore? From your brother...'

'It's nothing you can't cure.'

She was aware she was making herself vulnerable, her body beginning to tremble, but she couldn't back down now. And she was beginning to trust him—she knew he wouldn't do anything without her permission. Her mother had warned her against this, but surely one kiss couldn't hurt?

'Fine,' she sighed, as if it was a chore. 'One kiss.'

He sat up and took her hand in his, tugging her down to sit on the edge of the bed, and he shifted over towards her. She knew she should feign disgust at his closeness, but instead of pulling away, she found herself turning into his heat, wanting to get closer.

He began circling her shoulder with the tips of his fingers, sending goose bumps down her arms, making her shiver.

'I'll just close my eyes and wait for you to plant one on me,' he said, screwing up his face, scrunching up his nose, squinting one eye, and she gently punched him on the chest, laughing.

'Njal,' she said, and he caught her wrist and leaned in to kiss her softly, briefly. Laughter fled and fire blazed.

He lifted away slightly, to look into her eyes. 'Goodnight,' he whispered, his dark, heated gaze staring into hers and she felt a flicker of excitement as he tilted her head and lowered his lips once more, pressing them firmly against hers, and there was no way of pretending she was immune to him; that this wasn't what she wanted too, as her lips instantly yielded, parting, waiting for more.

His thumbs came up to stroke the corners of her mouth, to coax her lips open further, to allow his tongue inside, so he could caress hers. It was so tender, almost reverent, and she could do nothing else but meet him halfway, pressing her untutored tongue against his in return, in awe at the thrilling feelings rushing through her body.

Njal groaned and wrapped an arm around her waist, pulling her body closer to his, drawing her into his chest, seeking more intimacy, while his other hand trailed down her cheek, the sensitive skin of her throat, his thumb circling the pulse at the base of her neck.

His mouth moved against her skin, and her head tipped back, allowing him to leave a trail of delicate little kisses along her jaw, and heat coiled down from her stomach, between her legs.

She couldn't believe this was happening; how good it felt. And she brought her hand up to hold his back, her fingertips feeling the warmth of his smooth, solid skin.

He gently lowered her down onto the bed, hovering over her, resting his forehead against hers, giving her a moment to get used to what was happening, but her hands roamed over his shoulder, up his neck and into his hair, raising her head off the bed and pulling his down towards her, wanting more. And he kissed her again, more deeply, more urgently.

His strong, gentle hand held her at the waist, his fingertips tracing circles, before trailing up to the base of her ribcage and back down. She felt her nipples harden, chafing against the material of the tunic, and she willed him to touch her there. It was maddening when he didn't. He just kept grazing her side until she placed her hand over his, flattening his palm, drawing it up her body to curve over her breast and heat blazed in her stomach. His thumb circled her nipple through the material and she felt her eyes roll back in her head. It felt incredible, as he teased the taut peak to exquisite, aching life.

His lips continued to plunder hers, and when his hand moved, trailing down over her side again, skating lower, the instant his fingertips touched the bare skin on her thigh, her excitement escalated. She felt liquid heat pool between her legs.

His hand came round the back of her thigh and lifted her leg, raising her knee and drawing her closer, as his fingers curled beneath her bottom, beneath her tunic and grazed her bare, moist skin, so lightly, so skilfully, she felt dizzy with desire. She gasped at the intimate touch, and all at once his body came over, between her legs, as if his resolve had snapped and he couldn't wait any longer. She felt the weight of him on top of her, the hard ridge of him pressing into her hip, as he rucked up her tunic, exposing her lower half, and she suddenly realised where this was going—what would happen if she didn't stop him. Her eyes flew open and she gasped, pushing gently at his chest.

'Njal, stop!'

He stilled and lifted himself away slightly, his heated blue eyes staring down at her.

'You said just a kiss!' she threw at him.

He raised his chest off her, raking a hand through his hair, sighing. 'Sorry—I thought you wanted this. More... You seemed to like it.'

'No!' she said, reeling, amazed her bruised, burning lips could speak, trying to scramble out from beneath his large body, demurely, tugging the tunic back down over her damp, trembling thighs.

'Just to be clear. You are saying you don't want this to happen.'

'No. I mean yes,' she said shakily.

'How the hell can you say that, when you were kissing me back like that?' All hint of a smile had gone now. He seemed angry. 'When you were encouraging me to put my hands on you, writhing beneath me.'

She gasped. 'We made a compromise.'

He blew out a ragged breath. 'Why are you fighting this?'

She knew she wasn't being fair. The feelings Njal had brought about in her had shocked her. When she'd felt the hard ridge of him, pressing against her, elation had ripped through her that she had caused that—that she had made him feel like that. That he wanted her. And she had burned for his touch, willing him to place his hands on her, everywhere. She did want him, just as much as he seemed to want her, and she was lying to him and herself.

But how could she tell him that she couldn't have him kissing her like that, touching her like that, making her feel these things, because if he carried on that dangerous path, she would give in to him. She was so close to surrendering and letting him discover her secret. The truth of Leof's parentage…and now, in this moment, she wasn't even sure why she thought that was so bad. Yet he would surely think she was terrible for lying to him. For deceiving him. He would see it as a betrayal.

She shook her head. He couldn't know. It had gone too far.

He pulled himself up the bed, so he was sitting beside her, resting his back against the wall. 'When I kiss you, you kiss me back. When I touch you, your body comes to life. You think I can't feel that you're wet with desire for me?'

'What?' she gasped.

'Why deny it?' He turned to face her, and took her hand in his, bringing her fingers up to his lips. 'It's nothing to be ashamed of.'

'I'm not,' she exploded, her face burning.

'Then why don't you explain it to me—help me to grasp what's going on.'

She shook her head again. 'I can't.'

His brow furrowed. 'You know, you never told me what happened with Leof. About the birth.'

'I don't want to talk about it,' she said, wrenching her hand out from his.

'Maybe not, but I think we should. I told you about Synnove. It might help me to understand…'

He clearly thought that the birth was one of the reasons why she was keeping him at arm's reach. Another thing to feel shameful about.

'How bad was it, Cwen?'

But maybe if she told him, it would make him back

off for a while, give her the space she needed to cool her own desire—to get a grip of herself again.

There was a long pause before she answered, thinking carefully how she should respond. 'It was long. It went on for a day and a night.'

'Your husband was there?'

'Yes.' Feran had been supportive, wanting to help, and she'd been glad, as she'd been afraid. She had sent him on endless errands and he had maintained a steady watch at the door, making sure they weren't disturbed.

'It was traumatic. I'd never known it could be so painful. The baby was breech—it hadn't turned.' But there had been no healer there. They couldn't risk it. No one could know the queen was having a baby. Not even the king.

'It was a long struggle. Messy. Loud. More terrifying than I'd ever imagined, but it's true what they say—when the baby is born you forget everything. Leof made up for it all.'

And she had loved him instantly, knowing he was going to be hers to raise.

When she had married Feran, they had agreed it would be a union in name only. That they wouldn't consummate their marriage. She understood his reasons; respected them, and had been happy for their relationship to be platonic. She hadn't felt that way about him either. Not the way she was feeling about Njal. So over the years she'd had to come to terms with the fact that she would probably never have a child of her own.

When Leof was born, she had been overjoyed, knowing she would love him as her own, that they had been given a gift, but there had also been heartache, as it had reaffirmed the fact that she would never get to give birth to a child herself. And when you're told you can't have something, wasn't it funny how you suddenly wanted it all the more? But she had sworn to protect her mother's life. And Leof's, by keeping the truth hidden. And not even finding a man she thought she might be able to care for could make her betray that confidence and put them at risk. Yet she was so sick of lying. Especially to Njal.

And she had put him through the heartache of telling him he would never be a parent, just like Feran had done to her.

She lay down, rolling onto her side. 'I'm ready to go to sleep now. Can you blow out the candle?' Her throat was thick with emotion, and to her horror, she felt tears swim in her eyes.

He sighed, and she felt wretched—bad about her wanton behaviour, the way she'd writhed against him, bringing his head down to hers, encouraging him, and then pushing him away, telling him to stop. She felt bad for lying to him, as he had been nothing but honest with her.

Cwen felt Njal's body move off the furs. She lifted herself onto her elbow. 'Where are you going?'

'We made a deal, remember? If you kissed me, I'd take the chair. So I am.'

She collapsed back onto the bed, feeling even worse than before. 'It's fine,' she said, sighing. 'You can stay in the bed. I don't mind. I won't be able to sleep with you in the chair either. I'll just worry about you being uncomfortable.'

'You'd worry about me?' he asked, in that familiar mocking tone. 'I didn't know you cared.'

But she was glad when he got back into the bed and blew out the candle.

She felt miserable. She was lying here, staring into the darkness, wanting him to touch her, but too afraid to tell him, too afraid of the consequences of what would happen if they went any further. She had a responsibility to her loved ones to keep them safe. And yet, she was starting to wonder if she had a responsibility to herself to be happy too.

She had been a good mother to Leof, going out of her way to fulfil all his childhood needs. She had sacrificed a great deal—her own freedom—to be his mother, and she wouldn't change it. But should she sacrifice what she was feeling for Njal? It had been attraction at first sight—just one shared look and it had changed her. She had been his. And it was becoming harder to stay away from him. She was beginning to feel his pain. Being around him and never being able to kiss him, touch him, was torture. Suffering nights like this for the rest of their lives would be horrific...

Suddenly, he moved, his body coming up against hers, curving around her spine, his hand coming round her front, over her arms, and he pulled her back into his chest.

'What are you doing?' she gasped.

'Holding you. That's all.'

'Why?' Her voice sounded strangled.

'Because I think we both need it. And tonight, I'm not taking no for an answer.'

Chapter Nine

The intense rain was still pelting down, monotonous and heavy and depressing, and the weather matched Njal's mood. He felt irritable and short-tempered, a pounding in his head and his groin. There had been torrential rain in the night and the river had risen even higher, undoing all their good work from yesterday. When Bjorn had knocked on their door early this morning to tell them things were worse, that their scouts had seen Caedwalla's army not two days away, he and Cwen had raced out of bed, pulling on their clothes as quickly as possible.

All around him, people were once more trying to bail out water. Was this divine punishment for their behaviour these past few years? The outer buildings were totally submerged now, and people had become trapped in buildings, or stranded and forced to swim for their lives.

Cwen had shown him there were boats in the boatyard, and they sent out a few vessels to fetch anyone left standing, to bring them back to the safety of the great hall. But even that was still ankle-deep in water. They'd need to come up with a good drainage system, and fast.

And a plan to stave off Caedwalla's army, which was

drawing closer by the day. Two days. Was that enough time to get their defences ready? It would have to be.

Njal was also aware of the absence of his brother and his men. They could have done with their help, and he knew at some point this morning he would have to go and speak with them. Just the thought of it was blackening his mood.

He was keeping a closer watch on Leof today, feeling responsible for what happened last night. And yet, despite all that was on his mind, he was unable to think about much else other than Cwen.

Kissing her last night had been incredible—and when she'd drawn his head closer to hers, deepening the connection, his pulse had raced. He'd pulled her into his body, wanting to feel her soft curves crushed against him, and he'd needed to touch her—everywhere. The feel of her soft breast in the palm of his hand had made him so hard, and when he'd stroked the pale silky skin on her thigh, he had almost lost control. She made him feel things he'd never felt before, not even with Synnove—she set off a kind of frenzy of desire in him, and he'd moved his body between her legs, wanting to claim her at last.

He cursed himself. He had thought he was winning her over with his words, but when he'd tried to show her how much he cared with his body, she had made him stop. He'd taken things too fast. He'd scared her off. And now he felt miserable. He'd told her he would just kiss her, making her believe she could trust him, and then he had ended up doing a whole lot more.

It was unbelievable how much he wanted her. And when he'd touched her, her sensitive skin had been slick with her own excitement—he could feel how much she wanted him too. So he couldn't understand why she kept pushing him away. Her secretive actions unsettled him. It made him feel as if there was something she was keeping from him, something he wouldn't like.

Her father had recovered sufficiently enough for him to travel now, and as Caedwalla and his forces were drawing ever closer, it was time for Cwen's parents to leave. Was that what was upsetting her, perhaps, strengthening her resolve against him? That he was separating them; forcing her to say goodbye? Yet he knew they weren't especially close, and she had known this was part of the deal when they had wed.

Her signature floral scent drifted under his nose, alerting him to the fact she was nearby, and he glanced up from the table and saw she was helping an elderly couple into the hall. She met his gaze and he felt his heart clamour. He wasn't sure how much more of this he could take. Would she ever succumb to him, or was he to suffer for eternity?

And yet, after it all, he had been amazed how content he had been just to hold her. Thankfully, she hadn't fought him on that, and she had eventually relaxed in his arms, allowing him to draw her closer still. She must have felt the hard ridge of him pressing into her bottom most of the night, and yet still she hadn't tried to move away. She had even drifted off to sleep, and due to her nearness, for once, he hadn't had another nightmare.

Telling Cwen about Synnove had brought back all the usual feelings of inadequacy and shame—and hate. And he realised he'd been angry with his former lover for a very long time. Her betrayal had prevented him from developing deep relationships with anyone—maybe even his brother. But incredibly, talking about it, sharing it with Cwen had helped. At least to let go of some of his rage, and his guilt.

By the afternoon, they'd got the flood situation under control once more, and he knew he couldn't put off speaking to his brother any longer. He'd dealt with Ove's friends, and they'd all been contrite, swearing their loyalty to Njal from now on, blaming their actions on the ale. And they'd promised to make amends to Leof and Eadhild.

But with Ove segregated in a room of his own, Njal found it harder to take the steps to confront his brother. He unlocked the door to the small room at the back of the barn and found him lying on a bench, his hand over his chest.

'Get a good night's rest in here?' he said, looking around the dank and dingy room, the water creeping under the door.

'I thought you were going to leave me here to drown.'

'Tempting, but no,' Njal said.

'How's your lip?'

Njal grimaced and sat down on the bench opposite. He'd tried to swallow his anger so they could talk. 'Fine. Thanks for that.' He sighed. 'Look, I don't want to fight with you. You're my brother. I love you. I don't understand what's happening here.'

Ove kicked his legs out and spun round, sitting up on the bench, facing him.

'You've changed. That's what.'

'Me?' Njal said.

'Since the moment we got here, when you got what

you wanted, you gave in. You turned soft,' Ove said. 'You put aside all we fought for. You couldn't bring yourself to kill our biggest enemy. The murderer of our kin. And now you're about to set him free. We're wondering why you get to choose?'

'You and your men are questioning my command?' Anger kicked up in his veins.

'And you chose a Saxon over me. A woman and her child,' Ove said, looking into his eyes. 'Blood is thicker than water, or have you forgotten that?'

Njal shook his head. He felt conflicted. 'I haven't chosen anyone over you. It's always been the two of us, first, before anyone else, since this whole thing began.'

'Until you met her. Now you're neglecting everyone else. Neglecting the cause.'

Njal felt a prickle of guilt. 'That's not true.'

'It is. You're different this week.'

'A lot has happened. We won the battle. There was no need to fight any more.'

Ove shook his head. 'It's not that. It's her. The princess. She's changed you. You can't even think straight. You were like this before, with Synnove. Look what happened then. You weren't there when we needed you the most.'

It was a low blow, and it hit Njal where it hurt most—right in the heart. He rubbed his chest.

Was Ove right? He knew the lust he was feeling for Cwen was consuming him, but had his desire for her overtaken everything else? He didn't think so. This had always been about finding peace for his people to live here safely.

'She's turned your head so much, you're even going to

name her son—a Saxon—as heir, instead of me, a Dane, your own flesh and blood. Why? I deserve this, after what the king took from me. I was there by your side in battle after battle. I struck the final blow. I've earned it. What has she done? She stood by and let her father massacre our people. How can you forgive her for that?'

'She didn't know about it,' Njal said, clenching and unclenching his fists.

'Really? Just like Synnove? She's deceiving you, Brother, using you for her own advantage.'

Njal didn't want to believe it. And yet, if he thought about it, he'd been played for a fool by Cwen already. She had married him, but she was still keeping her distance. She still wouldn't let him touch her, and he didn't understand her reasons. The magnitude of what he'd given up to be with her was great—he'd given up his chance of having children. And for what?

Was any of it real?

Perhaps he'd got it wrong. Perhaps she would never be able to return his affections and his desire as he'd hoped. Perhaps she would never be able to warm to him, care for him, like she'd loved her first husband.

He suddenly felt frustrated. Was she weakening him with desire to such a state where he couldn't see the facts? Might he miss something important, like he had all those years before, with Synnove?

'I hope she's worth it, Brother,' Ove said.

Njal stood, raking his hand through his hair, feeling desperate to get his brother back on his side, missing their camaraderie, and wondering if it was all his fault their lines of communication had broken down. Perhaps he had been neglecting him. 'I wouldn't know,' he said. 'Our wedding bed remains cold.'

Ove stared at him, shocked. 'You have not taken her?'

'No.'

And then his brother threw back his head and laughed. Njal rolled his eyes and stood.

'If you're not man enough to bed her, Brother, I will happily do it for you,' Ove added, roaring.

Njal paced away, feeling frustrated with Cwen, with Ove, and with himself, for being so loose-tongued. 'I wish I had not told you.'

'I'm glad you did,' Ove said, standing and slapping him on the back. 'It's made me feel a whole lot better.'

Njal shook his head. 'Keep it to yourself. Our position is still precarious in Jorvik. It's imperative Cwen and I are portrayed as allies,' he said. 'I'm going to let you out of here, but I don't want any more trouble, all right? Of course things were going to change. We achieved what we came here to do. But everything's at our feet now.'

Ove nodded. 'You may have got what you wanted, Brother, but I haven't. Not yet.'

'And what is that?'

'Death to all Saxons.'

Njal stared at him, his mouth drying. 'I hope you're jesting.'

Ove shrugged. 'I'm not done with fighting yet.'

'Who do you want to fight?' Njal said, exasperated. 'Innocent children? Unarmed women? And what for? We can't keep hurting each other—moving from one battle to another. It's not living. We have succeeded in what we came here to do. Now we have to let our anger go.'

* * *

Cwen felt a change in Njal at the meal in the hall that evening. He was quieter than usual, eating his food in silence, and he hadn't asked her anything about her day.

Was he angry about last night? She knew she'd behaved recklessly, leading him on, teasing him, then making him stop at the last moment. But he had held her in his arms afterwards, so she didn't think he could have been too upset. And she had liked the feel of his strong arms around her, holding her, keeping her safe. She had nestled in closer, and when she had felt the hard ridge of him pressing into her, even that hadn't scared her. She knew now it just meant he desired her—not that he was going to force her to do anything.

She took a sideways glance at him. Was he all right? He seemed preoccupied; more pensive than normal.

She was aware he'd let his brother and his men free, and she was irritated he hadn't spoken to her about it first, so she could have had some warning before she'd come face-to-face with Ove and some of his men in the hall.

One or two of them had approached her later, as she'd served their meal, offering their apologies for their behaviour yesterday, and she'd accepted their words, graciously. But not Ove. He hadn't said a word.

Did Njal think they had learned their lesson from being put in a cell overnight? She wasn't so sure. She saw something darker at play, but it wasn't her place to say. If it had been Leof who had done something wrong, she would have forgiven him in a heartbeat.

As she put Leof to bed later on, tucking him in, her heart was hammering in her chest about going back to their room and being alone with Njal again. Something was different about him and she couldn't be sure what. Would he still treat her kindly?

Procrastinating, she checked in on her parents first, making sure they were ready for their journey on the morrow. They were both ill at ease about leaving their home, but their trunks were packed and they'd said their goodbyes to their closest friends.

Finally, Cwen plucked up the courage to face Njal, and as soon as she knocked on the door he pulled it open before stalking away, leaving her to let herself in. He was bare-chested and he sat on the bed, undoing his boots. He pulled one off, then the other. She closed the door behind her, gently.

'Where's the barrel gone?' she asked, looking around.

'I had it removed.' His voice was cool. Too cool.

'Did you have a good day?' she asked, wringing her hands.

He shrugged. 'As good as to be expected.'

'I hope we don't have as much rain tonight.'

He sent her a look, and she knew she was reaching—talking about the weather. But she felt as if she had to fill the silence, his mood was setting her on edge.

'Is everything all right?' she asked.

'Everything's great,' he said sardonically.

She went over to the table and poured some wine, before turning back to face him.

'If something's wrong, you should just tell me,' she said, fiddling with the ring on her necklace, giving her fingers something to do, but she instantly realised she'd made a mistake when Njal caught sight of it. He stood, and his hand reached out to take the band between his fingers, and his eyebrow rose. 'Will he always be between us?' he asked.

'What's it to you?' she said.

'Perhaps I don't want to see that constant reminder that you belonged to someone else.'

She snatched it back.

'Especially when you haven't yet been mine.'

She could sense his frustration, and she felt it too—and an increased awareness of him. His scent. His heat. His beautiful body swimming before her eyes.

Could she really deny him again, for a third night? Did she want to?

She knew now, they couldn't continue like this…it was too hard. Maddening, even. Perhaps if she spoke to him, opened up to him…but she couldn't. She had her mother's voice ringing in her ears, telling her what was at risk, saying she could never tell a soul. It would ruin them; end them. It would all be her fault.

And yet, when Njal stared down at her like this, with those piercing blue eyes, full of need, she wanted him to kiss her again, to put his hands on her again, and touch her between her quivering thighs, and her thoughts terrified her, making her heart race.

'Do you want to play a game?'

'No. I'm not in the mood for any more games tonight, Cwen,' he said. He took a step towards her. 'The way I see it, we have two options. I can leave now, go and find another place to sleep, and to hell with what anyone else thinks. Or two, you will give in and let me touch you—because that's what we both want.'

She licked her lips, her heart beginning to pound so loud she felt sure he could hear it.

'But as for standing there looking like you want me to kiss you, and then you teasing me a little before pushing me away and saying no, that's not going to happen again.'

He came closer, and she swallowed.

'I won't be taken for a fool.'

'Please, Njal...'

'Please what, Cwen? Please touch you, or please go?'

She shook her head. 'Why does it have to be one or the other? Why can't you just stay and we talk a little, get to know each other a bit better?'

'You want to talk? All right.' He closed the distance between them and she edged backwards. 'We can talk first. What do you want to talk about?'

She tipped her chin up. 'Why didn't you tell me you'd let Ove free today?'

His eyes narrowed on her.

'It was a shock to me and Leof when I saw him in the hall. Did you not stop to consider my feelings on the matter?'

'Do you ever stop and think of mine?'

Her back hit the door and he loomed over her.

'What is the matter with you today?' she said, raising her hands up.

'What do you think?'

'I don't know—you tell me.'

'You. You are the matter with me.' He placed his hands on the door either side of her head, trapping her against the wood with his body, and he was so close, she had to tip her face up to look at him. 'I want you so badly I can't think straight.' His one hand came down to hold her jaw, his thumb pulling at the corner of her mouth, and he leaned in. 'Make your choice.'

And she caved. She wanted this. She couldn't deny them both any longer, and she pressed her lips against his, before pulling back, shocked by her own fervour. He let out a growl and hauled her to him, bringing his lips down onto hers, hard, and she gasped at the fierce passion behind his embrace. Her arms came up to hold his head as she kissed him back, frantic with need, wanting more of his tongue in her mouth, wanting to taste him fully, to get closer.

He pressed his whole body against her, bringing his hands up to cup her breasts, and he squeezed, making her gasp. She felt sure he could feel her erratic heartbeat thudding against his chest. Stepping away from her for a moment, he pulled back, and began tugging at her pinafore straps, teasing them down her arms, easing the material over her breasts, letting it fall to the floor, and then he was pulling at the tunic beneath, loosening the tie, smoothing his hands over her chest to widen the opening so she was exposed to him, so that he could see her. And he stared down at her in wonder, his breathing ragged, his look hot and heavy, and her arms came up to his shoulders, as he stared at her.

'Njal...'

'You are extraordinary,' he whispered.

And then he bent his head, pressing his hot mouth to her breast, his beard softly grazing her, and she cried out at his eager passion, her hand stealing into his hair, holding his head in place as he took one rosy peak into his mouth. She felt swollen, as he kissed and sucked her, first the one breast, then the other, every lick of his tongue causing a new coil of heat to lash between her legs, and she moaned. She had never felt anything like it.

He pulled away and his lips met hers again, his hands coming up to cover both her breasts, and it felt glorious to be held by him, his thumb flicking over her nipples, teasing and tweaking. And then he was rucking up the material of her tunic, impatient, as if he had got a taste of her and now he wanted more, and it was all she could do but to try to keep standing on her trembling legs, wrapping her hands around his neck, pressing herself harder against him, telling him she wanted this too.

He was still kissing her as his large, unsteady hands ran up the bare skin on her leg, behind her knee and up over the back of her thighs, curving over her bottom, and he squeezed, drawing her closer. She felt her flesh quiver and his hard shaft press into her stomach.

And then his palm stole round, over the front of her thigh, and her breathing halted. His fingers were right there, at the apex of her thighs, and before she could stop him, he curved his palm into her intimate curls. His fingers stole lower, delving between her soft, wet folds, parting her, so gently, she thought she might crumple. As if he knew, he pushed a knee between her legs to hold her up as he began to stroke her, intimately. Her head fell against his shoulder and she could have wept with pleasure as he circled her, purposefully, making her legs feel like water, and all thoughts were suspended. She never knew anything could feel this good, and she never wanted him to stop, until his finger slid lower, deeper, and pressed inside her body. It felt so intimate, she choked out her surprised cry, gripping onto his shoulders for dear life.

'I told you that you were wet for me,' he whispered, and her face burned.

He slid his finger out before doing it again, torturously slowly, and she whimpered. 'Njal.'

'Does that feel good?'

'Too good.'

'Then let's lie down,' he said. 'I want to take off your clothes and look at you spread out beneath me. I want to be free to touch you with my body, not just my hands, right here,' and he plunged inside her again, deeper than before, showing her where he meant, and her breathing quickened, and the sensations tipped her over some precipice, making her cry out in ecstasy as her body shuddered and climaxed around him.

'Oh, Njal, Njal.'

He stared down at her, grinning, as she fought her emotions, trying to get them in check. What had just happened? She felt shaky and breathless. Dizzy. He had made her body soar with pleasure, but now he was dropping her skirts, taking her hand, leading her over to the bed.

'If you think that was good, wait till you see what else I can do,' he bragged. 'Let us make tonight the wedding night we didn't have. Lie down, Cwen,' he whispered. 'Let me undress you.'

But as she looked between him and the bed, she faltered, her satisfaction finally bringing with it some reason, allowing her to think, to be rational, for just a second.

'Cwen...it's all right,' he said, reaching for her face, smiling down at her.

She looked up at him, her eyes wide. Was it? Could she do this? Suddenly it all felt overwhelming. She liked him, she realised. Too much. And she was in danger of telling him everything. *Giving* him everything.

But what if she did, and there were consequences? What if they were to conceive a child of their own? It was possible. Within her grasp. She knew it was what he wanted. It was something she had always wanted.

But was she really willing to reveal the truth about Leof to him, and let down her family, just so he could lay claim to her and take ownership of her body? Was she being selfish? What if something happened? What if Leof got hurt? Or her parents? Would she ever be able to forgive herself? And she shook her head, miserable. She knew she had to sacrifice both her dream of having children and her relationship with Njal for the sake of her secret.

'Njal... I thought I could do this, but I don't think I can,' she said, biting her lip.

She took a step away from him, pulling her tunic back together. 'I know you're going to hate me. I hate myself...'

'Cwen?' he said, seeing her hesitancy, looking confused.

And then her back hit the door. 'I know I'm letting you down. And I wish I could explain it. I wish things could be different. I'm so sorry,' she whispered.

His brow furrowed with the realisation that she was saying no to him—again, and as she watched the feelings of hurt and betrayal creep across his face, she reached for the door handle, pulled the door open and ran through it.

Njal stood there for a long while, looking at the wooden panel, shaking in the frame where it had been slammed shut.

What had just happened?

Had Cwen really just rejected him for the third night in a row?

She had kissed him, pressed her body up against him, writhed against him, encouraging him on, and she'd even let him touch her, intimately, taking her own pleasure—and then she'd pushed him away, denying him his own.

And his body, his thoughts, were tied up in knots. He'd wanted to spend the rest of the night giving her more satisfaction, and sating himself inside her.

Now he was at a loss. He didn't know what to do. All he knew was he couldn't keep going through this every night. He couldn't keep convincing her that she wanted him, not if she didn't. He thought it would destroy him.

Had he scared her off by leading her over to the bed, telling her he wanted to see her naked? Was she shy? He didn't know why. He had been given a glimpse of her body and she was beautiful. She had perfect, round breasts with upturned rosy nipples that he'd fondled to tight, swollen peaks. He'd felt her silky thighs, and her soft, intimate places, but it hadn't been enough. He'd needed to see her naked in her entirety. She had made him wait too long for fulfilment and his restraint had snapped.

He drew in a ragged breath. He was livid. There was no excuse for her behaviour. None. Perhaps Ove was right and she was just like Synnove. But he wasn't sure. He didn't think she meant to betray him, and he was certain she hadn't faked her pleasure. Had he been too forceful? Too rough? Too frantic? He didn't think so. She'd moaned with pleasure and climaxed hard. Her entire body had trembled from his touch.

No, it was something else that was preventing her from giving in to him. But what?

He thought back to the look on her face when she'd backed away from him, heading for the door—she'd looked torn. Bereft. As if she was fighting a war within herself, not necessarily with him. She'd even apologised...

He sank down onto the bed and buried his face in his hands, and he could smell the sweet scent of her on his fingers. It stirred his emotions, and he knew he would have to go after her. He couldn't let this lie.

Chapter Ten

Cwen lurched down the corridor, blinded by her own tears. She needed to pull herself together. To focus on something else apart from Njal and her needs. She couldn't go on like this. It was like being offered the thing you desired most, and then having it snatched away from you. It was too cruel.

She checked on Leof and he was asleep, and she was envious of his peaceful slumber—she didn't think she'd slept properly in weeks. Perhaps if she left it long enough, Njal would be snoring softly too when she returned.

But could she return? She had let him down. She wasn't being fair—to him or to her. What man would put up with this indefinitely? He would resent her. End up hating her. What she'd done was despicable. She'd encouraged him, letting him put his hands on her, squirming against him, and she'd taken her own pleasure, finally got some satisfaction, without giving him any of his own. And she knew he must need it. She had been teetering on the edge for days, and her release had been more powerful than she had ever thought possible. She never knew such feelings were possible.

She had been a coward, running from his arms rather than telling him the truth. Would he ever forgive her? And if he didn't, what would that mean for them, and for their people?

Would he cast her aside, and find comfort in the arms of another woman? She felt bile rise in her throat at the thought. But what man would stay with a wife like her? A wife who couldn't fulfil his needs.

She knew now he would never be so cruel as to have her and Leof killed. But might he send her away? Might he divorce her? She had heard rumours that Danes could do that...

She headed to the kitchens. And what about her needs? Was she really going to deny herself the happiness of a full relationship her entire life? With Feran it had been different—she didn't know, or want to know, what she was missing out on, but if Njal could make her feel like that with just his fingers, she was starting to have an idea that having sex with him would be amazing.

She was beginning to care for him, she realised. She liked him a lot. Who would have thought it? That she would feel this way about a Dane. She knew she was fortunate, as not many wives felt that way about their husbands. Her mother hadn't about her father, and that's what had led to all the trouble in the first place. Was she really going to throw away what she and Njal had because of a secret she'd promised to keep years ago, before she'd even met him?

All was quiet as she poured herself a drink of ale and smeared some honey on some bread. She ate it slowly, chewing it as she dwelled on her misery.

Surely Njal would keep her secret? He was a good

man—the best she had known. She didn't think he would use it against her, or the monarchy. And he seemed to care for Leof, she didn't think he would do anything to put him in danger.

Perhaps he would just be delighted that they could be intimate, and could even have a child of their own. And she wanted that. Why shouldn't she have it? Leof had shown her how incredible it was, being a mother, but he was also the cause of her never knowing the pleasure of carrying and loving her own child. It was paining her to deny Njal that experience too—knowing he wanted to be a parent as much as she did. And he would make a good father. He had won a place in Leof's heart so easily, and he cared so greatly for his brother who he'd raised these past few winters. He was so generous and forgiving of him, while trying to show him the right path.

If she could just go back there and tell him, trust him, be truthful, breaking her vows to her mother, perhaps everything would be all right. It could be her salvation—her way of getting what she'd always wanted, after denying herself for so long. Maybe she should take a chance on Njal, like he had on her, despite his deep mistrust of women after Synnove. The sweet comfort of the honey raised her spirits. How could honesty ever be a bad thing? she decided. Njal's father was right—if the relationship wasn't honest, it had no future, and she wanted a future with Njal.

Washing up her bowl and putting it away, she now knew what she had to do. And she was determined about her new course of action. She even felt a spark of excitement that she was taking control. That she was finally doing something for herself. She would return to their room and she would be brave. She would tell him everything. She just hoped Njal would stick around long enough for her to get her words out.

She leapt out of her skin when she saw a lone figure coming towards her, through the door.

Njal?

No. She instantly knew who it was and her skin erupted in goose bumps. Out of anyone she should meet, alone, at this time of night, he was the last person she would want it to be. Especially trapped in here, with him blocking the way out.

'Ove. What are you still doing up?' she said, trying to keep her voice steady.

'I could ask you the same thing.'

Her skin at the back of her neck bristled. She suddenly felt foolish for leaving Njal's side; the safety of his bedroom, and the irony wasn't lost on her. For the past three days thoughts of being alone with him had terrified her, but now there was nowhere else she'd rather be.

How easily she'd allowed herself to be distracted by her thoughts of him. In just a few days she'd all but forgotten how these warriors had fought their way across lands of ice, seas and settlements to get here. How some had raped and pillaged across the country, eventually taking control of the fortress and all the people in it, her included. Why had she thought she would be safe walking around the place at night on her own? Because she hadn't been thinking. Her desire for Njal had consumed her. He had convinced her to let down her guard.

But she knew this man wasn't like his brother. She'd seen the hatred in his eyes on one too many occasions, and tonight was no different.

She shuffled backwards, stepping away from him, retreating against the tables.

'Are you avoiding my brother?' he sneered.

'I just came down to get a drink,' she said, glancing over towards the door. It seemed a long way away. And he was obstructing her exit.

He lifted up his tankard. 'Great minds.' But by the way he staggered towards her, she knew he'd had too many already.

'Well, Njal will be waiting for me, so I'd better get back.'

'You know your secret will get out eventually,' he said, and she froze.

What was he talking about?

'You don't need to pretend to me.'

'What do you mean?' she said, her voice taut.

'Well, it's not as if you're going to do anything anyway,' Ove said, coming closer, looming over her, and she could smell the stale stench of ale on his breath. 'He told me you two haven't consummated your marriage.'

Cwen's blood ran cold.

Why would Njal confide in Ove about that? Why would he share that information with anyone, betraying her trust—it was between them.

She couldn't understand it, especially as he had told her it was imperative people thought they had slept together, for the good of their alliance. That they had to put on a united front.

It winded her, especially as she'd just decided she would tell him everything.

Had Njal been that frustrated by their situation that he'd been moaning about her—or worse, laughing about her, behind her back to his brother? She suddenly felt ashamed, but also wounded, and furious with him all at once.

Why would he share the intimate details of their relationship? It made her feel vulnerable and exposed, like perhaps she couldn't confide in him after all. If he'd shared that, what else would he reveal? Maybe she'd got him wrong. Maybe she couldn't trust him.

'I told him, I wouldn't have given you the choice.'

She froze. She had heard the underlying threat in his voice and knew she had to get away from him. She went to go, but he was right there, in her way, and suddenly, he gripped her wrist in his clammy hand, roughly pulling her up against his chest, and she bristled, recoiling from his touch.

'Let go of me.' Her senses screamed in disgust. She needed to get away, right now.

She wished Njal was here. Whatever he'd told his brother, she knew he wouldn't want Ove touching her. He would still protect her.

Was this young man really his kin? They seemed so different. For she knew Njal would never hurt her. She had known it from the moment she'd first seen him.

She tried a different tack, trying to stall Ove—whatever he was about to do—and appeal to his better nature. There must be some ounce of good in him, if they shared the same blood, the same parents.

'Njal cares about you. A lot.'

'What do you know of me and my brother?' His voice hissed between his teeth.

'I know before you came here you were inseparable. And I know he wants you to be happy.'

He sneered. 'Does he? I'm not so sure. But maybe you could make me happy instead.'

He grabbed her breast and squeezed and she gasped, trying to push him away. It was nothing like Njal's gentle caress. 'Don't touch me! Get off me! You're hurting me!' He held her to him with his one arm and with the other his hand groped all over her, as she tussled with him, trying to fight him off. She felt sick. Panicked. He was too strong for her.

'Do you know what I want? A legacy for myself.' Fear and dread pounded through her as he spun her round and shoved her up against the table, bending her over the wood and pushing himself between her legs. He reared over her, his one hand still holding her body in place while the other moved to the fastening of his breeches, his nostrils flaring. 'Perhaps if I put a baby in your belly, my own child on the throne...'

Her whole body trembled as she realised she was stuck, pinned beneath him, and something life-shattering was about to happen.

She lashed out, trying to scratch and hit him, kick him with her legs, attempting to fight him off—and the churning feeling inside. She wished she had her sword. But his grip became more aggressive, harder, as he tried to hold her down and ruck up her tunic. She was aware of him ripping her necklace from her neck, sending it flying across the floor—Feran's ring bouncing once, then twice, before disappearing beneath the cabinet.

And suddenly, she wished she had let Njal touch her. She should have stayed in his room and let him make love to her. She didn't want her first time to be like this. She had always wanted it to be with someone she cared for;

who was gentle. But now it was too late, she realised with a sob. She wished she had told Njal the truth, that she'd opened up to him, as right now, she wasn't sure what she had been afraid of. Nothing was as terrifying as this.

'Get *off* me. What are you doing? Let me go!' She sobbed.

He was lifting her tunic, trying to spread her thighs, forcing his large body between them.

And then suddenly, he was yanked backwards, away from her.

'Get your hands off her!'

Njal.

She slumped in relief—until she glanced back over her shoulder and saw his eyes. They were cold and hard and furious. She had never seen him look so angry.

'You might not have been man enough to kill her father, or man enough to bed her, but I am.'

Smack! Njal punched him with such force, it sent Ove reeling.

'Are you hurt?' Njal yelled at her, running his hands over her, checking her over, his eyes wild. 'Answer me!' he roared.

'No.' She shook her head and he gripped her elbow, pulling her off the table, launching her forwards.

Ove was picking himself up off the floor, curling himself upwards. 'Are you going to let a woman come between us, Brother? Are you picking her over—?'

Njal swung again, and this time his fist cracked into Ove's jaw, cutting him off mid-sentence, and the beast fell to the ground, silent. The force of Njal's blow had knocked him out—Ove was lying unconscious on the floor.

And then they were moving. Njal was propelling her out of the hall and down the corridor, so fast, she felt disorientated; light-headed. Her legs felt wobbly—she wasn't sure how they were keeping her up, and her skin felt bruised and dirty where that brute had squeezed her flesh.

She wasn't sure if Njal was angry with Ove, or her, his rage literally rolling off him in waves. And she just let him lead her, in shock, and she was certain he must be stunned too, to have come looking for her and to have found...*that*.

They got back to the room and he practically flung her inside, his breathing coming in serrated breaths. He slammed the door behind them and leaned against it, while she lowered herself down onto the edge of the bed, unable to stand any longer. Her whole body was trembling. She couldn't believe what had just happened. How close Ove had come to...to... Thank God Njal had got there in time.

Njal had known something was wrong.

Wondering where Cwen had gone, after what had happened between them, he'd gone looking for her. He'd wanted to appease her, to tell her perhaps they should drop this whole pretence and if she really wanted to they could have separate rooms. He didn't want to force her to be in his company every night if she didn't want to be—it wasn't doing either of them any good. But as he'd walked down the corridor into the hall, he hadn't been able to find her among the people camping out. He'd checked her father's state rooms, wondering if she'd gone to curl up in one of the big benches in there, by a warm fire, but he'd found them empty. He'd started to feel concerned when he considered she might have gone to get a drink. And when he drew near the kitchen and had heard noises, voices he recognised, alarm had raced through his blood.

When he'd pushed open the door and seen Ove bent over her, his hands on her, hurting her, and Cwen fighting him off, anger and fear in her beautiful grey eyes, Njal's whole body had contracted in shock.

His outrage had been instant, and in that moment, he realised he no longer had a brother.

He'd been endlessly frustrated by Ove's behaviour of late, it had been testing their relationship to its limits, but now he was enraged. This was too much; he'd gone too far. Cwen was his wife, and his and Ove's bond was broken for ever.

He wasn't sure how he reached them so fast, his rage launching him forwards, and he'd pulled Ove off her so fiercely, he reckoned he must have dislocated his brother's shoulder.

He felt sick. Those images would haunt him for the rest of his life. And he berated himself for not seeing this coming. He had thought if anyone was going to betray him, it would be Cwen—he had never thought his brother would stoop so low. And he was glad he'd punched him so hard he'd knocked him out cold.

He had half a mind to pick up his sword, go back there and run him through, but he didn't want to leave Cwen alone right now. He was a fool for having let her out of his sight at all, allowing her to walk round the fortress on her own at night. He should have known something like this might happen.

He closed his eyes briefly, trying to get his anger—and his breathing—under control. When he opened them, Cwen was sitting on the edge of the bed, pale and trembling, her lips pressed together. The air was thick with tension between them. He didn't know what she wanted; what she needed—whether to go to her or keep his distance.

'Are you hurt?' he asked her again.

She shook her head, as if she couldn't form any words, and drew her legs together, rubbing her palms across her clothes as if trying to get her hands clean.

What if he hadn't got there in time? He couldn't bear to think about it.

'I should never have left you alone.'

'You should never have told him we haven't been intimate,' she spat, turning on him, making him reel. 'Why did you do that?'

'What?'

'You told him you hadn't touched me. It must have spurred him on. He said he'd be the one to put a child in my belly,' she said, her voice breaking at the end.

Fury whipped through Njal and he cursed. 'I can't believe he said that.' He had thought he'd known his brother. He had thought he could control him. Obviously not. This was despicable. Unforgivable.

'Why? Why did you tell him that?' she asked, accusingly.

'I don't know,' he said, raising his hands, his body thrumming. 'I was frustrated.'

'How do you expect me to trust you?' she said bitterly.

'Or I you?'

Her head shot up, her eyes filling with tears. 'What did I do?' she gasped. 'You think I wanted this to happen?'

He raked a hand through his hair and blew out a breath, and he turned away from her for a moment to collect himself. No, he didn't.

'I told you he was dangerous. You didn't listen. You said you would protect me,' she said.

'Maybe I could if you were with me, not wandering the halls at night to get away from me!' he roared, and she reared back, her eyes narrowing on him. When she lifted her hand to swipe a tear off her cheek, he instantly felt guilty for raising his voice. '*Helvete!*'

His anger, these feelings he had for her...it made him feel out of control. He wanted to kill Ove. His own brother. And he was being much too harsh on Cwen, after the ordeal she'd just been through. But he was so wound up.

He wanted to reassure her that she was safe with him, that he would never let anything happen to her, but how could he say that, after what had just happened? He seemed incapable of protecting anyone. Deep down, he felt like he had failed her, like he had failed his family and his settlement.

He should be holding her, comforting her, tugging her into his chest and stroking her hair, reassuring her she was safe, and yet, he didn't think she wanted him to. She had never wanted him to. How many times did he have to hear her say she didn't want him until it began to sink in? Why had he ever thought she would? It was obvious now, and he had pushed and pushed, giving her an ultimatum, forcing her into kissing him, marrying him, into sharing his bed, and now she'd been attacked.

He was doing everything wrong—had done everything wrong since he'd arrived here. He should never have got involved with her and made this personal. He was disgusted with himself and Ove—after all, he had raised him since their parents had died. How could he not blame himself? Somewhere along the line he must have got something very wrong, for he had made him the man he had become. His mother and father would be so ashamed.

Even though he thought that Cwen's feelings had been beginning to thaw towards him, this would no doubt solidify her opinions of the Danes. How could she think they were anything but brutes? This would destroy the alliance they had built up. And had this just reinforced what she thought of him? She must think the worst now.

He wanted to reach out and hold her, but he was too afraid of what her reaction would be and he had to protect himself from further rejection. More disappointment. But he also wanted to do the right thing by her—give her what she needed.

He pulled himself upright, the path suddenly seeming clear.

'Stay here,' he fumed, and he pulled open the door and stormed through it, slamming it shut behind him.

He must do what he should have done when he first arrived here.

Cwen didn't want to be alone right now.

Where was Njal? She needed him here. She wanted his comfort.

She had been pacing, wondering where he had gone, growing restless, the events of the evening going over and over in her mind. She still couldn't believe what had happened. She kept reliving the feel of Ove's rough, sweaty hands on her body, the weight of him on top of her, and the bile rising in her throat when she'd heard him unfasten his breeches.

Thank God Njal had come after her.

And yet, the way he had behaved when they'd got back here, to their room, was bothering her. He had been vibrating with rage. She had wanted him to come to her, hold her and comfort her, but he had kept his distance, as if he couldn't bear to touch her after what he'd seen.

She had been attacked by the brother of her husband, the one he continually protected. She was sure he was in just as much shock as she was. She was desperate for him to return, to tell her he had had Ove thrown into a cell. She wanted him to pull her close and tell her that he would never let anything bad happen to her. And she knew that now. He had rescued her tonight. And yesterday. And perhaps when he married her, saving her from Caedwalla and a lifetime of misery.

She realised what a fool she'd been—that she should have fought for what she wanted. She couldn't believe she hadn't let Njal near her—that she had denied him, and herself, from consummating their marriage, even though it was what they both wanted. She had thought she'd had to keep him at bay, to do as her mother had said. She'd never been allowed to be selfish, to do something for herself, but now that the worst had happened, she had to question why she had been so restrained with a man she did want, who made her feel the way he did. Why was she wasting time?

When Ove had tried to violate her, to take control of her body without her consent, something inside her had snapped. She was the only person who should be making decisions about her body, and who got to touch it. He had tried to take that choice away from her, and she determined it would be the last time anyone would get to assert authority over her.

Her mother had behaved recklessly, sleeping with a man who wasn't her husband, and Cwen had been paying the price for it ever since. But now Cwen was married, she was the new queen, and her mother was still controlling her, forbidding her daughter from sleeping with her own husband, all to protect her secret. How was that fair? Why shouldn't she have a fulfilling relationship, children of her own, when everyone else kept using her for their own gain?

And yet, Cwen hadn't done it for her—she'd done it for Leof, to keep him safe. She hadn't known the heart of Njal, but she did now, and she believed if she told him the truth, he would protect them both.

After two nights of being in Njal's company, it felt strange to be in this chamber on her own. She wanted to go looking for him; she was starting to worry, but he'd told her to stay put, not to leave the room, and after what had happened earlier, she thought she should probably do as he'd asked.

A knock at the door made her jump, and she padded over to it, relieved he was back. But when she opened the door a crack she saw it wasn't Njal, but his man, Bjorn.

'Your Highness,' he said. 'Njal sent me. Are you dressed?'

Her brow furrowed. 'Yes.'

'Then come with me. You'll need your cloak. Quickly now.'

She shook her head, wondering if she should believe

him—that maybe this was a trap. But she knew Njal trusted him. And this man had treated her and her people with respect since he'd got here. She'd witnessed his loyalty the other night, when he'd come to tell them about Ove taking Leof.

She grabbed her cloak and threw it on, following him down the corridor. 'Where are we going?'

'Njal thinks it best if you leave the fortress under cover of darkness.'

Her heart slammed in her chest. 'We're leaving?' She couldn't believe it. Did Njal really want to leave the fortress he now ruled? The one he'd spent so long trying to take control of—and build back up?

'He's concerned for your safety. Unfortunately, Ove and his men have disappeared. Caedwalla's men are advancing. The danger is great.'

Did Njal think they were about to be attacked on two fronts—by Ove and Caedwalla? But shouldn't they stay and fight? 'What about the people? We can't abandon them.' She had so many questions.

'I'm sure Njal will explain everything, Your Highness, but we don't have much time.'

'Where is he? I must speak with him. And where's my boy?'

'Leof and Eadhild, and your parents, are waiting for you by the boat. Njal too.'

'Boat?'

When they'd navigated their way through the hall, past all the sleeping families camped out, they took the steps down into the waterlogged courtyard and began to wade through it, towards the back gate.

She saw Njal and she let out a breath she hadn't realised she was holding. He was there.

Her mother and father were already climbing down into the boat, and as she drew closer in the darkness, she watched Njal pick up her boy and pass him down into her mother's arms. Eadhild was next, and then she was there; it was her turn.

She looked up at him, questions in her eyes. This didn't feel right, like they were abandoning their people, running away, but she wanted to trust him. He must know what he was doing.

'Ready?' Njal gripped her hand and she sought strength from his firm grip as he helped her down into the boat. Then he let her go.

She took a seat on the bench and looked back up expectantly, waiting for him to get in. When he didn't, her heart began to pound. Instead, Bjorn jumped down into the hull and picked up the oars.

'Send word when you get there,' Njal said to his right-hand man, a look of grim determination on his face.

'We will,' Bjorn said.

And panic exploded in Cwen's chest. She leapt out of her seat on shaking legs.

'You're not coming with us?'

'No.'

He couldn't bring himself to look her in the eye.

'But you wish for me to leave?' Realisation dawned, and a sickening feeling of dread unfurled through her stomach. He was sending her away from him. He wasn't abandoning his new home, or his people—he was abandoning her.

Why?

Had he had enough of her pushing him away?

Did he no longer want her—after tonight?

'I should have sent you away when we first arrived. Tonight's events have shown me you are not safe here.'

He was going back on the vows he had spoken just days earlier. He had promised to love and to cherish her, till death us do part, but had he not meant it? He couldn't have if he was rejecting her, discarding her so easily. And she realised, after trying to keep her distance from him for the whole week, the panic she could feel rising in her chest was because she now didn't want to be parted from him.

What of their alliance? They had agreed to rule here together—was he going back on that too? And what did that mean for Leof and his heritage? If he wasn't going to be heir, if they were all headed into exile, what had it all been for?

'That isn't what we agreed.'

'It's for the best.' His voice sounded strange. Cold.

'For who?'

He gave her a long last look. 'I'll be in touch.'

And as the boat pulled away from the jetty, Cwen crumbled like sand back onto the bench. She felt bereft. Chilled to the bone. She couldn't even bring herself to shed any tears. She felt empty, as if everything was ending. As if all the good was fading from her life.

She watched Njal standing there, alone outside the mist-shrouded fortress on the jetty, until he grew small and smaller in the distance. Finally, he faded into blackness.

Even though she was surrounded by her family, she had never felt so alone. She shivered, and she tugged

Leof closer, to keep them both warm. She knew she had to pull herself together, for his sake. But she felt broken inside.

'Where are you taking us?' she said, turning to Bjorn.

'Njal said to take you to Bamburgh, Your Highness. He said you knew it well and had friends there. That you'd be safe.'

She nodded. Njal had listened to her. That was some comfort to her at least.

She tried to concentrate on the bends of the river, the familiar buildings lit up by the moonlight, as she had made this journey once or twice before.

She told herself she should be relieved. She loved Bamburgh and she had longed to return. She knew they would be welcome. She could live there with Leof in peace, away from Caedwalla's army and Njal's unruly brother. She could spend her days pleasing herself. She wouldn't have to be around Njal and lie any more. And yet, none of that made her feel any better.

She still couldn't believe Njal had done this. She had just suffered a terrifying ordeal at the hands of his brother and instead of offering her comfort, holding her close all night, making her feel better, he had sent her away. He had made it clear he couldn't bear to be in the same fortress as her, let alone the same room.

She felt as if something was sitting on her chest. Something akin to grief. And that she'd failed everyone. Her people. Her family. Njal. But mainly, herself. She had been the queen of Northumbria, Njal's wife, for less than a week.

Chapter Eleven

How many moon cycles had it been since they'd been here? The days were beginning to blur into each other and Cwen felt as if the walls were closing in on her and she had to get out, to walk, to shake off some of her restless energy.

She'd asked Eadhild to watch Leof for a while and had trudged along the cliff path for miles, the sight of the wild, rolling waves crashing onto the shore down below raising her spirits, until her feet had grown tired and sore, and she'd taken a path back inland, through the fields, to make her way home. She knew Bjorn would be cross with her, going off without telling him of her whereabouts, but she had needed some time alone. She had told Eadhild to tell him that she'd promised to make it back before dusk, as they were hosting a feast tonight for Hāligmonath, to celebrate Bamburgh's successful summer's crop.

She doubted Jorvik would be celebrating in the same way, not after the dreadful floods.

It had been a long journey via river and then sea to get here, and her mind and heart had been in turmoil. When she'd finally seen the grand fortress rising up from the beach, the sight of her old home had lifted her heavy heart just a little.

The people of her former settlement had been delighted to see them all, and welcomed her back with open arms, honoured to have the former king of Northumbria stay with them, and their new queen. The ealdormen and ladies had filled her in on the various skirmishes between local settlements, some summer raids, but on the whole, they had been able to live in relative peace.

They had all settled into a new routine. Cwen spent her days stitching, playing with Leof, and helping with the work in the fortress and out in the fields—she wanted to keep busy. But she couldn't seem to find the same contentment she'd felt when she'd lived here before. She felt as if she'd left a part of herself behind in Jorvik, and she was constantly wondering what was happening there, whether the people were safe, and what Njal was up to. She felt as if she was missing out on something. Something huge.

Leof seemed to like it here, being back by the ocean. He loved splashing in the waves, building fortresses in the sand, and having the space to roam free. There was so much more open land here than in Jorvik, where the people all seemed to be crowded, living on top of each other—even more so after the flooding.

Leof often asked after Njal, whether he would be coming to visit, or when they could go and see him, and when he did, it was as if someone was reaching into her chest and clenching her heart. Had he grown to like the Danish warrior just as much as she had?

There had been no news from the fortress—she would ask Bjorn every day if he had heard anything, and as every sunrise and sunset went by, she became more agitated. Njal had said he would be in touch, but there had been no word. Were they supposed to wait here indefinitely, in limbo, wondering if he'd ever send for them to come home? Did Njal not feel alone, without Bjorn and her? Had the floods receded, and had Caedwalla's forces come? And what about his brother—had they tracked him down or was he still on the loose? Even Bjorn was getting restless, she could tell, worried about his friend, and she had asked him why he hadn't returned to be with the king. Apparently, he was under strict orders to never let her out of his sight, to keep her safe. And it gave her hope…it almost sounded as if Njal cared. And if Njal wanted to be reunited with his right-hand man, wouldn't he have to see her again too?

Or had he forgotten her?

Her hurt and upset over how Njal had discarded her, casting her aside so brutally, had turned into anger, and she had vowed never to forgive him for his mistreatment of her. He had married her, forming an alliance, saying they'd rule over Jorvik together, then disposed of her when things had started to get difficult. He had broken his word; her trust. And after she had been attacked. Her—not him! At the hands of his brother. How dare he treat her this way?

The floods had barely touched them here in Bamburgh. The fortress was on much higher ground, sat on tough dolomite rock, and it was as if the devastation in Jorvik had never happened. Just like her time with Njal. Like it had all been a dream.

Even her father seemed to have forgotten that he'd lost his throne, quite content to be in their new surroundings. He seemed to be concentrating on healing, as she was trying to do, only her wound had been to the heart, and she felt as if it could be irreparable.

As Cwen came into a clearing she stopped dead, seeing two huge deer stalking towards each other, making loud bellowing noises, each trying to deter the other. As they drew closer, their antlers clashed and a mighty fight ensued. It was incredible to watch, these majestical creatures competing for a mate—and she wondered, was every animal the same, whether deer or human? Was there no end to the fighting over a mate, or land or domination? Finally, after a brutal battle, one came out as the victor and the other stalked away into the trees. As she lingered a while, she saw the champion claim his doe, and for some reason it made her feel sad. This was nature. This was how it was meant to be. And yet she had fought against every natural instinct when she had found her own mate, continually pushing him away. She had said her vows to him, and then denied him. She must have hurt him, badly. Had she done irrevocable damage? If she had just shared her secret with Njal, told him the truth, might it have made a difference?

And yet, he had hurt her too. After everything that had happened, he had taken away her freedom of choice, sending her away without even asking her if that's what she wanted. He had pulled the strings as if she were a puppet, once again controlling her, just like her parents, just like Ove had tried to do. It was the worst thing he could have done.

Bjorn was rightly livid with her when she came back through the gates to the stronghold, ranting and raving how Njal would never forgive him if anything had happened to her—that she was putting his life on the line. But she had to wonder if Njal would even notice or care. It had been many moon cycles now since she'd seen him. She tried to appease Bjorn by saying there was no harm done, and she would serve him extra meat at the feast tonight. She had grown fond of him, and could tell a bond was forming between him and Eadhild. She wanted to encourage it. Someone deserved to find happiness around here!

She was helping in the hall, peeling potatoes, when people started calling out from the courtyard, and their words made her stop dead in her tracks.

'He is here! The king! The king is coming!'

Bjorn met her gaze and raised his brows, instantly getting up out of his seat, charging outside to see if it was true. She could tell he was desperate to see his friend again.

'The king—Njal—has arrived from Jorvik, Your Highness!' Eadhild said, rushing back into the hall. 'He and about thirty men. Some look to be wounded.'

Cwen's heart lurched and she raced over to the door, trying to catch a glimpse of the men on horseback; one rider in particular. She hoped he wasn't hurt.

All around her, the hall sprang to life, a whirlwind of activity, as tables were dusted, benches straightened, floors swept. The fire was stoked and the courtyard cleared, just in time as the royal team of horses pulled up at the gateway and the men came into view.

And then, she saw him. Sat atop his horse, he looked weary, slightly older perhaps even though it had only been months since she'd seen him, but every bit as attractive as she remembered. His hair had more silver streaks than ever before, and it was longer. His armour was covered in dried blood and mud, as were his boots, but he looked robust. More handsome than ever.

It was such a surprise to see him, her legs gave way beneath her and she sat down on a bench to try to recover herself. But it was all she could do to try to remember how to breathe.

He was here. He had come.

And then Leof tore past her, heading out to the gate. 'Mother, Njal is here!' he said, delighted, excited. 'Are you coming outside to welcome them?'

Her gaze followed after him. 'I'll be there in just a moment,' she said.

She watched through the door as her son raced over to the men, straight up to Njal, and he descended his horse and stooped to pick up the boy, smiling.

Cwen's heart was in her mouth. How had he won over her son so quickly and so completely?

She knew she should act normally, as if she wasn't fazed—pretend to be busy with work, or something, but she could barely move. Her fingers trembled, her knees felt weak. She didn't know whether to run or hide. And yet she couldn't tear her gaze away, as next he embraced Bjorn, pleased to be reunited with his man.

Would he be as pleased to see her?

She absent-mindedly raised her hand up to touch her hair, patting over the braids, to check they were neat.

She watched as the people of the settlement gathered round to welcome their new king, and even though she knew she should, still she could not bring herself to go outside. She could hear him instruct his men to deal with the horses, and she had just made it to her feet, thinking she would continue with the potatoes, when he entered the hall, Leof tugging him along.

A mixture of excited awe and dread swirled in her stomach.

And when his eyes lifted and locked with hers, her heart fluttered, almost taking flight.

It was wonderful to see him again. He was a sight for sore eyes. He looked incredible, if a little tired. Had they had a long ride? How had the summer they'd spent apart not dampened her body's reaction to him? And why had he come?

'Hello, Cwen.'

She was so relieved to hear his voice, she almost wilted.

'Hello.'

His penetrating gaze regarded her carefully.

Part of her wanted to reach out and embrace him, tell him she was glad he was here and find out how he was, but he didn't deserve such a warm welcome. Her smile faltered, and she crossed her arms over her chest. 'This is a surprise.'

'We have been fighting Caedwalla's forces for months, out in the fields, pushing them further away from Jorvik. The city is safe for now. But the last fight... we lost a lot of our soldiers. When Erik said we were nearer to Bamburgh than home, we decided to come here and rest the horses. Some of my men could do with being patched up, and a good meal, if it's not too much trouble.'

Disappointment lashed through her. So it hadn't even been his choice to come? He hadn't missed her, or wanted to see her. He had come purely because it was the closest settlement? This was more than she could bear!

She nodded. 'Of course, it's no trouble,' she said, swallowing down the lump in her throat.

Suddenly she noticed her mother and father were in the back of the hall, watching them, and she guessed they would now make themselves scarce. He would not wish to dine in their company, or them in his.

'Tell your men to come inside. They're all welcome. Warm yourselves up by the fire and we'll prepare some food,' she said.

Njal and his men seated themselves at the tables near the central hearth and listening to them talk, it was all about their battles, their victories and their wounds.

Cwen tasked some of the women to tend to each of their injuries, and she had their glasses filled with what she was sure was much-needed ale.

'The pottage won't be long,' she said.

She was aware Leof was filling Njal in on all the mackerel he had caught since he'd been here, and telling him about the seals he'd swum with in the sea. The boy even clambered onto his lap, and she saw Njal wince. She narrowed her eyes on him. Was he hurt?

'Leof, don't bother Njal,' she chided him.

'It's all right. I want to hear about it,' he said, dismissing her comment, and she felt jealous at the easy connection the two of them had, whereas she felt as if he was treating her as if she were merely an old acquaintance. As if they were strangers who had gone so long without seeing each other that it wasn't easy to talk about the small day-to-day things, what they'd been up to, so they struggled to find anything to say at all.

They had been apart for months—had he missed their long, torturous nights together, or had he replaced her with a woman who was more willing? The thought made her stomach churn. Surely not? And yet, why shouldn't he? Apart from the fact they were tied together in marriage, it wasn't as if she had meant anything to him. It wasn't as if she had given him what he'd needed.

'Have you had any trouble here?' Njal asked, looking between her and Bjorn.

'Trouble? No, why? Should we be expecting any?'

Njal coughed to clear his throat, and he looked back at Bjorn, giving him a knowing glance. 'My brother didn't return to the fortress the night you left,' he explained, seemingly unable to look her in the eye. 'He took his men and fled, but they rallied a force of their own and struck us a few days later. It was a deliberate subversion. A small band of them, hitting the fortress at various points. They chanced upon us a few days ago, so we know they're this far north.'

The breath left her body. She couldn't imagine how Njal must be feeling, now having to fight his brother on the battlefield as well as Caedwalla. He must be suffering, struggling with the fact that his own flesh and blood, the boy he had raised alone after his parents had died, had turned so completely against him. But it wasn't her concern. He hadn't wanted her support and she knew she must hold on to her anger against him. She must not forgive him for his cold treatment of her; for sending her away.

'Why would he come here?' she asked.

'I don't know. But I'd like to double the defences on the battlements, just in case.'

She shuddered. She didn't like the thought of Ove and

his men coming anywhere near Bamburgh. She didn't want them to bring any trouble to these peaceful lands.

As he sipped on his ale, Cwen took the chance to study Njal. He was a strong man, but she could tell the fighting of late had taken its toll. Close up, she could see his colouring was paler than before, his face almost drained of blood, and he looked shattered, the dark circles under his eyes giving it away.

When the pottage was served, the men ate in almost silence, grunts of praise and satisfaction rippling around the table, but Cwen couldn't manage her own. Njal had made no effort to speak with her again, but instead had turned to talk to the ealdormen from Bamburgh and she felt as if he was shutting her out, excluding her, and she felt her rage surge to the surface. This was her home. He had chosen to come here. And yet, he was treating her as if she didn't exist. He might have felt he could behave this way in Jorvik. But not here. She would not have it. And she determined before the night was out, she would demand an explanation for his actions. And an apology.

Despite Cwen's words, it wasn't welcome Njal saw in her eyes when she'd ushered them into the hall, but wary apprehension and judgement. He knew that he'd made a mistake; they shouldn't have come. Cwen didn't want him here.

Cwen didn't look pleased to see him, and he couldn't blame her after what had happened the last time they'd been together. He wondered if his very presence reminded her of his brother and what he'd done, and the last thing he wanted was to make her feel uncomfortable. This was her happy place—where she'd been content with her late husband. And he was a fool to have thought that she'd want him here, tarnishing those memories.

She looked beautiful. Much more relaxed in these stunning surroundings. The scenery here was incredible—wide, open skies and vast beaches, with the blue surf rolling onto the shore. She'd had her shiny dark hair cut shorter, and it suited her, resting on her shoulders. She had a healthy glow of colour in her cheeks, and the moment he saw her, he knew the summer apart hadn't extinguished the flame of desire that licked inside him whenever she was around. It had just made it burn fiercer than ever before.

Back in Jorvik, he hadn't been able to concentrate when she was around, constantly distracted by her presence, but when she had left, it had been a whole lot worse. She'd consumed his thoughts. He'd avoided having conversations about her and tried to keep busy. He had even been all right with having to go back into battle again, as it was a distraction from his misery of having let her go.

Had it only been a summer? It felt like a lifetime.

He was so glad to see her. He had needed to. It had been too long. Every day he'd spent apart from her had been torture. He was desperate for the fighting to be over so he could finally try to make amends and win her back. But he wouldn't put her in jeopardy again. He had to rid Northumbria of their enemies first.

On their journey here, Njal had taken furtive glances behind him, to check that no one was following them. He had been reluctant to come because he didn't want to bring more trouble to Cwen's door. But when Erik had suggested it, saying they were just a half day's ride away, and they could all do with the sanctuary, he hadn't been able to get the thought out of his mind. He had been desperate to see her again. And knowing that Ove could be on his way here, that she might need his protection, had just reinforced his decision. He needed to know she was safe. But having to tell her Ove was on the loose, and possibly heading this way, made him feel like a failure all over again.

He didn't like the way things had been left between them that night. He'd felt terrible for the way he'd touched her, giving her an ultimatum about whether she wanted to be with him or not, and then he'd felt responsible for what his brother had done.

He'd been so worried she'd been hurt.

He'd known he had to get her to safety, away from whatever was going on between him and Ove. Away from the ever-advancing Caedwalla. Away from him and his insatiable desire.

Looking around the hall now, at his men's hunger-sated faces and Cwen, so serious, trying to make sure they had everything they needed, he pushed out his chair and stood. 'Perhaps we should make a move. Find somewhere else to sleep tonight.'

Cwen's head shot up to look at him, her eyes narrowing.

'You want to leave? Now?' Bjorn said, shocked and obviously displeased.

His men all turned to look at him in protest, disappointed by his suggestion. They were enjoying the company of the people of Bamburgh, the safety and comfort the fortress offered, the warmth of the fire, their full bellies and the flowing ale, if only for a night.

'I just thought if we left now we might make good headway on our return journey.'

'Or we can leave in the morning when it's light and we've all had a good night's sleep,' Erik said.

Njal glanced at Cwen.

'You're all welcome to stay,' she said, though her mouth was taut, the expression in her eyes dark and unreadable.

He sighed. 'All right. If you're sure. We'll go in the morning. I'm going to take a look around—get the lie of the land. Check the fort's defences.'

'You don't need to do that. I have secured the ramparts,' Cwen said.

'Nevertheless, I'd like to check them out for myself.'

He made his way through the hall, and when he thought no one was watching, he swiped a needle and thread from one of the tables. He crossed the square, winding his way down the grassy slope towards the sea, but not before Leof caught up with him.

'Where are you going?' the boy asked.

'Just for a walk.'

When they'd come upon the coast earlier today, it had lifted his spirits—to see the ocean again. He hadn't realised how much he'd missed it these past few years. He saw the boat tied up on the jetty that he'd put Cwen and her family in the night he'd sent them away from Jorvik, the boat that had taken her away from him, and he felt a pang of regret in his chest. Standing there on the jetty, her boat moving further and further away from him, he'd never felt so alone.

It was beautiful here. He could see why she liked it. The fort sat on huge cliffs that loomed over the ocean, making it a difficult stronghold to attack. There was only one way in or out, and from inside, on the ramparts, you could see across the plains for miles. Fortunately, there was no sign of either enemy army.

'You broke your promise,' the boy said.

'How?' he asked him, stopping in his tracks.

'You said you wouldn't hurt my mother. That first day we met. You promised me.'

'I didn't hurt her,' Njal said.

'When we left Jorvik, she cried for weeks. You did hurt her—you broke her heart.' And then the boy was gone, racing up the path, back towards the hall.

Had he? He couldn't believe it to be true. For him to have broken Cwen's heart, she would have to have cared for him. Surely that wasn't the case? Was the boy talking nonsense?

Reaching the sand, he looked up and down the beach. There was not a soul around. He tugged off his boots and his chain-mail, and it felt good to discard the heavy garment. He untucked his tunic, pulling it up and off over his head, grimacing, and looked down. The wound was deeper than he'd thought. He'd need to wash off the blood to see it properly before he tried to stitch the skin back together. He tugged off his breeches and waded into the water. The icy, salty surf felt incredible against his aching muscles, but excruciating against the deep gash to his stomach. He swam a few strokes, before the smarting was too great and he decided to get out. But as he drew closer to the shore, he saw a figure standing there, waiting for him.

Cwen?

Her hand was resting against her forehead, guarding her eyes from the evening sun, and his pulse kicked up.

'You might want to turn round,' he said, projecting his voice as he drew nearer. 'I've got no clothes on.'

'Of course you haven't,' she said, rolling her eyes, immediately turning her back on him.

And he smiled. He padded up the sand and reached for his breeches, then pulled them on. He was pleased she still had her spirit. 'What are you doing out here?'

'I came to find you,' she said, turning to speak to him over her shoulder.

That sounded promising. Perhaps she didn't hate him as much as he thought. Was there some truth to what Leof had said?

'How was the water?'

'Freezing.'

'I know. I've swum every day since we came back here. You're bleeding,' she said, turning round fully, just as he pulled on his tunic.

'And you're not meant to be looking.'

'I knew you were hurt. Is it bad?'

He shrugged. 'Just needs a stitch.'

'And you were going to do that yourself, I presume? Not tell anyone, or ask for help?'

'I didn't want the men to know. It's not good for their leader to be wounded. It's bad for morale.'

She tutted. 'I'll do it for you, although I'm not the neatest with a needle. Over there?' she said, gesturing to some boulders at the edge of the sand.

He nodded, his heart lifting in hope, and he picked up his boots and mail coat, following her.

When they came to the first rock, she gestured for him to sit.

'You'll need to take that back off,' she said, nodding to his tunic.

He did as he was told, gingerly peeling the material away from the wound. It was already bleeding again, and he cursed.

'Did you think you could hide it from everyone?' she frowned.

He shrugged, passing her the needle and thread. 'It was worth a try.'

'I saw you take this.' She threaded the needle and then came towards him. 'It looks nasty. This is going to sting.'

He nodded grimly. 'Just make it quick.'

She set to work with the needle, pulling the skin tight, and he bit out a curse. It helped to take deep breaths, drawing in lungsful of her sweet floral scent. He'd missed it. He'd missed her. He was so glad she'd followed him down to the beach. Why had she come?

'Have you been all right here? Leof seems happy.'

'He is. But he was pleased to see you today.'

He swallowed. He had missed the boy too. He'd felt bad for abandoning him.

She paused what she was doing and looked up at him. 'Njal, why did you send us away?'

In that moment, he didn't know. He was a madman. He wished he hadn't. It had been torture being away from her.

'I told you, I thought it was for the best.'

'But why?'

He raked a hand through his wet hair. 'I felt awful about everything that had happened. Attacking your home, your father getting hurt, forcing you into marrying me… Then what happened with my brother. It sickened me. I'm so sorry about what he did, Cwen.' His voice broke with emotion as he spoke. 'It was my duty to protect you. I felt as if I'd let you down. Just like I did my family. And I thought you'd be better off away from Ove. Caedwalla. Me. All these men who would use you for their own needs.'

'By sending me away, you made me feel I was at fault, that I'd done something wrong.'

'Ah, hell, that was not my intention,' he said, dragging a hand over his beard.

'You were angry with me.'

He cupped her chin in his hand, forcing her to look at him again, so she'd know he meant it. 'No,' he said. 'I wasn't. I was angry with Ove. With myself. Not you. Maybe I took it out on you—that was wrong of me. But when I saw his hands on you, I lost it. I just wanted you away from there. Out of harm's way.' He stared down into her eyes. 'I sent you away because I thought that was what you wanted. What you needed.'

'But it wasn't, Njal,' she said. 'You got it wrong.'

He nodded, accepting that. 'Tell me.'

'When you sent me away, I was so angry with you. You didn't talk to me, discuss it with me. When we married, we came to an agreement. We said we were going to rule Northumbria together, but you took that away from me. My home. My loyalty to my people. You took away my choice. Just like your brother tried to do. Just as my father has always done.'

He stared into her eyes, shocked by what she was telling him, realisation dawning, and he felt worse than ever.

'Oh, God. I'm sorry, Cwen,' he said. 'You're right. I hadn't thought about it like that. I'd just wanted to get you out of there, to protect you. I didn't know where Ove had gone. He was on the loose, dangerous. He still is. Please believe me, it was for your sake, not mine. I really felt like everything I'd done from the moment I'd arrived in Jorvik had made you hate me.'

She bent down and drew another stitch and he winced. He would take it as punishment.

He waited for her to sit back up before he carried on.

'You slept next to me night after night, making me feel like a bad person for wanting to touch you so much. Why didn't you just say no to marrying me?' he said.

'I didn't regret marrying you, Njal. The reasons to go through with it were right—they still stand. But you expected me to sleep with you immediately, when I didn't even know you, or whether I could trust you, when I knew you only wanted me for my crown.'

'Is that what you thought? I wanted you for you, to hell with the crown.' He pinched his nose, trying to keep calm, be steady.

'So, after Ove attacked you...what if I hadn't left the room that night? If I hadn't sent you away, but instead if I'd have asked you what you needed, what would you have said?'

She looked up at him. 'I would have asked you to hold me. To offer me comfort. To tell me everything would be all right.'

He reeled, sitting back, shocked. 'I thought that was the last thing you wanted.' He bravely lifted his hand to touch her, to graze his knuckles down her cheek. 'You were like a butterfly that had landed in my hand.

It comes and sits there for a while, but you know you can't make it stay. It's too beautiful to trap. You have to set it free. I honestly thought you were indifferent to me. Afraid of me.'

'No, Njal. After Ove tried to force himself on me, I needed you more than ever. I was beginning to care for you, and I thought the touch of someone I trusted would be healing.'

She continued to stitch him, and he hoped she was almost done. He wanted to focus on her, and what she was saying. He wanted to know what she needed from him now.

'So you don't think I'm like my brother? You're not afraid of me?'

'No. I know you're not like him, Njal. I knew from the moment I met you. I'm sorry for what he's putting you through,' she said. 'It must hurt a great deal, after all you have done for him. But as for me being afraid of you...' She reached forwards and put her palm against his cheek. 'I'm only terrified of the way you make me feel. The things I want to do, when I'm with you.'

He stared down into her eyes, stunned.

'What?' he whispered. He couldn't believe what he was hearing. And then he quirked an eyebrow. 'What *do* you want to do?'

'Njal,' she said, smiling, gently swiping his chest, embarrassed, but he caught hold of her wrist, hard.

'Be very clear.'

Her cheeks flushed with colour and her eyes looked up into his.

'What are you saying, Cwen? That you've missed me?'

He didn't make any move towards her. He wouldn't—not until she told him what she wanted. He had to be sure.

'Yes,' she whispered. 'I missed you. Ridiculously.'

'It's not ridiculous. I missed you too.'

He softened his grip just a little, his thumb gently stroking her skin on the inside of her wrist. He was breathing hard—and so was she, her chest rising and falling, and he could see her tongue nervously run across her lips. 'So, just to be sure. You *like* me?' His lips curled up for the first time in weeks. The weight on his chest lifted.

She rolled her eyes, frustrated, and tried to back away. 'Njal.' But he held her in his grip.

'I'm just trying to understand. I want you to be truthful. Just tell me how you feel—what you want. You don't think all Danes are brutes? And you don't want me and my men to leave?'

'Let me just finish this last stitch,' she said, and he reluctantly released her, knowing he mustn't push her.

She bent her head and pulled the last of the skin together, closing the wound, so it would have a chance to heal. She tied a knot in the thread and sat back to study her work.

'Is that all right?'

He looked down and nodded. 'It's good. Thank you. Better than I could have done.'

She put down the needle and thread and went over to a little rock pool to wash her hands, while he pulled his tunic and boots back on.

When she came back to him he stood, and reached out to take her hand in his.

'So you were saying?'

'No, I don't think all Danes are brutes. And no, I don't want you to leave.'

'You like me.'

'Didn't I say that already?'

He grinned. He tilted his head to look at her. 'You can tell me again. Do you want me to kiss you?'

'No, I don't want that,' she said, shaking her head.

He stepped back, frowning, disappointment crashing over him. 'You don't?'

'I don't want you to *just* kiss me, Njal. Not any more.'

He couldn't believe what he was hearing. He pulled her up against his chest, hard. 'Are you sure about this?'

'Yes. From now on, I want to make my own choices. I need you to let me. And right now, I want to do this, with you.'

And suddenly he was overcome with desire to get closer. All his dreams were coming true. She was giving him permission to kiss her and a whole lot more. At last.

He pulled her right up against him, not caring about the smarting of his wound, and he slid his hands up and down her arms.

He took her face between his hands. 'Here? Or do you want to go inside?'

The summer apart from him had given Cwen the time she'd needed to think about this. And she was ready. She wanted to do this.

Perhaps that was why she had followed him to the beach. She had seen him try to take the needle and thread, discreetly, and had been instantly concerned, needing to know he was all right. But she'd also known she had to talk to him, to ask him why he had sent her away, and get the answers she craved. She'd wanted him to apologise and he'd given her that and more, telling her he had only sent her away because he'd wanted to protect her, because he felt bad about everything that had happened, and he'd thought she didn't want him. But now he knew the opposite was true. She did want him. Badly. And hearing that he'd missed her as much as she'd missed him had been glorious.

'My room,' she said.

But she didn't know whether her legs would carry her there, they felt weak with desire.

It was a steep climb back up the hill, but she barely remembered it, her need carrying her forwards. He led her towards the great hall, but then she took over, taking his hand and bypassing the door and all the revelry going on inside, past the stables and the horses gently neighing, and round the back of the building to the keep, up the winding stairs to her room.

She pushed open the door, letting him inside, and the moment they were alone, he turned to face her. The air was thick between them, with anticipation and desire. And he reached out and took both her hands in his.

'Are you really sure about this?' he asked.

And she nodded, although she felt giddy with nerves.

When he gestured to her to come closer, she went into his arms willingly, and the moment was huge. But she could no longer stay away. She had kept him at a distance, pushed him away, trying to fulfil everyone else's needs, but now she needed to see to her own. She wondered whether she should tell him the truth now—about Leof and her ability to have children.

But then he took her face in his hands and looked

into her eyes before bringing his lips down onto hers, and she didn't want to prolong their intimacy any longer. It felt incredible to finally have him kiss her again. He smelled of the sea. His skin was cold but his mouth was warm on hers, his lips both tender and firm. And he took his time, as if savouring the taste of her, introducing his tongue to her mouth slowly, making her shiver.

His kiss was like him, she thought. Hard on the outside, soft on the inside, each stroke of his tongue making her melt further into his arms.

She had grown up thinking that wanting things for herself was selfish. She'd been taught about duty, and putting the monarchy above all else. But since the moment she'd met Njal, she had *wanted*. She had tried to put him off, choosing what was safe, to protect those she loved over her own feelings. But she couldn't stay away from him any longer. She could no longer pretend she was happy with how things were—acting as if she didn't want him, lying about being unable to have children to protect Leof and her mother—when she wasn't. She couldn't keep living by someone else's rules.

She lifted her arms around his shoulders and her fingers curled around his neck, bringing his head closer, deepening the kiss, and he groaned.

He pulled away from her to look down into her eyes. 'Do you know what you do to me?'

'I have a pretty good idea.'

He kissed her again, his tongue stroking hers, more insistent, delving deeper, his hands sliding down her back, and they settled on her hips. He tugged her soft curves against his body, binding her to him, so they were chest to chest, his knee parting her trembling thighs, and when she felt the hard ridge of him pressing into her stomach, her excitement soared. She was so relieved he still wanted her, like she wanted him.

She pulled away from him slightly to look up into his eyes. 'I thought you might have found satisfaction in the arms of someone else after you sent me away.'

She needed to know he hadn't.

'And break our marriage vows? Never,' he said. 'Besides, I don't want anyone else. Only you.'

She smiled and kissed him again, and wriggled against him, bravely, letting him know she wanted to do this, and his hands roamed down, over her bottom, cupping her buttocks and moulding her against him, his kisses becoming fiercer, more urgent with need.

'No one has ever made me feel this way before,' he said. 'I've never wanted anyone this badly. There have been times where I've felt like I'm going out of my mind.'

'Me too.'

She wondered if she ought to tell him she had never done this before—would he be able to tell? But then his mouth trailed down along her jaw, and she lifted her head, encouraging him to explore further. She was lost to her desire. He released a hand to bring it up to curve over one of her aching, swollen breasts straining against the material of her tunic, and she whimpered.

'I want to undress you, to see you,' he said. And she knew he was asking for permission. 'I don't want there to be anything between us. Just my skin against yours.'

And she nodded, her excitement escalating, her throat dry. 'I want that too.'

He stepped away slightly to tackle the brooches holding up the straps of her pinafore, and even though he unclasped them easily, skilfully, she noticed his fingers were trembling. Good—she must be having the same effect on him as he was on her.

When the straps tumbled down, he gripped the material at her waist and began to ruck it up her body, navigating it over her curves. He drew her arms up over her head, and then the pinafore was gone, discarded on the floor. His hands came back to her tunic, and he did the same again, raising her arms so he could lift it off her, only this time when she brought her arms back down, she was left standing there in nothing but her breeches. She felt exposed—vulnerable—but the dark hunger in his eyes told her he liked what he saw. And so she didn't try to cover herself up. She wanted to please him. She refused to disappoint him again.

'You are exceptionally beautiful, do you know that?'

She shivered, her naked skin exposed to the air, the peaks of her nipples tilting upwards, as if towards him, yearning for his touch, and he complied, raising his hands to cradle her swollen breasts. He caressed them gently, his thumbs circling the tips, teasing them with his thumbs, and she swayed in pleasure, her eyes fluttering shut. 'Njal...'

And then he was rolling down her breeches, over her thighs, until they pooled at her feet on the floor. She was utterly naked, completely at his mercy, standing before him trembling. 'Njal,' she whispered again, her knees almost giving way with the heavy weight of her desire.

'You are remarkable,' he said. 'You can't even tell you've carried a child—your body is...perfection.'

His words flashed a warning in her mind, that perhaps she should say something. But she was frightened of ruining the moment, and when he kissed her again, his hands lightly trailing down to rest on her hips before grazing over the quivering flesh of her buttocks, all reason fled. She just wanted… And then he took her hand and led her over to the bed.

She was grateful to sit down and rest her unsteady legs, and he sat beside her and brushed her hair over her shoulder. He dipped his head, lifting her breast to meet his mouth, and he trailed his hot tongue over her chest. She felt her eyes roll and she lay back, her hand coming round his head, bringing him down with her.

She let her fingers trail up over his shoulder, and as he lifted his head to kiss her on the lips again, she ran her hands round the front of his chest, flattening her palms against his solid muscles, and felt the peak of his nipples through the material of his tunic. She brushed aside the opening, wanting to see and feel more of him, and with her other hand, she tugged it, lifting it up. She needed to touch his warm, ink-covered skin, and he helped her, pulling the garment over his head and casting it off.

Her hands roamed over his chest, freely exploring him, taking in his ink. She'd missed seeing the now-familiar designs. He was magnificent. All muscle and hardness, and yet he was being gentle with her, taking things slow, and she was grateful. 'You are beautiful too,' she said.

'I've never been called that before.'

His hand reached down to untie the fastening of his breeches, and her stomach tightened in anticipation, her cheeks burned. He pushed them down his solid thighs and came down to lie beside her, and her eyes bulged at the sight of him.

'Nervous?' he asked, stroking her cheek.

'Yes,' she said, chewing her lip.

'Me too.'

'You?'

He shrugged. 'It's been a while. Since…'

'You haven't done this since that night?'

'No, I haven't,' he said, and tucked her hair behind her ear. 'It put me off women, because while I was there, doing that…my family were being hurt…' His forehead creased. And she could see it tortured him. He felt guilty. But it wasn't his fault.

She brought her hand up to hold his jaw. 'Are you sure you want to do this now?' she asked.

And he grinned at her. 'Definitely,' he said.

He started kissing her again, more passionately than before, and she couldn't think past the pleasure he was bestowing on her with the flick of his tongue in her mouth, the delicate touch of his fingers on her naked skin.

He trailed his hand between her hot, swollen breasts, flattening his palm over her taut stomach and down, running his fingers through her triangle of soft curls. She writhed impatiently, knowing what exquisite sensations lay in store if he moved lower, and then his fingers curved downwards, and she gasped at the intimate touch. He looked into her eyes, as if wanting to watch her reactions as his fingers gently parted her soft folds and stroked between them. With every melting touch, any concerns she had began to fall away. It was unbelievable. He was unbelievable.

Her hand flew up to her brow. It felt incredible. She wanted more. And she wanted to please him in return. She reached out and trailed her fingers lightly over his body, being careful not to go near his wound, and lower. He stalled his fingers between her legs in anticipation of her touch. She knew she must satisfy him too, but she wasn't sure how. She had no idea what she was doing; she'd never touched a man before.

She ran her fingers over him lightly, touching the tip, and he bucked, so she thought he must like it, and she did it again. But he clamped his hand around hers, wrapping her fingers around the base of him, and showed her what he liked, moving her hand up and down him. He was all heat and hard silkiness. He groaned, pressing his forehead against hers, letting her continue on her own while his fingers stole back between her legs.

She didn't think there could be anything better than this, lying next to each other, skin on skin, touching each other, exploring each other, pleasuring each other to their heart's content.

Just thinking about what he was doing to her made her pulse race, her excitement build, his fingertips opening her up, circling her, and heat burned through her.

'Does that feel good?'

'Yes,' she whimpered, burying her head into his shoulder.

And he gripped her chin, forcing her to look at him. 'Describe it to me,' he said, as he slid a long finger inside her.

She shook her head, knowing she wouldn't be able to put something so amazing into words. Her breath quickened, the need building, and then he was moving, forcing her to let go of him, as he dragged his lips down her body, kissing her breasts, her stomach, still stroking her, intimately, and he pushed her knees apart.

She was still holding his bearded jaw as he looked up at her.

'What are you doing?' she asked, her eyes wide.

'Spread your legs,' he whispered. 'Wider.' And as she obeyed, like a flower unfurling its petals, he dipped his head so he could taste her, his tongue gliding along her so tenderly, making her shiver, and she cried out in ecstasy. She stretched her legs, pointing her feet, her hips rising off the bed to meet his mouth and the exquisiteness of the teasing caress of his tongue.

He lifted his head and smiled. 'I've wanted to do this to you since the moment I first saw you. I thought it might frighten you off if I told you,' he said.

'I haven't ever—'

'Never?' he asked incredulous.

She shook her head.

His other hand came up to cup her bottom, holding her in place, bringing her closer to him, as if he wanted to deepen the intensity of what he was doing to her, and she threw her head back and succumbed to all the sensations he was lavishing upon her. Her hand was still trapped between his moving jaw and her thigh, but she needed to keep hold of him, to ground her—she felt she was floating. She couldn't believe what was happening, his tongue lashing against her, building the dizzying pleasure that was tearing through her, and she never, ever wanted this feeling to end. But suddenly her climax came in a great surge and release, overwhelming her, making her thrash and scream until she could take no more and she begged him to stop, to come back up to her.

He came up over her body, on his elbows, grinning, looking down at her. His deep blue eyes were focused on her in the soft evening light, and she flushed, but there was nowhere to hide.

She didn't trust her voice to speak—she had no words to describe the things he had just done or how he'd made her feel, and so she raised her head to his, placing a kiss on his lips.

'Thank you,' she whispered.

'Thank you? I haven't finished with you yet, Cwen,' he said, gripping her wrists and placing them either side of her head. 'I've only just begun.'

Her pulse raced.

She liked the weight of him on top of her, the feel of his solid body against hers, pinning her down, their bodies mirroring the shape of the cross on his chest. Her hands ran over his smooth, broad back, and down, over his buttocks, pressing him to her, not wanting him to ever move from here.

'I want to be inside you,' he said. 'I want to make you mine.'

She nodded. 'I want that too,' she said. 'I want to be yours.'

She felt him straining against her, pressing into her stomach. And he raised himself off her a little, to reach down and guide himself between her legs. Fire burned in her stomach. She hadn't thought there could be anything more intimate than his mouth on her down there, but this...this was wholly different. His most private, sensitive parts stroking against hers, caressing her, opening her up with the tip.

Instinctively, she wrapped her legs over his, opening her hips wider, and she felt him right there, at her entrance. She gave an impatient wriggle, and he growled, and with fierce urgency he finally entered her with one long, thick thrust, and where she expected to feel pleasure, she felt a sharp spasm of pain, and she sucked in a breath, her body tensing.

He went very still, his brow furrowing, and she cringed. She shifted beneath him and he raised his head a little, to stare down into her eyes.

'Cwen?' he asked, confused.

She looked up at him, blinking back tears, her face aflame. 'Don't stop,' she said. 'I want this. You.'

'Are you all right?'

'Yes.' She nodded, moving her legs further up, around his waist, encouraging him on.

He brought his hand up to her jaw and kissed her, tenderly, deeply, until she began to relax around him, and he adjusted his position slightly, before he moved inside her again, slowly, more gently this time. With the next careful thrust, her body allowed him all the way in, and she cried out in pleasure. The feeling of him filling her up completely, impaling her limp body on the bed, was intense, incredible, and she wanted more. She gripped his buttocks, trying to pull him closer as she ground against him, and he groaned.

'You feel so good,' he whispered.

'So do you.'

He began to quicken his pace, and he deepened the intensity of his thrusts. Her whole body trembled and she cried out in pleasure, so he did it again. And again. And he couldn't stop. And she knew he would not stop until he'd wrung every last inch of enjoyment from her body. She began to move her hips, matching his thrusts, his erotic rhythm, wondering if she was doing this right.

But she must have been, as his next surge took her over the edge, and she soared, screaming, thrashing, biting down onto his shoulder, and his own intense climax followed swiftly after, had him roaring out her name as he emptied himself inside her in thick wave after wave.

They lay there like that for a while, trying to catch their breath, until he eventually, reluctantly, withdrew from her body, making her wince, and lifted himself off her. He lay beside her on the bed, pulling her to him, and she nestled into his shoulder. The speed of his chest rising and falling began to slow down as every moment passed, and she lifted her head to study him, to rest her palm against his cheek. He was the most beautiful man. It had been a beautiful experience. Everything she had wanted.

Was he sleeping? She didn't think so. But his eyes were closed so she couldn't see into his blue depths and know what he was thinking.

She knew there would be questions, and she had to prepare herself to answer them. And after the things they'd just done, she knew she couldn't lie. She didn't want to. Not to him. Not any more. Not after they'd just been so intimate.

Cwen's curves felt so soft resting against him, and Njal struggled to get his breathing back to normal. His hand began to lightly graze her cooling skin at her hip.

His muscles ached from the vigour and passion of their lovemaking. He felt alive. It had been incredible, better than he'd ever dreamed it would be. She'd felt as if she was made for him and just lying here thinking about it, her body moulded to his, he already wanted her again.

But also, questions tore through his mind. His emotions were a tumultuous mix of elation and bewilderment, satisfaction and doubt.

They had to talk.

For he was in shock. The moment he'd entered her, he knew, no one had been inside her before. He had stilled, at first concerned by the obvious breach and the spasm of pain that had flashed across her face. He'd been momentarily confused, but as comprehension had dawned, and she'd wriggled against him, encouraging him to continue, he'd been unable to help the spark of triumph that had coursed through him.

He was her first.

He was the only man to claim her.

He was overjoyed.

And yet, he was struggling to understand it, what it meant. Of only one thing was he certain—she had lied.

She stroked her hands over the ink on his chest, following the lines and patterns, and down over his stomach, making his muscles clench. He knew the markings fascinated her. Or maybe she was just trying to distract him from asking her questions about the things she must surely realise he would now want to discuss. If he didn't stop her roaming fingers, it might just work.

He opened his eyes and placed his other hand over hers.

'What we just did—you hadn't done that before.'

Her fingers stilled. 'No. I hadn't.'

He gave a slow, disbelieving shake of his head.

'Cwen, you should have told me... I would have been gentler. I would have explained how things were between a man and woman. Did you even know what to do?'

'I do now,' she smiled.

He swore softly and gripped her chin, tipping her face up to look at him. 'That's not funny. Did I hurt you?' He'd thought she was ready, that she was experienced—he'd taken her much too fiercely, and he was ashamed. Had he known...

'No, you didn't, Njal. It felt good,' she said, resting her hand against his jaw. 'It was everything I'd hoped it would be and more.' And looking into her flushed, radiant face, her bright eyes, he wanted to believe her. 'And I did know about it. I'd just never actually done it.'

His brow furrowed. 'Then you've been lying to me,' he said.

She bit her lip.

'For God's sake, why?'

'Because I didn't know you, or whether I could trust you until now.'

And she had trusted him with her body. She had allowed him to remove her clothes and take ownership of her, to possess her, completely—and right now, the memory of that and how amazing it had been was the only thing helping him to keep his anger in check.

He shook his head. 'But how can it be possible? I don't understand. You were married. You have a son...'

She ran her tongue over her lips. 'I know I have a lot of explaining to do, and I want to tell you. I'm ready. It would be such a relief to have you know. I don't want to hide it from you any more.'

That was something at least. He nodded. 'Let me pour us both a drink and you can tell me.'

He swung his legs off the bed and walked over to the table and poured them both some wine from a carafe. He carried the cups back to her and handed her one, but not before he saw her eyes rake greedily over his body. He felt the stirrings of desire again, as he stood there, letting her look at him, taking a sip of the liquid. But he couldn't let her distract him. He couldn't take her again without knowing the details of her deception.

He lay back down, relaxing against the cushions, pulling a blanket over his lower half. She sat cross-legged on the bed, facing him, pulling the furs over her body, holding them up to her chin, and he was glad. He would be able to concentrate far better if her perfect body wasn't exposed to him, tempting him.

'So Leof...?' he said, putting his cup down.

'Is my son in every sense of the word. I love him more than anything. I just didn't give birth to him.'

His mind raced. 'Then...who?'

'I couldn't tell you, because nobody knows, not even my father. I swore I would never say anything. But you see, in actual fact, Leof is my brother.'

He stared at her for a long moment, letting the information sink in. He took the cup from her hands and set it down. 'Tell me everything...' he said.

'Well, I think I told you that my marriage to Feran was arranged. We were forced into it by our parents,' she said, twisting her hands in her lap. 'We had been childhood friends but we weren't in love, so there had been a fair amount of reluctance on both sides. In the end, knowing our fathers weren't going to back down, we bonded over our shared resistance. But Feran confided in me right from the start that he didn't find me attractive.'

Njal's eyebrows shot up. 'How can that be? You're stunning.'

She shook her head, smiling, blushing, looking up at him. 'Thank you. But you see, Feran liked men, not women.'

Njal felt his eyes go wide as he allowed this new information to sink in. He rested his head back against the wall. The man he'd been jealous of all this time had liked men, not women. 'Is that even lawful here?' he asked.

'No,' she said, 'So I was the perfect foil. And I was relieved. Because even though I liked him, as a friend, I didn't want to share his bed. And he didn't want me in that way either, so at the beginning, everything was good. We lived contentedly here for a while. I overlooked whatever he got up to at night in the privacy of his own room, and I was happy with my daily chores and all the people who became my friends here. But when my father started pestering us for a grandchild—a male heir for the throne, to strengthen our lineage—the cracks started to show. Because I had come to realise I did want a child of my own, to love and to cherish, and I was trapped in a marriage where I could never have that.'

'What happened?' he said, encouraging her to carry on.

'My father was away, fighting in the south, and my mother came to see me one night, distressed, arriving at the wicket gate. She had ridden all the way from Jorvik, on her own. She said she had been hiding a terrible secret, and she couldn't contain it any longer. And as she removed her cloak and her pinafore, I saw the swell of her stomach and knew she was with child. I couldn't understand why she wasn't elated, and then she told me—it wasn't my father's child.'

Njal sucked in a breath.

'She had fallen in love with one of the ealdormen in my father's witan. She'd had an affair, and the baby was the consequence.'

Njal cursed, and raked a hand through his hair.

'It was adultery. It was treason. And she hadn't seen my father around that moon cycle, so she couldn't say that the child was his. She was terrified that if he learned the truth, he would have her, the baby and her lover killed. She hadn't told anyone up until then, but her stomach was starting to swell, and she was frantic with worry. We talked through all the options, all night long, and we agreed—she would stay with me and Feran in Bamburgh, tucked away, until she had the baby. She asked me if I would start wearing wool beneath my dress, to make it look as though I was with child. And when the child was born, I would say it was mine and Feran's. I became her greatest accomplice.'

'She should never have asked you to do that,' he said, angry with the former queen. 'It's not right. It's not fair.'

'What other choice did she have? And my mother's safety was more important to me than the truth.'

'And what of your safety—she's forced you to lie for her, for years. What of your happiness?'

'But I was happy,' Cwen said. 'Selfishly, it helped with mine and Feran's predicament. I was being gifted this beautiful baby boy. It seemed like fate. And Feran was a devoted father from day one.'

'So when you were describing the birth to me, you were describing your mother's delivery?' he said, displeased.

'Yes.'

'And from the day she had the baby, you raised Leof as your son?'

'Yes.'

'Your mother did not mind that?'

'She was grateful to me—relieved. My father was on his way back to Jorvik, and her lover had been killed in the fighting. She was forced to put her grief aside and go back to doing her duty. It was a solution for us all, and she still got to see Leof often.'

'Did your father ever suspect anything?' Njal asked.

'No.'

Just like him, he thought.

'He was simply delighted to hear of his grandchild. He'd thought my mother had come to stay with us to help me with the baby. And since she returned to him, my mother has loyally stayed by his side. So yes, I raised Leof as mine. He is mine, in every sense of the word. I never want him to know the truth of his true parentage.'

'He looks just like you.'

'Thankfully. He actually looks just like my mother too, don't you think? And now you know why I kept it secret. My father, and the people, cannot know the truth. For Leof's sake, for my mother's sake—to keep her safe. And mine. I don't know what would happen if they discovered we had lied. It would hurt my father and Leof.

And people would lose trust in us—it would destroy my lineage, topple the monarchy.'

'So you've fooled the kingdom. Fooled me,' Njal said, bristling.

She reached out and held his face. 'No, I was never going to be able to fool you. Not if I wanted to do this with you, get this close to you.'

And the moment he'd entered her flashed through his mind again—the way she'd tightened around him, the way he'd breached her wall, her body exposing the truth. There were even a few spots of blood on the furs—proof he'd taken her innocence. And despite his anger, his hurt that she had lied to him, he wanted to take her again.

'I wish you had told me, before. It might have helped me to understand why you behaved the way you did. Why you kept pushing me away.' Although he wasn't sure he still completely understood it.

'I'm sorry,' she said. 'I was torn up inside. I hated myself, what I was denying myself, denying you, but I couldn't see any other way.'

'You could have trusted me. But I know, after everything that had happened, that must have been hard to do.' His thumbs circled the corners of her mouth. 'Do you trust me now?'

'Yes.'

But did he trust her?

'What of your needs?' he said. 'Did you never feel like you were missing out?'

She moved closer towards him. 'I honestly didn't know what I was missing out on, not until I met you.' She looked up at him from underneath her lashes. 'I never *wanted* before I met you. That day in my father's study room when you were talking about why we should wed, about desire, I hadn't even known what desire felt like until that moment.' She leaned in and pressed a soft kiss against his lips. 'And I can tell I still have a lot to learn, but I was hoping that you'd teach me.'

His lips parted, yielding to her sweet seduction, and she pressed her tongue inside his mouth. He groaned.

How could he say no to that? He might still be cross with her for keeping the truth from him about Leof, but he still wanted her. More, with every passing moment. She was offering herself up to him again, letting the furs fall from her skin, asking him to show her more of what he could give her, and he wanted to comply. 'I will enjoy that,' he said.

Chapter Twelve

Telling Njal was like releasing a big, dark cloud that had loomed over Cwen for years. He had listened intently, and it felt good to be honest. By revealing her transgressions, admitting the truth, she felt as if she had unburdened her heart—and she felt liberated; lighter, as the heavy feelings of guilt and shame lifted.

Once she'd had Feran to share all this with, but since he'd died, she'd had no one to talk to about it, and it felt cathartic to open up to Njal, the one person whose opinions she cared about more than anyone else, and have him accept her wrongdoing. He had been so good about it all and she felt cautiously optimistic. He had every right to be livid—she'd been deceiving him since day one, but she hoped he understood why.

He had become so important to her in such a short space of time.

And as he drew her down onto the bed, kissing her, touching her again, everywhere, frantic with need, it was as if he couldn't get enough of her, like she couldn't get enough of him. And when he rolled her onto her stomach and thrust inside her from behind, so easily this time, no barrier to halt his entry, she felt as if this was where he was meant to be. It felt so right.

As he lifted her up by the hips, pulling her up onto all fours, powerfully storming her body, she thought back to those deer she'd seen mating in the fields just yesterday. The way he was moving inside her, reared over her, their bodies slick with sweat, it felt animalistic, wild and raw. He cupped her breasts and pulled her up, back against his chest, and he continued to caress her, his fingers circling her nipples, as he kissed her neck, all the time moving in and out of her body with long, thick, relentless strokes. He was merciless in his need to give her pleasure, and as he took her to the brink and she cried out her climax, he surged inside her one more time, bellowing out his release, spilling his seed inside her.

He lay on top of her where they'd collapsed, breathing hard, his head facing hers on the furs, but he lifted himself away from her a little, as if suddenly realising something.

'So when you said you couldn't have children...was that a lie too? Or did you just mean you wouldn't have children with me?'

He was so close she could see the flecks of flint in his hurt blue eyes. She swallowed. 'I thought I'd explained all this,' she said, trying to think fast, wondering what she could say that would appease him.

He withdrew from her body and moved to lie to the side of her, and she felt bereft. She missed him already. Yet she could feel the remnants of their lovemaking coating her inner thighs.

'Don't you see? I had to tell you that,' she said, her pulse picking up with panic. 'I didn't think I would ever be able to share the truth with you about Leof, so I never thought I'd be able to have a child,' she said. She kept talking to fill the silence, trying to explain, knowing the realisation had only just dawned on him that she hadn't only just lied about Leof not being her son, but about not being able to have children.

His children.

'I had to come to terms with the fact I would probably never have a child of my own, and when you asked me to marry you, I knew I had to lie, as I thought if I told you I couldn't have children, it might mean you would keep your distance—that you wouldn't want to be intimate. That there would be no need. I wasn't counting on you wanting to do this anyway. I didn't appreciate that it was just as much about pleasure as it is about making a baby.'

He pulled away a little bit further, propping himself up onto his elbow, staring down at her, his face hard. 'So, can you? Have children?'

'I don't know. I hope so.'

'So I might have got you with child, just now?'

His face twisted, and in a sudden, forceful movement, he heaved himself off the bed. He turned around and she sat up, watching as he began pulling on his breeches, roughly, concealing his beautiful body from her, putting himself out of her reach. She was reeling from the sudden turnaround in the atmosphere between them. Just moments ago he had been buried deep inside her body, and now, it was as if the distance was increasing between them at an alarming rate. He fastened the tie with an air of finality, anger rippling off him.

'Where are you going?' she asked.

'I can't believe this,' he said. 'So not only did you

lie—deceive me—you married me knowing you were going to deny me becoming a father, when you knew that's what I longed for. What I dreamed of. Do you realise what a torment that was for me? The magnitude of what I gave up—for you? How I wrestled with that decision? The grief I felt at the thought of never having a child of my own? And how that lay heavy on my heart, but that I thought you were worth it? How could you put me through that—watch me suffer, knowing just how that felt—when you knew it was possible all along.'

'I'm sorry. It was a mistake,' she said. 'But I didn't know you. Not like I do now.'

'No, it was a choice. You chose to lie to me. To deceive me. To betray me. Whereas I—I chose you, over my dream, my legacy, over a child to call our own, to outlive us. I wrestled with myself, my own needs, and my desire for you, to make that choice and come to terms with it—that was huge. When I didn't need to. And for what? All to protect a child who wasn't yours?'

His eyes were like steel.

'That's not fair,' she said, defensive. 'He's my brother. I raised him. Like you raised Ove after your parents died, and would do anything for him.' She came across the bed, trying to reach him. 'Njal…?'

'Don't touch me!' he said, stepping backwards, raking a hand through his hair. 'I need to think about this. To think about what you've done. Because right now, I'm wondering whether every woman is the same and just lies and lies to get what she wants. It's making me question everything you've ever said and done. But mostly, you've made me question myself and what I want. Whether I would even want to have a child with you. If I even have a choice now.' He pulled on his boots. 'I'm going to get some air.'

An icy draft passed over her as he opened the door and walked through it, slamming it shut, leaving her sat there naked in the middle of the bed, all alone.

Cwen waited and waited, but Njal didn't return. Instead, after putting Leof to bed, she spent the longest night of her life alone, tossing and turning, wondering what she could do to make it up to Njal. To show him he could trust her, that she was worthy—and that she cared. She wished she had told him that she loved him, because she realised now, she did. She had fallen completely in love with him from that first moment when he had saved her father on the battlefield, and their eyes had connected. But would it make any difference now? Did he love her back?

He had made love to her like he did, but then he had withdrawn from her body and her bed so quickly, after taking what he'd wanted, and been so cold. But she knew she deserved it.

As she made her way down to the hall the next morning, she was nervous, unsure what she would find— whether he would want to speak with her. And the sight made her heart hammer in her chest. Njal and Leof, sat to a table, gutting fish—and Leof had a huge smile on his face.

Leof jumped up when he saw her, and raced over to her, smiling. 'We went fishing! Njal woke me up really early and we took the boat out, and we caught all this mackerel. Look!'

'I can see it! That's wonderful,' she said, and she

looked over at Njal, grateful for making Leof happy, despite what was going on between them.

She walked with Leof back over to the table, wary. 'Thank you,' she said to Njal.

But he wouldn't meet her eye.

She had made herself vulnerable to him, she realised. She was now at his mercy. He could reveal the truth, taking away the threat of a Saxon heir to his throne if he so wanted. She would be ruined, as would her mother and father—more so than they were now. He had already taken her body, her heart. He could take everything for himself if he wanted.

Would he?

He must know she had risked her son, her title and her family by trusting him, wanting to be with him. Would he reveal the truth of her son, ruining her reputation, her father's line for good? She hoped he wouldn't betray her now.

She didn't know what he was thinking, and she hated it. She loathed the fact that she was the cause of more hurt in his life. He had been betrayed by her father, his lover, his brother, and now her, his wife. She would do anything to go back and change it. And if he'd let her, she'd spend the rest of her life making it up to him.

'Njal, can we talk?'

But all of a sudden there was a commotion outside.

'They're here! Soldiers! An army is approaching!'

Njal was up out of his seat like a shot. 'Stay here,' he said to her and Leof.

'To hell I will,' she said. 'This is my fortress.'

He slanted her a look and incredibly, he inclined his head and conceded. 'Fine. It's your choice,' he said.

And his words carried such significance. He knew that decisions had been made for her in the past, and despite their argument last night, he was still willing to give her the autonomy to make her own choice. It meant a lot.

She followed him as they raced outside, and in the distance, out on the plains, she could see them—an army approaching.

'Is it Caedwalla? Or Ove?'

Njal turned to look at her. 'Both.'

The breath left her.

'Rally the men,' he said. 'Everyone who can fight must take up a sword. Cwen, get the women and children inside.'

She shook her head. 'I can fight.'

'No,' he said, turning on her, finally looking at her. 'I don't want you fighting.'

'This isn't up to you. I want to help. To show you that I'm on your side, because right now, I don't think you believe it.'

He went to walk away from her, but she gripped his arm. 'Njal.'

'What?' he said, turning back to face her. But his voice was lethal. 'Don't worry, I will keep your secret, Cwen, if that's what you're worried about.'

She shook her head. 'It isn't. That isn't what I meant.'

And then she had a thought. 'Can you even fight with your wound?'

'I'm fine.'

'Maybe you should tell your men…'

'No! Keep it to yourself. That shouldn't be too hard for someone like you to do.'

* * *

Njal would never forgive himself for bringing a battle to her door.

Was there no end to his brother's ambition? But when he'd seen those soldiers crawling across the plains towards the fortress, to attack Cwen and her people, a new determination had settled in his stomach. He had to end this, today. He'd had enough betrayal to last a lifetime.

He braced himself and the rest of the stronghold for battle. He sent word for the people in the surrounding villages to come into the fortress, and he called upon every able-bodied person to find a weapon, and to fight. Whether they were Saxon or Dane, they couldn't continually live in fear. That's why he'd started this in the first place, why he'd gone to war—to achieve peace.

As he and Bjorn and the rest of the men threw on their armour, sharpened their weapons and ascended their horses, he gave instructions for those on the battlements to defend with arrows and fire. He knew that being on higher ground made them safer, but he didn't want the fight to take place here, in Cwen's home. No, he and his men would meet the enemy, halfway, out there, on the plains beside the ocean.

He was still reeling from last night. It had been the best night of his life, in so many ways, but when he'd emptied himself into Cwen for the second glorious time, he'd suddenly realised the extent of her deception—that it ran even deeper than he'd first thought, and it had thrown him.

Could anyone be trusted?

The gates to the fortress opened and they spurred their horses on, to wind down the hill towards the wide, open fields, their hundred-strong enemy approaching on the horizon. Caedwalla had a formidable force, but with Njal's men and Cwen's soldiers combined, they might just be able to hold their own. Ove's men? He wasn't so sure. He knew they could fight. He knew they would show no mercy.

As the men lined up in a shield wall, he could see his brother drawing closer, and he wondered how it had come to this. Where had it all gone so wrong? Had he done that bad a job raising Ove these past years, or had the damage already been done—the wounds of the massacre irreparable?

And if he had planted a seed in Cwen's body last night, if he'd put a child inside her, would he fail that child too?

Ove's men hammered their shields with their swords, and the ground vibrated with the force of their stamping feet. Njal raised his sword into the air, signalling to his men to get ready to charge.

What would happen if he encountered his brother in combat? Would he have the stomach to fight him?

And then he lowered his sword and they were charging into the fray, and all thoughts fled his mind. He had to focus. Metal clashed against metal, horses bayed and the battle commenced, as bloody and brutal as ever. Njal took down one opponent then the next, desperate to just get this over with now. He engaged men he knew and men he didn't, not stopping to think, as that would get him killed.

On and on he fought, and looking around, he felt they were making progress, the ground covered with the limp, lifeless bodies of their enemy. And then he looked up and saw Cwen fighting, and his blood ran cold. He didn't want her anywhere near the horrors of the battlefield. He didn't want her anywhere near Caedwalla or his brother.

And yet, he knew he must allow her to make her own choices, and if this marriage was going to work, he had to support her to do so. He could not send her away. She had just as much right to be here as anyone, to fight for what she believed in.

But he could try to protect her. He could fight at her side. Whatever she had done, whatever lies she had told, right now, he didn't care. He could forgive her. He loved her.

The realisation hit him so hard in the chest, he faltered, giving an opponent the chance to slice their blade into his arm, and he roared in pain. He swung back.

He loved her, and he didn't want her to get hurt.

Violent blows rained down on him, but he fought harder, fiercer, pushing the men back, disposing of one, then the next.

If he lost her now…

Fighting for vengeance was one thing, but he realised fighting to protect someone you loved was a hell of a lot worse, because you had something to lose.

He loved her.

He loved her and he'd made love to her, taking her innocence, and he hadn't even told her how he felt. Yes, he'd hoped he'd shown her, by the fierceness of his actions, the strength of his desire, but he hadn't said the words.

He had been hurt by her deception, felt fearful of the emotions taking over him, when he realised he might have got her with child, that he might become a father and let down that child too. He was scared, he realised.

But now, none of that mattered. He loved her, and he hadn't told her. And he was terrified he might never get the chance.

Another man veered towards him, and he sliced his blade through the air, but he couldn't take his eyes off Cwen, fighting someone off herself. He needed to get to her.

Yes, she had lied to him, but he understood why she'd done it. He had attacked her home, her father, then given her an ultimatum—marry him or be banished. To save her family, she'd agreed to tie herself to him, yet she'd known she would have to keep him at arm's bay, to protect the true identity of her son.

He struck down one warrior then another, all while she was in the throes of an intense encounter, and when she finally emerged victorious, he let out a breath.

But was it possible she hadn't been able to stay away from him, like he hadn't her? That as they'd got to know one another, she had wanted to tell him the truth, but before she could, he'd coldly sent her away? And then, when he'd come here, bringing more devastation to her door, despite her fears, she had trusted him enough to let him inside her body, inside her heart, but he hadn't trusted her enough to stay. He'd callously pushed her away. Again.

In the heat of his hurt, he'd thought she was like Synnove, but she was nothing like her. She was warm and kind and would do anything for anyone else, even sacrifice her own happiness.

He was a fool.

If their lovemaking had resulted in him planting a seed in her, a child of their own, he wanted that, with her. A future. A family. And he would make sure he was a damn good husband and father.

He had almost reached her side when Ove stepped between them.

He froze, but his brother didn't. Ove wasted no time in raising his blade and Njal was forced to lift his own in defence. Every jab and thrust was a wound in itself, Njal not wanting to really hurt him, but having to protect himself at the same time, shocked. He couldn't believe the discord and animosity between them, the aggression behind his brother's blows. Where had it come from? Njal's emotions were conflicted—he had to fight, but he didn't want to.

And then he managed to knock the weapon out of his brother's hand, but Ove lashed out, hitting Njal with his fist. Njal dropped his own sword and punched him back, and a vicious struggle ensued. They wrestled and tussled with each other, a tangle of limbs, like they had done when they were younger on the beach, when Njal had taught him how to fight, and there was a small part of Njal that wanted them both to start laughing, for them to hug it out like their father had always told them to do. And yet he knew that would never happen. It was too far gone. This was a fight for their lives.

All around them, he realised men were fleeing the scene, saying Caedwalla was dead, that Njal had won, and Ove's men began to drop their weapons too, knowing they'd lost. And Njal was glad because he was aware he was flagging, the inner struggle and exertion of each strike making it a monumental effort to keep going. He could feel his stitches had come undone and he was bleeding again.

He dealt a blow that sent Ove reeling, and his brother lay back in the mud, as Njal wearily got to his feet. He picked up his sword again and stumbled over to him, looming over his brother's limp and bleeding body. He knew he had to end this, but the storm of grief that churned within him was immense. Yet he couldn't let Ove continue to hurt the people he cared about. He couldn't let him constantly bring destruction to these lands; their home.

Ove grappled around, trying to find his own weapon, but Njal kicked it away. Ove's death was inevitable now. He had to sacrifice him for the good of Northumbria, to ensure a peaceful future. And yet Njal felt broken inside.

He stoically raised his weapon, ready to bring down his sword and deal the fatal blow and Ove looked up at him, his eyes wide, shocked his brother would actually do this; what he'd brought him to. And then Njal realised Cwen was there, rushing towards him, pulling off her helmet and throwing herself against him, wrapping her arm around his shoulder and putting her hand on his wrist, increasing the pressure, preventing him from making the final strike.

'I'm here. It's over.'

He had done the same to Ove that day, to save her father. And in that moment, he realised she was reminding him that love—and forgiveness—was a powerful alternative to hate and revenge.

He didn't need to do this. He dropped his sword and his hands came round her waist, holding her tight, burying his head in her neck, never wanting to let go.

'I love you,' she whispered. 'So much.'

As he stood there holding her, his men crowded Ove, securing him. And as he pulled Cwen closer, wrapping his arms around her, he told her he loved her too, whispering the words, over and over again.

Chapter Thirteen

It had taken the whole day to clear the battlefield. There had been too many lives lost, but Cwen had been glad of the outcome—and so grateful their home hadn't been tarnished. Caedwalla's men had fled the scene, and Ove and his last remaining men had been rounded up and taken to an outhouse, while Njal decided what to do with them.

Cwen and the women had tirelessly patched up wounds, and she was aware Njal was still bleeding and hadn't let her see to his yet, but he was determined to clean up the mess first. He wanted there to be no lasting memory of what took place here today.

Finally, come twilight, he and Bjorn returned to the hall and she insisted he sit down while she took a look at his wound.

'Best do as you're told, else you'll be in serious trouble, and we've both seen what an expert she is with a sword. You don't want to cross her,' Bjorn said.

And Njal slumped down onto a bench, his eyes on her. 'Let me eat first. I need to regain my strength before dealing with you and a needle again,' he teased her.

And she rolled her eyes, placing some steaming bowls of stew in front of them.

She couldn't believe he'd told her that he loved her. She felt a whoosh swoop through her body every time she thought of it, a rush of love every time she looked at him. She kept thinking back to the way he'd held her so tightly, as if he'd needed her to help him stand, to breathe, to live—and she had felt just the same.

She had seen the confliction on his face as he'd edged towards Ove, raising his sword, and she hadn't wanted him to live with the decision of taking his own brother's life. She'd wanted to save him from that, as he'd saved Ove from killing her father, so she'd rushed forwards, halting him.

Leof came over to them and handed Njal and Bjorn a drink, before sitting next to Njal and nestling into him. 'You're not going to die, are you?' he asked.

'Not a chance. I've got far too much to live for,' he said. 'Your mother's going to patch me up and I'll be like new in no time.'

'Good,' Leof said. 'Because, well, I like having you around. And I know Mother does too.'

Njal grinned. 'That makes three of us.'

'Run along to bed now—Eadhild is waiting,' Cwen said, brushing something out of her eye.

'Are you all right?' he asked.

'Shouldn't I be asking you that?' she said.

'It's been quite a day for everyone.'

'I'll be better when I know your wound has been seen to,' she said.

She busied herself while the men ate, and she asked her maid to arrange a bath in her room, just as Njal had done for her that time back in Jorvik. It would be good to clean his wound and he deserved a little bit of indulgence. He was a man who put everyone else's needs before his own, and she decided that had to change. It was time for him to have some of the things he wanted. He'd earned that.

He found her in the kitchens a while later, when they were boiling the last of the water on the fire, and the moment she saw him, leaning against the door, her pulse kicked up.

'I'm ready for my torture,' he said, grimacing.

'Finally,' she said. 'But first, a bath. We need to keep the wound clean.'

He quirked an eyebrow. 'Are you mothering me?'

She shrugged. 'Someone's got to look after you.'

She helped him back to her room and he stood there as she removed his clothes. She knew he was looking at her with heated eyes, wanting to stir her attentions, and he wouldn't have to try too hard, but right now, she wanted him to wash the blood and dirt from that gash. It was worrying her.

He clambered into the barrel and as his body submerged beneath the steaming water, he tipped his head back and relaxed. She came round the back of him and massaged his shoulders, kissing him on the forehead.

He opened his eyes and she looked down at him.

'Thank you, for today,' he said. 'For stopping me from doing something I know I'd come to regret.'

She nodded. 'I was just reminding you who you are. Who the man is that I fell in love with. Have you decided what will happen to Ove now?'

He sighed. 'I need to think about it. At least he's locked up and can't hurt anyone tonight. I shall go and speak to him shortly, before bed. Get it over with.'

'What will happen to Caedwalla's throne in Mercia?' she said.

'I guess he has an heir, or someone next in line? Hopefully they'll be content to stay down in Mercia and not cause us any more grief.'

'And you? Will you go back Jorvik? You know, you haven't officially been coronated yet.'

He sat up in the water and looked at her. 'You mean we. Will we go back to Jorvik?'

Her breath halted and she stopped massaging him and came round the barrel to face him. 'I didn't want to be presumptuous.' She bit her lip. 'I'm really sorry I lied to you, Njal. I should never have done that.'

'No, you shouldn't. But I understand why you did. You didn't know me. I had to earn your trust.'

'When I started to fall for you, I really wanted to tell you, to confide in you. But I was scared. I'm so glad you know everything now.'

'Me too.'

'I'm not like Synnove.'

'I know that, Cwen.'

'And I won't ever lie to you again.'

'I know that too.'

She swished her fingers through the water, swirling them about. 'Why *did* you choose to marry me even though I told you we couldn't have a child, when that was your dream?'

'Because I wanted you more. If it was a choice between having you and having children, I wanted you. My dream changed. You were it. *Are* it. I love you. I loved you from the very first moment I met you. The way you handled yourself on the battlefield. The way the men looked up to you. I just knew.'

'I love you too,' she said, grinning helplessly. 'Do you still want children, after everything that's happened?'

'Yes,' he said. 'If it's a possibility. Do *you* want a child of your own? With me?'

'Yes,' she said. 'Although I feel guilty—I don't want to dismiss my relationship with Leof.'

'Nothing could take away what you two have, Cwen,' he said. 'After what's gone on with Ove, I'm worried I won't be a good father.'

'I've seen what you're like with Leof. I can promise you, you are. He adores you, we both do. Now get out of there and let me stitch you up, so I can show you how much.'

His eyebrows rose. 'I like the sound of that.'

He launched himself out of the tub and she roughly dried him off, rubbing down his shoulders, his chest, thighs and his legs, and she could tell he was already thinking of his reward. He stood against the table, naked, looking magnificent, as she gathered the needle and thread together, and he reached over for his breeches, fumbling in the pocket.

'Here,' he said, pulling something out and handing it to her.

She looked at it. It was Feran's ring. The one she had lost in the kitchen that night.

'I found it, after you left. I thought you'd want it back. It's good to have something to remember someone by.'

'Thank you,' she whispered, taking the ring and placing it on the table. It was good of him to give it to her, and she was pleased to have it back. And yet she didn't think she needed to wear it any more. If she needed to draw on someone's strength, it would be Njal's. But she would put it away and keep it safe.

'Right, no more procrastinating—let's get this done.'

She sewed his skin together once more, and he winced, but she knew he could handle it. He was the strongest, but also the kindest, fairest man she knew.

When she'd finished, she washed her hands in the cooling water and dried them off, before coming back to him.

'So, how are you going to show me how much you adore me?' he said wickedly. 'Tell me what you want to do.'

She flushed, and he wrapped a hand around her neck, tugging her closer. 'And remember, you promised to never lie to me again.'

Her cheeks burned. 'What you did to me the other night, with your tongue.'

'You want that?'

She shook her head. 'Does it work the other way round?'

And he laughed. It was the most glorious sound after the stresses of the day. 'You can do whatever you want to me, Cwen,' he said with outstretched arms. 'I'm yours.'

Hers.

This incredible man was hers. It was almost too good to be true.

'Will you show me how to satisfy you?'

He swallowed down a groan. 'With pleasure.' And he gently placed his hands on her shoulders. 'Get on your knees.'

She bravely moved herself down his body, not breaking eye contact, running her hands down the backs of his thighs, then up again, to cup his buttocks. 'Is this your way of getting me to bend the knee to you?' she teased him.

He took himself in his hand and lifted himself towards her lips.

She wrapped her hands around him and leaned in and kissed the tip, reverently. And then instinct kicked in and she curled her tongue around him, inquisitively, wickedly.

And he moaned. 'Dear God, what do you do to me, woman?'

When she took him in her mouth, drawing her lips up and down him, his grip on her shoulders intensified, holding her tighter, telling her she was doing it right. She increased her speed and he thrust, losing control, crying out her name as he exploded on her tongue.

She sat back on her knees and looked up at him. That's how she liked him, out of control with desire and love for her, as she was for him.

He pulled her up to her feet and wrapped her in his strong arms, and she held him back.

'That was... I have no words. I want to repay the favour, and take you to bed and make love to you all night long, but first, do you mind if I go and speak with my brother? I want it finished; dealt with, so that all I'm thinking about when I'm with you, is you and your pleasure. Will you wait here until I get back?'

'I'll always be here.'

And he kissed her, passionately, on the lips. 'Thank God for that. You know, I was lost before I met you,' he said, tucking a stray tendril of hair behind her ear. 'Loving you saved me.'

***

Njal pulled on his clothes and headed down the steps and out to the gatehouse, where he spoke to one of the men. Then, with a heavy heart he went to the outhouse where Bjorn had put his brother.

Ove was sat on the dusty floor, his hands bound to one of the wooden beams, his legs outstretched. He looked up when Njal walked in, and his face was riddled with bruises. Njal was reminded of that boy of fourteen he'd found hidden beneath the floorboards, dirty and frightened.

'You look how I feel.'

Ove grimaced.

'Have you been fed? Watered?'

'Yes.'

Njal came down and sat opposite him, resting his back on the wall, stretching out his own legs.

'So Caedwalla is dead. Most of your men are dead. What do you plan to do next?'

Ove shrugged. 'You should have just killed me and put me out of my misery. I could have been at peace—seen Mother and Father again.'

'Is that what you want? To see them again?'

'Don't you?'

'One day. But I want to live my life first. I want to be happy. I want that for you too.'

'I can't. I'm not like you. I can't forgive the Saxons for what they did. I can't live here and forget it. It eats me up, makes me bitter—I'm so wrapped up in my hate. How can you excuse them for it?'

'Because I don't want to spend my life being angry, it doesn't help anyone. It only causes more pain. I try to understand why Ælfweard did what he did—maybe he was scared. Maybe he felt threatened—that we had come here to his lands and our people had been known to hurt his. I know it's no excuse, but being bitter won't bring our parents back. It won't change anything.' Njal dragged a hand over his beard. 'Why did you turn against me, Brother? We used to be inseparable...'

Ove shrugged. 'Something changed in you when we got to Jorvik. You started to forget. You started to be cheerful. I resented it. I didn't want you to put aside all we had gone through. I wanted you to feel the same as me. You suddenly had everything—power, wealth, love...and I had nothing. And no one wants to be number two.'

'I'm sorry I made you feel that way,' Njal said, shaking his head sadly. 'It wasn't my intention. I only ever wanted the best for you.'

Ove looked up at him, his eyes swimming with tears. 'It wasn't your fault. How can you speak to me, forgive me, Brother, after the things I've done?'

Njal felt a lump swell in his throat.

'Because love is more powerful than hate. And I love you. I always have. I may not like you, or the things you've done, but I will always love you, in spite of everything. When we started out on this journey, we were angry, we wanted vengeance, but did any one of those lives we took, any one of those battles we fought, make you feel any better? No. I've realised only love can do that. And I certainly don't want to live with the guilt of your blood on my hands. Forgiveness brings peace, and I forgive you for everything, and hope that you can forgive me for not taking you away from here after it happened, for not finding us a better life, rather than dragging you into the conflict, making this your existence.'

'Then you wouldn't have ended up here. And you are content here, I can see it in your eyes. So maybe all of it was for a reason. You really love her—the princess?'

'Yes.'

'I'm sorry, you know, about what I did.'

'You should be.' He inclined his head. 'I'll tell her.'

Njal curled himself upwards, getting off the floor. 'Everything hurts. Thanks for that.'

His brother tried to smile. 'Same. So what happens now?'

'I'm sending you home. Back to Denmark. A boat will be waiting at dawn. My man will come to fetch you.'

Ove stared up at him.

'I think it'll do you good to get away from here. Start afresh. Put all this behind you.'

Njal headed towards the door.

'Will I ever see you again, Brother?'

Njal rested his hand on the doorknob. 'Probably not,' he said, his voice thick with emotion.

Ove nodded. 'You're a good man, Njal. The best brother. You'll make a good king to these people. A good husband—and father.'

Njal opened the door and gave him a last look. 'Be happy, Brother.'

Njal walked along the beach, in the moonlight, trying to get his emotions in order. Even though Ove still lived, he felt he was grieving the loss of his brother. He looked out across the dark, inky ocean, towards Denmark. He knew he was doing the right thing, sending him away where he couldn't cause them any more pain, and hopefully finally feel free of his own grief, but it didn't make it any easier.

Njal shucked off his boots and rolled up his breeches, wanting to feel the icy surf between his toes. He would miss the sea if they returned to Jorvik. Yes, it was the capital of Northumbria and had a lot to offer, but it didn't make you feel alive quite like the beauty of this place. And yet he knew with Cwen and Leof at his side, he would be content anywhere.

A sound behind him made him flinch and he turned. Cwen.

'Are you following me?' he said, grinning.

'You'd been gone a while. I came to check you were all right, after your chat with Ove. I can go if you'd rather be alone.'

'Rather be alone than be with you? Never,' he said, reaching out and taking her hand in his. 'Mind if we walk a while?'

She shook her head.

'I was just thinking about where we should live—what would make us happy.'

'Oh? I'd just assumed you'd want to go back to Jorvik.'

'I'm not sure. Maybe we could spend our time between both places.'

She nodded. 'That sounds good.'

'What of your parents?'

'They're going to go to Caester. My father has friends there. And it's not so far that I can't visit in the not too distant future. If I'm allowed.'

He raised a brow at her. 'Who is going to stop you?'

'You?'

'I wouldn't deny you seeing your parents, Cwen. Or your mother seeing Leof. And since when have you asked for permission for anything—apart from to pleasure me, which, might I add, felt pretty astounding. From now on, I won't assert my authority over you at all. I will allow you to make your own choices, I promise.'

He stopped walking and turned to her, bringing her into his arms, resting his forehead against hers.

'Are you sure you're all right?' she asked.

'Yes. I'm sad. But speaking to Ove also made me realise I'm lucky. I'm lucky that grief and anger no longer consume me, as it does him. He pointed out that it seems something far greater, far better, has taken its place. Love.'

He took her face between his hands and pressed his mouth to hers, softly at first, slowly and sensually, wanting his kiss to affirm his words. His tongue caressed hers, until passion took over and she kissed him back, hard, so unrestrained, her arms wrapping around his neck, and it left him breathless.

'I want you,' she said.

'Here? You're insatiable,' he laughed. 'I won't deny you. Whatever you want, it's yours. Your choice.'

She began frantically untucking his tunic from his breeches just as he began rucking up her skirts, backing her up the beach until they could no longer walk, and tumbling into a laughing heap on the sand. Her skirts around her waist, he groaned, and pushed his knees between her legs, sliding his hands up her thighs before putting his hand to the waistband of his breeches, setting himself free, wanting to be inside her, now.

He pulled her up so she was sitting, then drew her further up, onto his lap, so she was straddling him. He reached beneath her bottom and hoisted her up, before lowering her down again, impaling her on him, and she cried out in wonder. She rested her hands on his shoulders as he squeezed her buttocks, showing her how to move herself on top of him, grinding against him, as he thrust into her. He was mad for her, pulling her closer, harder and faster, wanting to be one, until she screamed out into the night sky, and his own orgasm rolled over him like the waves, taking him over and then under on an almighty crashing tide of overwhelming love and passion.

Chapter Fourteen

They'd returned to Jorvik a month before, and Njal had been pleased to see the floods had receded and the stronghold was still undergoing repairs, just like his heart after Ove had left these shores, but it was most definitely on the mend. Cwen was helping with that, every morning, every night, and the hours in between. Even the wildflowers in the meadow that had been trampled during the battle had sprung back to life.

Njal had been relieved that the people of the city had welcomed them back, pleased to see him as well as Cwen and Leof, Bjorn and Eadhild, and now everyone was busy preparing for the coronation the following day.

Njal had been enjoying keeping busy during the days, mainly helping to work the land, doing what he had always loved, and at night, he was enjoying playing games with his wife, teaching her new skills and strategies. But tonight she seemed quiet, as they lay there in each other's arms, breathless from the things they'd just done together.

'Are you all right?' he asked, lightly stroking her arm.

'I've been thinking about Leof. And I think I want to tell him the truth, about his parentage. I'm ready.'

Njal sat up, shocked. After all she'd gone through to keep this secret—to protect the boy from finding out the truth, it seemed like a huge and sudden turnaround. 'Why?'

'Because I don't want him to ever hear about it from anyone else.'

Did she not trust him to keep the truth hidden? 'I will keep your secret, Cwen. I would never betray your trust. I wouldn't want any harm to come to you, or Leof. Ever.'

'I know that,' she said. 'But I've been thinking a lot about what we've been through, and I love that our relationship is built on trust—that there are no secrets between us. No lies. And I want that to be the same for me and Leof. I always feel like I'm hiding something from him, and I think I'm ready to tell him. Like your father said, honesty is always the best course. I know it will probably hurt him, to begin with, and that it will take him some time to come to terms with it. He might be cross with me, and my mother. He might be confused. He will have questions. But I feel between us, we could cope with it, and make sure he knows he is loved, and special, and secure. If he won't talk to me, I know he will open up to you.'

Njal nodded. He and the boy had become very close these past weeks. They were inseparable.

'I know there's a risk he might tell someone, but I don't think he would. And I think it will ease some of the pressure for him. You know he never wants to be king—he wants to be a fisherman,' she smiled.

'Or a farmer, like me, he's said.' Njal grinned. 'I've converted him to my ways.'

Cwen smiled.

'He keeps nagging me for a brother, so that we have another heir, other than him. He reminds me of me. I never wanted this either!' Njal said.

'But you're so good at it. So well regarded.' She reached up and kissed him on the lips. 'The people love you. I love you. You won your right to live here—your place on the throne, and in our hearts,' she said, changing her words from the first day they met. 'I would never have been strong enough to tell Leof before, on my own, but with you by my side, I feel able to do anything. And this is something I feel I ought to do.'

'All right,' he said, his brow furrowing. 'If you feel it is the right thing, then it must be. When do you want to do this?'

She bit her lip. 'I don't know. Before the coronation? And will you be there, with me, when I do it?'

'Of course.'

They told Leof the next day. They sat him down and explained to him that while Cwen would always be his mother, and Njal, his father, if he would accept him as such, Cwen hadn't been the one to actually give birth to him.

He'd stared at her, wide-eyed at first. 'So I didn't come out of your tummy? You didn't make me?' he'd asked.

'No,' she'd said, brushing away her tears. 'But you were given to me, like a gift—the best present I could ever have wished for—as your birth mother couldn't look after you as well as she wished to. She had too many duties. So I have done the best job I can.'

'You've done a very good job,' Leof said.

'Thank you,' she'd said, her throat swelling with emotion. 'You are a very good boy. You've made it very easy for me. And I want to continue being your mummy for a very long time, if that's all right? I just wanted you to know the truth.'

He'd nodded. He hadn't asked about his real mother and she thought perhaps she'd revealed enough for now. It was a lot to take in. He would ask her in his own time. And when he did, she would be ready with the truth.

It felt as if a weight had been lifted. Njal had come into her life and set her on a new path to liberty and truth and love, and she was now ready to embrace her new title of queen, and be the woman she and the people wanted her to be. Someone they could look up to.

There was a huge attendance of representatives of both Saxons and Danes in the church for the coronation ceremony, unified Northumbrians, and later, in the hall, as she and Njal were crowned king and queen of the realm. Finally, they had united their peoples and brought peace to their kingdom. They hosted an enormous feast in the great hall to celebrate. There was so much food, enough ale to cause another flood, and singing, dancing and much merriment. But Cwen couldn't wait to have her own personal celebration with her king and husband alone. And by the way he was looking at her across the hall, he couldn't either.

They managed to slip away a little after dark, and they barely made it down the corridors to their old room—having decided they liked that one far more than the royal chamber. It reminded them of the nights they'd spent in torturous close proximity, wanting to touch each other but being unable to. It reminded them of how far they'd come.

His mouth was on her neck, his tongue tracing the rim of her pinafore even before they reached the door, and as she pushed open the wood, they fell inside, against each other, laughing, kissing and breathless. Njal kicked the door to and his hot mouth was back on hers, seeking, plundering, as his hands roamed down, over her back, cupping her bottom, hauling her into his body.

His fingers to her brooches, he ripped them off in haste, tugging down the straps and the material, letting it drop to the floor, before he tackled the silk tunic.

'I want you naked in my arms.'

And she was only too happy to oblige.

She stood before him naked, just like she had that first time, but tonight, she had nothing to hide. His fingers delved between her legs, eager to touch and torment her, to see how much she wanted him. And her hands came up to rest on his shoulders, pushing him down gently, wanting his hot mouth to join his fingers, and he grinned at her, knowing what she was after. He was compliant, sinking to his knees, laughing against her stomach, and she squirmed in anticipation, his hot lips brushing her skin on his way down.

'I wish we could go back to that day we met when you asked me to give you my reasons why we should marry. I would have given you only one,' he said, his eyes shimmering up at her.

'And what would that have been?'

'Love. You should only marry for love. And I fell in love with you the moment I saw you on the battlefield. I was changed, instantly. I wanted you. I wanted you to be mine. I wanted to love you, for the rest of my days. That's why I wanted to marry you.'

'And I loved you from the moment I first saw you too. That's why I surrendered to you, why I said yes to marrying you. Not because I had to—but because deep down, I wanted to. Saying yes was the best thing I ever did.'

And as he dipped his head, she cried it out over and again. 'Yes, yes, yes.'

Epilogue

Eight months later

Njal held Cwen's hand and squeezed, offering her reassurance as she gave one last final push and the baby arrived. He kissed her forehead, her lips, telling her well done; that she was so brave and strong—that he loved her.

'Congratulations, you have a son, Your Highness,' the healer said. 'A beautiful boy.' She wrapped him up and placed him in Cwen's arms.

Njal tried and failed to blink back his tears. 'He's perfect,' he said. 'Just like his mother.'

'Just like his father,' Cwen said, raising her hand to his cheek and pulling him down for a kiss.

'Just like his brother,' Njal said. 'Shall we call Leof in? He'll be waiting outside, desperate to meet him, and worried, wanting to know you're all right.'

Cwen nodded.

Leof burst through the door moments later, bounding up to them, excited to meet his baby brother.

'He's so tiny,' he said. 'Look at his little fingers and toes. What's his name?'

Cwen looked up at Njal. 'Merewen,' they said in unison. It meant happiness. And this scene, right here, the four of them all together, was that. Pure happiness.

But Njal now knew it wasn't just a name like Njal Salversson that would make a great legacy, it was family, and his love for them, that would last for eternity.

* * * * *

*If you enjoyed this story
then you're going to love
Sarah Rodi's other captivating romances*

One Night with Her Viking Warrior
Claimed by the Viking Chief
Second Chance with His Viking Wife
"Chosen as the Warrior's Wife"
in Convenient Vows with a Viking
The Viking and the Runaway Empress
Her Secret Vows with the Viking

HARLEQUIN
Reader Service

Enjoyed your book?

Try the perfect subscription for Romance readers and get more great books like this delivered right to your door.

See why over 10+ million readers have tried Harlequin Reader Service.

Start with a Free Welcome Collection with free books and a gift—valued over $20.

Choose any series in print or ebook. See website for details and order today:

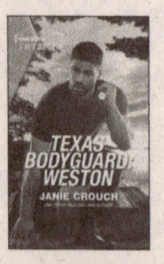

TryReaderService.com/subscriptions

RSBPA24F